W9-BZP-433

GRIND JOINT

A new casino is opening in the rural town of Penns River, Pennsylvania but just where the money is coming from no one really knows. Is it Daniel Hecker, bringing hope to a mill town after years of plant closings? Or is the town's salvation really an opening for Mike "The Hook" Mannarino's Pittsburgh mob to move part of their action down state? Or could it be someone even worse?

When the body of a drug dealer is dumped on the casino steps shortly before its grand opening, Detectives Ben "Doc" Dougherty and Willie Grabek have to survive their department's own inner turmoil and figure out not only who's behind the murder, but what it means to whoever is behind the operation itself. Between the cops, the mob, and the ex-spook in charge of casino security–Daniel Rollison, a man with more secrets than anyone will ever know–Grind Joint is a mesmerizing mix of betrayal, police action, small town politics, sudden violence and the lives of the people of a town just trying to look after itself.

DANA KING BIBLIOGRAPHY

Wild Bill (2011)
Worst Enemies (2012)
A Small Sacrifice (2013)
Grind Joint (2013)

GRIND JOINT

BY DANA KING

Introduction by Charlie Stella

STARK
HOUSE

Stark House Press • Eureka California

GRIND JOINT

Published by Stark House Press
1315 H Street
Eureka, CA 95501, USA
griffinskye3@sbcglobal.net
www.starkhousepress.com

ISBN: 1-933586-52-4
ISBN-13: 978-1-933586-52-6

Cover design and layout by Mark Shepard, www.shepgraphics.com
Proofreading by Rick Ollerman

*The publisher would like to add his thanks Rick Ollerman
for his work with the author on this project.*

First Stark House Press Edition: November 2013

Reprint Edition

To Charlie Stella:
Listen to me. He's a friend of mine.

Acknowledgements

No book, even a work of fiction, is written in a vacuum. The author draws upon all experience, memory, and interactions with others when creating his fictional world. There are a few individuals and groups who stand out:

First, Charlie Stella, without whose efforts I can safely say you would not be reading this book today.

Declan Burke, who rounded up an internet posse to keep me from throwing in the towel.

The Beloved Spouse and First Listener, who submits to every chapter as it is finished and whose sense of what works is better than mine.

The Writers of Chantilly, where continuous support in semi-monthly meetings gave me the confidence to show my writing to people I didn't know.

John McNally and George Washington University's Jenny McKean Moore Writers Workshop of the spring of 2002, where I learned the craft of both genre and "serious" fiction was the same.

The handful of stalwarts from John's workshop who continued on in monthly meetings, for their support and for finding ways to improve everything.

My parents, to whom much of this entirely fictional work will seem vaguely familiar.

Greg Shepard, Rick Ollerman, Mark Shepard, and everyone associated with Stark House for making the process far better than I had imagined.

Those with knowledge of the Pittsburgh area may recognize the three small cities that inspired Penns River. Much of the area's prosperity left with the closing of the steel and aluminum mills. Subsequent improvements in Greater Pittsburgh's economy never seem to move northeast, yet the towns survive. They are proof that Nietzsche was right: what does not kill you makes you stronger.

Introduction by Charlie Stella

Amici:

The first time I read Dana King's work, I thought the publishing world was fast asleep. It wasn't the work of some untested wannabe. Quite frankly, it was brilliant writing. I had the pleasure of reading one of his early drafts to Grind Joint, and I couldn't have been more impressed. It was more than obvious this guy had slipped through the publishing cracks. I distinctly remember turning to my wife while reading in bed and saying, "This guys is terrific... Jesus Christ, this is good... how is this guy not published?"

Flash forward a year or two and I'm still in disbelief that this guy hasn't found a publisher. Enter Ed Gorman, a guy who can't do enough for others. Ed did me the favor of handing Johnny Porno to Greg Shepard a few years earlier, and a new relationship was born. I've never been happier with a publisher. Mutual respect, amici, is a beautiful thing. Ed convinced Greg to open the door to original publications and now Stark House Press has a true gem—Grind Joint, by Dana King.

Forget the industry mantra about mob fiction being dead. That's just bullshit. Sometimes it takes a while to find the right set of eyes to bring a project to fruition, but over time great writing will not be denied.

Dana King's debut, Grind Joint, is wall to wall great writing—fact.

No need to shock with gore and senseless brutality, or rapes or brutal murders, as way too many in the world of noir seem to depend on for shock value. Dana King does it the old fashioned way, with writing so good it reads like a documentary; narrative that sparkles, and dialogue as good as any in the game. My favorite mob fiction writers ultimately make a novel read like a documentary, and from the very first paragraph of Grind Joint, I'm hooked as if I'm watching it unfold on a 60" television screen.

The building used to be a mini-mall. Penney's on one end, Monkey Ward's on the other, with a handful of little local shops in between. Nail salon, barber, wing joint, liquor store. They closed years ago, boarded up the windows. The Blockbuster in an outbuilding went tits up last summer. The toy store next door saw half a dozen re-inventions before it managed to scrape by as one of those operations where everything was five bucks or less. That and the bank were all that were left. Kenny Czarniak would have thought it ironic, how only the bank and the discount store survived amid the shells of failure, but any sense of irony had left him long ago.

In that paragraph I not only see what is being described, I can hear Morgan Freeman providing the voiceover. And is there any doubt about the setting? It's all there in one neat and tidy paragraph—a town down on its luck, one that is ripe for the picking.

And if you're unsure of the title, *Grind Joint*, the author's clever dialogue makes it easy.

> ... *The bartender came by. Nick asked what was available in bottles and ordered another draft. "What's up with this casino bullshit? Are they serious?"*
>
> *"Oh, yeah. Not only will it make the owners rich, everyone in town is going to get well. Be the new Atlantic City."*
>
> *"AC's a dump."*
>
> *"Then we have a head start."*
>
> *Nick thanked the bartender for his fresh beer. "Seriously. That casino in Pittsburgh is supposed to be really nice."*
>
> *"You ever hear of a casino that wasn't supposed to be really nice?"*
>
> *"Point taken, but it's no grind joint, not with the kind of money they put into it and who's behind it. I drove by this place yesterday. It looks like an old Sears."*
>
> *"Uh-uh. Monkey Ward's and Penney's."*
>
> *"Even better. I'm not knocking Sears. I buy a lot of stuff there. It's not my first choice of venue for an upscale entertainment experience."*
>
> *"That's where your big city uppity-ness loses touch with the real world. They're not looking for an upscale experience. This is a grind joint, pure and simple."*
>
> *"A casino for the working man."*
>
> *Doc flashed to Kenny Czarniak, getting up at four AM to turn on the heat for people who actually did things. "Just what the working man needs."*

A casino in Penns River is the start of trouble for local law enforcement. Russian mobsters and gangbangers, and what's left of the Pittsburgh Italian mob are fighting over turf. Local politicians and a real estate mogul also have an interest. And then there's infighting among the cops. Mostly there's Ben "Doc" Dougherty, the man readers will take a quick liking to and stay with throughout this wonderful novel. Doc looks out for his friends, as well as the poor schmucks just trying to make it day-to-day. When all is said and done, you'll love Doc, and you'll look forward to more of him in the future.

Mob fiction is dead? Really? Me thinks the rumors of its death have been greatly exaggerated. The addition of Dana King to this particular niche in the literary world is a wonderful breath of fresh air all readers of fine writing will appreciate. For me there's simply nobody writing better mob fiction in the industry today, and that includes the master, Elmore Leonard.

Dana King's *Grind Joint* does for mob fiction what prohibition did for organized crime—it provides the juice for it to flourish in a world consumed with special effects and cartoons; graphic novels and journalists turned private investigators turned vigilante killers. *Grind Joint* is a touch of reality in a world dizzy with a glitz *de jour*.

A huge hat tip to Stark House Press for recognizing Dana's writing, for putting him in print, something long overdue for someone this good. The premier publisher of classic crime novels in the industry today has gone rogue yet again, publishing another original crime novel, Dana King's *Grind Joint*, and we the readers are very grateful beneficiaries.

Listen to me: Dana King is already one of the great ones.

CHARLIE STELLA
2013

A Pronunciation Guide

Western Pennsylvania has a rich ethnic heritage that is obvious from even a quick glance at the phone listings or any high school yearbook. Many of the names are hard to pronounce to outsiders who don't come across them often. Even for those who do, Western Pennsylvania natives have developed unique accents and pronunciations that bear little resemblance to how relatives in the old country would speak.

This is not a Russian novel. Below is a key to pronouncing some of the more difficult or unusual names. Tolstoy never met his readers halfway like this.

Czarniak	ZAR-nee-ak
DeSimone	dih-SIGH-mun
DeFelice	dee-fuh-LEASE
Dolewicz	DOLE-uh-wits
Dougherty	DOCK-ur-dee
Grabek	GRAY-beck
Lucatorre	luke-a-TOR-ee
Mannarino	man-uh-REE-no
Napierkowski	napper-KOW-ski
Neuschwander	NOO-shwan-der
Wierzbicki	weerz-BICK-ee
Zywiciel	suh-WISS-ee-ul

– Dana King

GRIND JOINT
by Dana King

*There is always an easy solution to every human
problem—neat, plausible, and wrong.*
-H. L. Mencken

[1]

The building used to be a mini-mall. Penney's on one end, Monkey Ward's on the other, with a handful of little local shops in between. Nail salon, barber, wing joint, liquor store. They closed years ago, boarded up the windows. The Blockbuster in an outbuilding went tits up last summer. The toy store next door saw half a dozen re-inventions before it managed to scrape by as one of those operations where everything was five bucks or less. That and the bank were all that were left. Kenny Czarniak would have thought it ironic, how only the bank and the discount store survived amid the shells of failure, but any sense of irony had left him long ago.

He parked fifty yards from the service door in back. Room for at least a thousand cars in the lot. Construction crews didn't need ten percent of the spaces, but casino management wanted the employees to get used to parking away from the entrances so customers could have the good spaces when the doors opened next week. Pulled his gloves on with his teeth and fished the casino keys out of his jacket pocket.

Some assholes had left bags of trash by the door again. Not everyone loved the idea of a casino in town. Some thought it hilarious to pull teenage harassments like dumping garbage or a flattened road kill in front of the doors. Never bothered to think the only person they inconvenienced was Kenny, who was just like them and didn't give a shit whether Penns River had a casino or not so long as he had a place to work.

He looked down to find the key and when he looked up he saw the pile of trash was actually a bum sleeping one off. They didn't often come this far from the old business district. Too spread out here, a five mile walk to the shelter where some of them took a bus into Pittsburgh to bum quarters off shoppers. Kenny'd nudge him awake and tell him to keep moving, point him west on Leechburg Road, town's that way.

Eight feet away and Kenny noticed the guy's face had an odd color. Leaned over for a closer look and realized the discoloration was ice crystals. Then he saw the bullet holes, one over each eye, and dropped the keys grabbing the cell out of his pocket.

[2]

The call came with Ben Dougherty face-deep in Anita Robinson's well-trimmed shrubbery. He'd hit the Edgecliff on the way home last night and there she was, her kids spending the night with their father, part of his combined visitation policy and twelve-step plan. Duke Robinson never drank when his kids were around—he'd always been a good father, drunk or sober, usually drunk—so they spent random evenings with him, after which he'd stop by the City-County Building to pee in a cup. This freed Anita and her still resilient breasts for occasional evenings of passion. Doc said he'd be there in twenty minutes and ran his face through the wash cycle an extra time.

He thought the corpse looked familiar, asked his partner if he knew him. Willie Grabek hawked up a wad of phlegm. "That's Donte Broaddus. He was small time downtown when I retired. I heard he'd moved up, had a nice section of the North Side all to himself." Grabek hunched his car coat higher on his shoulders. "I wonder who he pissed off."

"Me, right now. Too cold and dark and I was in the middle of something. Hey, Noosh? What's it look like? A .22?"

Rick Neuschwander down on one knee examining a stain on the ground with a flashlight. Did double duty as a detective and crime scene tech in Penns River, getting his in-close work done before the medical examiner from Allegheny County arrived. "Probably," he said, not looking up. "No more than a .25. Autopsy should be able to say. Looks like they're still inside."

"Not that they'll do us any good," Grabek said. "Rattle around in that hard head a few times, come out looking like either gravel or shrapnel, not worth a damn."

"It doesn't matter," Doc said. "He wasn't killed here. No blood at all. Actual crime scene could be anywhere. What do you think the odds are we clear it?"

"This was very professional. We catch this guy, it's dumb luck."

"It is professional, isn't it? Small caliber weapon, body dumped away from the scene. Sounds like Mike Mannarino's crew."

Grabek wiped his nose with a thumb and index finger. "Maybe. He doesn't do much heavy work, and he doesn't shit where he eats."

"He dropped Frank Orszulak on the steps of the Bachelor's Club last year. Fucked us big time on that Widmer case."

"That was a message. Orszulak did one of his guys without permission."

Doc nodded toward the body. "Maybe this is a message, too. Think Broaddus was selling here in town?"

"Never heard of anyone selling here, not worth mentioning. Can't shake those rumors the shit comes down the river to Pittsburgh through here, but far as I know that's all we are, a pass through." Grabek spat again. "Fucking sinuses. Besides, even if Mannarino did him for some drug thing, why dump him here?"

"Showing his ass, maybe. This joint can't be doing the Hook any favors, siphoning off his gambling business."

"He's smarter than that. This dump is small time compared to the Rivers and down the Meadows."

"This one's in his home town. Insult to injury and all that." Doc stamped his feet. "Just thinking out loud, but Mannarino's the only person within a hundred miles who does this kind of hit. The body could've been dumped anywhere, or disappeared. Leaving it here, a week before opening? You have to wonder."

They watched Neuschwander work for a minute. Grabek said, "You're the primary. What do you want to do?"

Doc took a beat to answer. He liked Willie all right, though he was the laziest prick Doc had ever worked with, and he'd worked with a few. Smart, saw things everyone else missed. Also missed things everyone else saw while he was reminding you how smart he was. Retired from Pittsburgh homicide over a year ago, worked in Penns River to supplement his retirement while his daughter was in college. If "work" was the word for what he did.

"Hey, Noosh," Doc said. "Find any ID on this guy?"

Grabek said, "I told you. It's Donte Broaddus."

"I heard you. Do you know where he lives?"

Neuschwander held up a wallet. "Here. License is inside. Not much else."

"No cash?"

"In his pocket. About a hundred bucks."

"Where's he live?"

Neuschwander scanned the wallet, thought. "Looks like Homewood somewhere."

"Give Willie the address before you bag the wallet." To Grabek: "That's your old stomping grounds. Go find his people. Break the news to the family. You know what to do."

Grabek looked like he'd have something to say if he hadn't already ceded control with the "primary" comment. "I'm gonna stop for breakfast first. No one's up yet, anyway, not in Homewood."

"Whenever. I'll help Noosh put together the reports after I talk to the guard that found him."

A Lincoln Town Car floated to a stop, quiet as fog. A man got out about Grabek's age, thinner, Burberry scarf tucked into a navy pea coat. He wore round glasses and showed as much expression as the Town Car's headlights.

"Oh, Christ," Grabek said. "Look who it is."

Daniel Rollison was a private investigator from Pittsburgh. Reputed to be a retired spook, willing to do things law enforcement wouldn't. Or couldn't.

A year ago he'd worked for Tom Widmer's defense team, Widmer a numb nuts stockbroker conned into killing his wife's former lover. Two people ended up dead because of Marian Widmer. Her husband got natural life; she got the house. No one could prove what Rollison got.

He stopped between the detectives, hands in his coat pockets. "Okay, then. What do we have here?"

"What's your interest?" Grabek said.

"Chief of Security for the casino."

"No shit?"

"What do we have?"

Grabek gave Doc a "you're the primary" look. Said he'd better get a move on if he was going to beat the traffic to Homewood and walked away.

"Seems to me this is kind of a come down for a man with your reputation," Doc said.

Rollison nodded toward the corpse. "What do we have here, Dougherty? That's three times I've had to ask."

"Donte Broaddus. Medium-time drug dealer. Lived in Homewood. Worked, we think, on the North Side. Shot somewhere else with either a .22 or a .25, then dumped here."

"Suspects?"

"Even if we had any, I wouldn't be at liberty to discuss them, you being a civilian and all."

"Don't be petty. I can help you. The casino opens in less than a week. Something like this is a blemish that's easier to erase sooner rather than later. Preferably before we open."

"You want to help, help. You know anything about this?"

"I just got here."

"So did I."

They made their own little Sergio Leone staredown for a minute before Doc said, "I have work to do. Let me know if you hear anything. Maybe we can share. Remove that blemish for you." He turned to the guard, standing near the corner of the building cupping a cigarette between his hands. "Mr. Czarniak, can I have a few minutes?"

Kenny took a last, deep drag and tossed the butt. "Can we go inside and talk? I been out here over an hour and I'm freezing."

"Sure," Doc said. He angled himself to allow Kenny to reach the door without disturbing Neuschwander and the medical examiner, who'd pulled in behind Rollison.

"Uh-uh." Rollison stepped between Kenny and the door. "No one but casino employees and contractors get in until we open. Company policy. You can talk to him right here."

"This is a crime scene," Doc said. "Police business supersedes your company policy."

"The crime scene is out here. Inside is still mine."

Doc gave him a look colder than Kenny Czarniak's fingers. "Fine. Mr. Czarniak, we can talk at the station. I'll drive and we'll get you some coffee on the way."

Kenny stopped walking. "I leave here, I don't get paid. Mr. Rollison?"

"You'll get paid," Doc said before Rollison could answer. "You're on the clock as long as you're with me." He turned to face Rollison. "Casino business, right?"

Rollison shrugged and went through the door, pulled it shut.

[3]

"You sure they'll pay me?" Kenny Czarniak sat in a straight-backed chair next to Doc's desk. He held a large Sheetz coffee with both hands. "I might need a new transmission."

"If you mean 'can I legally force him to pay you?' well, no." Doc tipped his own chair back a little. "He'll pay, though. The last thing they want right now is any more bad publicity, or local police coming and going through the casino like I guarantee you we will if he jerks us around."

They drank coffee until most of the color migrated from Kenny's cheeks back to his hands. "How'd you come to be night watchman at the new casino?"

"I'm not the night watchman. I start at five so I can turn the heat and lights on and open up for the work crews."

"Who'd you piss off to get that shift?"

"It's what they had." Kenny sipped his coffee, looked into the cup. "I worked twenty-eight years over at Osteen's in Tarentum as a master machinist. Got laid off about a year-and-a-half ago."

"This the first thing you found since?"

Kenny nodded. "Enough piecework here and there to screw up the unemployment. Not enough to live on." Another sip. Sheetz coffee ruled. This batch was hot enough to melt solder. "I keep reading how Pittsburgh's recession-proof now, everybody works in education and medical and things like that. I thought about telling that to the mortgage company when that jagov senator from Kentucky killed the unemployment extension. Anyway, my boy shows me a thing in the *Post-Gazette* about these guys in their fifties who might never work again, and the next day my wife seen this ad for the casino. I thought maybe I could be a dealer. I hear they make nice money and good tips. Hell, I'd'a been happy to tend bar. This is what they had."

Not the first time Doc had heard a similar story. He wanted to feel worse for Kenny, but he knew ten guys per block in what used to be downtown with stories at least as bad. "You didn't happen to know a guy named Mike Pelczarski over at Osteen's, did you?"

"Knew him to say hello. Why do you ask?"

"No reason. Me and his boy used to play ball together. Mickey had an arm like a cannon, throw it all the way from the fence to the catcher on a line. Of course, he was just as likely to throw it over the backstop, so his value was— I don't know—dubious?"

Kenny laughed, loosened his death grip on the coffee. "I know what you mean. I played some outfield in Legion ball. I might not look like it now, but I could cover some ground."

Doc had him talking now, time to get to work. "Can I get you anything else? A doughnut, maybe? We're cops. We got them everywhere."

Kenny laughed again and sat back as far as the chair would allow. "No, thanks." He tapped his chest. "Cholesterol."

"Me, too. Look, my partner's going to be all day in Homewood. Why don't you sit in his chair? It's a lot more comfortable. It's not like you're a suspect or anything."

Kenny's knees sounded like crinkled cellophane when he stood. He sat in Willie's chair, crossed his right ankle over his left knee.

Doc said, "Tell me what you saw."

The leather creaked under Kenny's weight. "I'd just drove around the building, like I'm supposed to. Check everything out." The casters squeaked as he shifted position. Doc had enough experience to know Kenny should have walked around the building. He considered asking, chose not to risk damaging their blossoming friendship. "I thought it was trash bags when I first seen it. They do that sometimes. Those ones don't want the casino. They're like little kids on Halloween, like they won't open the joint because people play kids' tricks on them. Anyway, I get a little closer and I see it's this guy, but he don't look right."

"Not right, how?"

"Got a face like a black guy—you know, with the nose and the lips—but he's awful light. I was thinking maybe he's one of them half-and-halfs you see around all the time now until I noticed he had like frost on him made him look funny. Then I saw the bullet holes and called you guys."

"What time was that?"

"Four-fifty-seven. I know because I looked at my watch as soon as I called in case it was important."

Kenny seemed pretty pleased with himself for that detail. Doc would've liked it better if the actual time for the 911 call hadn't been 5:06. Most likely Kenny didn't want to cop to being late to work, or his watch was slow. Doc still had to account for those nine minutes.

"You see anything unusual during your drive around? Out of place at all?"

Kenny shook his head. "Nope. Nothing."

"Any cars in the lot that shouldn't have been there?"

"You know what a parking lot that size is like. There's always a car or two sitting around. You know, didn't start, or two guys left work together. I'd a been more surprised if there weren't any."

"You didn't touch the body, did you?"

"No, sir. I watch all the cops shows, you know, like CSI and Law and Order. I didn't touch anything."

"Not even to see if he was dead?"

"He had ice on him and two holes in his head. I figured I didn't need to touch him."

Fair enough. "Can I see your hands, please, Mr. Czarniak?"

"My hands? What for?"

"I just need a look at them. It's a routine thing." Kenny half extended his arms and Doc snatched both wrists, turned the hands over to see the palms and backs. Machinist's hands, strong and scarred, no fresh marks. The time on his watch was dead on.

"Understand something, Mr. Czarniak. The person who finds the body and reports it is involved something like half the time. They think they're clever, calling it in like a good citizen, but it's stupid."

"Hey, wait. Do you think—"

Doc held up a hand. "You're good. You don't have any marks on your hands like you'd get from hefting around a body in this weather, and I watched you waiting this morning. You're either innocent or a hell of an actor. I do have to ask why you lied about the time you found him."

"I didn't lie. It was 4:57 like I said. Maybe 4:58, the hand was between two marks. No later than that."

"Mr. Czarniak," Doc using his name now, making it personal, "911 calls have automatic time stamps on them. You called at 5:06."

"No, I mean it. It was 4:57. Or eight. Maybe my watch ain't... synchronized with your clock here."

"It was a minute ago. When I checked your hands."

Kenny blushed. His eyes moved down and to the right. "I was ten minutes late a couple days last week. Mr. Rollison docked me an hour each time and said he'd fire me if it happened again."

"Fuck Rollison. You're working with me on this, and I'm not telling him anything he doesn't absolutely have to know to give me what I need." Kenny perked up every time Doc put Rollison down. "Now, are you sure about the time?"

"It was a few minutes after five. Like you said."

Doc kept his eyes on Kenny's. "When you talk to me, you have to tell me the truth. No fudging. Every lie you tell forces me to question everything else you say. There's dead guy on his way to the morgue right now. Someone's going to pay for that. You don't want it to be you."

Kenny didn't say a word. Doc knew from looking at him he'd made his point. "Is there anything else you can remember?"

"No. I told you everything. Honest to God."

"All right." Doc looked at his watch. "It's a little after nine. What say I buy you something to eat and we take our time getting back to the casino. I mean, you're on the clock, right?"

[4]

They walked into Bypass Motors like any other customers, stood around the Maserati cracking wise with each other in what sounded like Russian. Bypass was Mike Mannarino's "legit" business to keep Internal Revenue off his back. Always had at least one high end car on display to draw in locals who couldn't afford it if they sold their house and their neighbor's. They'd stop to gape and the sales team would pitch them some piece of shit made affordable mainly by its lack of provenance. The six-figure rides also allowed certain people of means from out of town a more or less legitimate excuse to drop in.

Art DeSimone came over to help them and the bigger one asked to see Mr. Mannarino. Said the Maserati was a "boo-ti-ful" car and they might have some business to discuss. Art said he could sell them the 'Rati if they were interested and was told they were interested in a lot more than buying one fucking car, please to see Mr. Mannarino, you wop cocksucker.

Now the Russians sat in Mike's private office. The door was closed, calls were held. Mike got them each a drink—vodka—and asked what they wanted.

The big one said, "You kill our nigger last night. What are you think we should do about this?"

Mike knew better than to play dumb. He didn't get to be the boss of Pittsburgh, as far as Youngstown, Erie, and Wheeling, by underestimating situations. "I'm guessing you mean Donte Broaddus."

"*Da.*"

"Then I think you should finish your drinks and get lost. Anything that happened between Donte and me was our business. He worked for me."

The big one drank half of what was in his glass. "Work-ed for you before, perhaps. This one was working for us since about six weeks now. We don't like no wop cocksuckers killing our customers."

Same thing Art said they'd called him. Mike hated dealing with people who didn't speak English at least well enough to vary their insults. "Donte and I had an understanding. He broke it. I guess you're the ones he broke it with."

"It was us, yes. Now, Mr. Mike the Hook, you and us will have understanding." Mike didn't mean to, but must have flashed something at the mention of his nickname. "We know much about you, yes. You like that people call you Mike the Hook because it makes you sound tough. People not knowing think you will hang them on meat hooks or put fish hooks through their testicles. I don't know what they think. I don't care. I know you are called that because you throw baseball at people. I am not afraid of baseballs, so I will tell you what to understand now.

"First thing is one black nigger less or more is nothing. There is always another to do business with. You kill too many, get to be inconvenience, then
we kill you. One wop cocksucker less or more is no big deal, too.

"Second thing is, doesn't matter what nigger wants to be in charge. He
buys from us, no one else. You try to sell to him, try to fuck with him, you
are fucking with us, and we kill you.

"Last thing. You do not ever make any noise around Allegheny Casino.
You do one more stupid like today and we will kill you. *Poymitye?*"

Mike's slow burn started with "so I will tell you." He felt his ears redden
and kept his concentration on the big one's mouth as he talked. He didn't say
anything when the speech ended. In part because he didn't trust himself, and
because he didn't understand what he'd been asked.

The Russian got tired of waiting. "Do you understand?"

Mike forced himself to make no sign of acknowledgment. "I'm just supposed to sit back and say that's okay with me. Aren't you even going to kiss
me?"

The Russian's face clouded. "Kiss you? Why would I kiss you?"

"I like to be kissed when I'm getting fucked. Even better, I like to have
my dick sucked. We can do that part right here if you want."

The Russian took a second to process. Then he smiled. "I think I see. You
are understanding what, but not why. You are big fish here, so you feel... entitled? Yes, entitled is the word. Okay. You are used now to being big fish,
no? Well, I am shark. Shark eats what he want, when he want. Shark don't
want no trouble with big fish, but will eat him, too, if he must. Is way of
world. Now do you understand?"

They weren't here to kill him, or he'd be gone already. That didn't mean
Mike couldn't talk them into it by saying the wrong thing. He stood at his
window, watched them walk to their car. Then he made a call.

[5]

Doc, Grabek, and Neuschwander chewed doughnuts in Stush Napierkowski's office, eight o'clock in the morning. Twice a week Stush brought in two dozen fresh for anybody who wanted some. He liked for everyone to get along and his insistence on maintaining the cop "tradition" of doughnuts was a running joke. For most, an affectionate one.

Neuschwander went first. "Victim is a twenty-two-year-old black male named Donte Broaddus. Address on his license is 630 North St. Clair Street in Homewood. Shot twice in the forehead with a small caliber handgun at close range, no more than three feet. Bullets are still in his head, so we'll know more when we get the coroner's report."

"Did they say how long?" Stush said.

"He said he'd try for this afternoon, but couldn't promise it. Tomorrow at the latest." An undercurrent of grumbling. Everyone in the room knew these reports took time, though they were instantaneous compared to getting DNA results. Still, the cop never drew breath that didn't think his case was more important than everything else, including presidential assassination.

Neuschwander went on. "As we suspected, he was shot elsewhere and dropped at the casino. It's an asphalt parking lot with a lot of foot and car traffic, so no tire tracks or footprints stand out. No blood or obvious fibers, except those from the victim. He wasn't assaulted or robbed that we can see, though I suppose it's possible he had more than the hundred bucks we found on him and the killer left it to throw us off." He closed his notebook. "That's all."

"Any idea when he was killed?" Stush said.

"Not unless we can trace his whereabouts before he died, maybe see where he ate. Coroner might be able to tell something from that. He was freezing— literally—when we picked him up. I'll try to extrapolate something from the body temperature at the scene and the ambient temperatures, but without knowing how long he was there... I don't think so. Too many variables."

"Thanks, Rickie. That's good work." No Penns River cop ever did bad work in Stush's eyes. There was good work, and there were disappointments. To most of his cops, disappointing him was like disappointing a favorite uncle. "Let us know when you hear from the coroner and if anything else shakes loose. Willie, what'd you find in Homewood?"

"Dick." Willie Grabek didn't have any favorite uncles. He knew too much to worry about favorites, and what he knew best was that he was the smartest guy in any room he walked into. "There's a 628 North St. Clair, and a 632, but no 630. I asked around some guys I know in Homewood, Point Breeze, Wilkinsburg, the usual places. No one had a fixed address for him, but he was definitely selling H on the North Side. Some coke, too, but heroin was his gig."

"I didn't think there was that much heroin sold in Pittsburgh," Doc said.

"It's not like Baltimore, but if you bought any north of the river, Donte had a piece of it."

"Someone making a move on him?" Stush said.

"Doesn't look like it. What I heard yesterday was business as usual. Same hoppers on the same corners, no disruptions. No one knew of any troubles down there, and the gang squad says things have been peaceful."

"So, nothing," Stush said.

"Maybe not quite nothing. There was one rumor. No one would stand by it, but I heard it a couple places. You know how we thought for a while now the jigs in Pittsburgh got the stuff from Mike Mannarino? Well, word is Donte and Mike the Hook had a parting of the ways. No one will say anything for sure, but it's possible—just possible, mind you—Donte was either going to switch, or had already switched suppliers."

"That would take quite a chunk out of Mannarino's income," Doc said.

"If it's true," Stush said.

"It makes sense," Grabek said. "We know the homies will shoot each other up for any reason down there. Talk to the wrong girl, wear the wrong color white tee shirt, doesn't matter. What they don't do is use small caliber weapons and transport bodies. These yos *want* people to know who they did. Some homeboy shot Broaddus, he'd have at least a nine millimeter hole in his head and would've been left where he fell. This is too professional. White guys did this."

Everyone sat for a minute looking away from each other. Stush asked Doc if he had anything to add.

"I talked to the watchman. All he did was find the body and call it in. Rest of the day I canvassed the houses that back up to the parking lot and wrote reports. No one saw or heard anything out of the ordinary."

"I didn't expect they would," Stush said. "They shot him wherever, so they could drop him off anytime they wanted. No rush, no commotion."

"Do we know what Broaddus drove?" Doc said. "We need to recreate his last day. Finding his car would make it a lot easier."

Neuschwander flipped some papers. "Nissan Maxima. Black. PA license O-G-R-I-D-E."

"Og ride?" Stush said.

"O.G. ride," Grabek said. "Original gangsta. O.G."

"Okay," Stush said. "What now?"

Doc re-established himself as primary before Grabek could speak. "Find the car. Willie, you know that area. You have the contacts. See what you can piece together about Broaddus's last day."

"What are you going to do?"

"I'll think of something."

Stush dismissed everyone but Doc. "I know you say you're okay working with Grabek, but I have to ask. He ever do anything makes you wonder about him?"

"In what way?"

Stush played with a pen on his desk. "The way he talks sometimes. You ever see him do anything made you think he has a problem with blacks?"

Doc sat. "It's hard to say. I mean, I've seen him come down on some, but now that I think about it, they're always suspects, and he comes down on white suspects, too. I was thinking for a second he's a little brusque with them once in a while, but he's like that with everybody once in a while. I can't honestly say he's worse with blacks than with anyone else. Of course, there's not a lot of opportunity, either."

There wasn't a lot of opportunity, not in Penns River. Seven percent of the population was black; less than one percent—combined—were Asian, Hispanic, or Other. The only American Indian anyone knew of in town was a cop, Lester Goodfoot, who liked working third shift because he claimed his heritage gave him better night vision than any criminal, though everyone knew he liked graveyard because no one minded if he grabbed a nap, so long as he responded when needed. Lester also claimed he could track a man across concrete and through the river. His primary endeavor was busting balls, reminding everyone he was the only Indian in town, how someday he'd scalp Eye Chart Zywiciel for calling him a godless heathen when he lost at poker.

"If you say so," Stush said. "You heard him just now."

"He's like that sometimes. I've never seen him do anything extreme, though. I try to go by what people do, not what they say."

"No, no, you're right. Willie's about my age. When we grew up, you still heard people call them niggers and coloreds. Not to their faces, of course, but I never had the feeling people meant anything by it. Some did, sure, but things were different then. You'd call a guy with a bum leg a gimp. Now you can't even say he's crippled."

"I'll pay attention if you want. I'm curious why it's bothering you now."

"The way he was talking. He sounds like he might just be going through the motions. I don't want him taking this case less seriously because it was some black kid got shot. He's already focusing on Mannarino, and we don't have a lot to go on yet."

"Willie's always been like that. Grabs a hold of a logical connection early and runs with it. He'll turn on a dime if something changes his mind and deny he ever thought the other way. Since you bring it up, you have any reason to think Mannarino didn't do it? Far as I can see, Willie's on the right track."

"No argument. I just don't want him—any of us—to get so locked on we overlook anything else. I hope it's not him. Mannarino, I mean. We'll never close it if he had it done, and we need to close this one. The quicker the better."

"Casino people on you again?"

"Not them directly, but they got people all over town ready to carry their water. All day yesterday I heard about what a big deal this is for the town, bring in money, bring in jobs. Christ, it'll bring in more sunny weather to listen to some of them talk about it. Maybe it will. Hell, anything that brings in the kind of money that follows a casino has to be good, doesn't it? The way things have been?" He blew his nose into a white handkerchief and inspected it. "You know what handkerchiefs are for, don't you?"

Doc knew, let Stush tell him. "A handkerchief is so you can carry something in your pocket you didn't want in your nose." Stush folded the handkerchief, put it away. "We can't let that change how we do the job. We need the guilty party, not the guy who looks best in the perp walk."

"You catching hell again?" Last year's double murders put Stush through the wringer. The deputy chief had been angling for the chief's job since the day he was hired.

"No more than usual." Stush folded his hands across his belly. The thread holding his lower shirt buttons stretched like a bow string. He took a deep breath, blew it out with puffed cheeks. "I'm sixty-two years old, Benny. Three more and I can collect my pension with a clear conscience. Two members of the council are ready to buy me out now. They get one more and I'm gone. Jack Harriger comes in here with dirty knees and a brown nose twice a week to size up my chair. I'm too old for this shit, but I'm a stubborn old Polack and I want going out to be my idea. This Hecker guy, owns the casino, he draws too much water. He doesn't get what he asks for and I'll be spending my days spreading mulch around Helen's trees. Is that what you want for your Uncle Stush? Make me a landscaper's assistant like some fucking Guatemalan rode up through Mexico hanging onto the bottom of a vegetable truck?"

Doc couldn't help laughing. "Okay, okay, I'll do my best. One thing, though. If it is Mannarino, I'm not sure we can touch him. His people do good work and he still has some juice of his own."

Stush's smile faded, but didn't die altogether. "I know."

"That might not be all bad. If Mannarino has a hard-on for the casino, and Hecker gets the wood for him because of it, then some of the people who think they run this town are going to have to make hard decisions."

"If it gets to be a pissing contest between Hecker and Mannarino, the best thing we can do is to keep our heads down until it sorts itself out. At least that kind of a fight shouldn't be a law enforcement problem."

Doc stood and zipped his windbreaker. "Let's hope not."

[6]

Tookie Harris knew he looked good. There was a time for hoodies and Tim-berlands, white tees and baggy jeans. Five-O come by, everybody fade away, all looking alike. Witness says, "It was a black kid with a white tee shirt and jeans, boots and one of those hood things over his head." Cop closes his note-book and says, "Thank you sir, we'll see you again soon." Other times you needed to come tight and represent. Like today, for his cousin Donte's view-ing.

His aunt Latonya up by the coffin, crying and screaming about how could this happen to her baby. How he didn't deserve this, these drugs were a plague, just like the locusts and such in the Bible. Like she had no idea Donte didn't pay for the CTS she rolled up in out of what he made at the drive-through window at Mickey D's, you want fries with that, motherfucker?

Coming to Pittsburgh was cool when he was a shorty. Aunt Latonya and Donte brought Tookie and his brother Eldon to the zoo and this place where they had model trains running, must've been twenty of them on a platform big as a house. Now he was a man in the life, and Pittsburgh minor league com-pared to where he cribbed in Baltimore. The women not dressed as sharp, not as many flowers, and they all just flowers. Maybe say "Son," or "Peace," or whatever. In B'more a man like Donte go down, you'd know he was some-body. The women looking fine and none of this pansy-posey flower bullshit. Maybe the straight ghetto relatives send some, but mostly it be floral arrange-ments, horseshoes and elaborate designs and shit. Here Donte just one more homeboy took out over drugs. Tookie couldn't wait to get back.

First, he had business. Killing his boy Donte wasn't right, no way, and Tookie had to look into that before he went home. Someone might have to feel some pain, and bringing pain was how he paid for his black E350 parked out front. He didn't know who to approach and didn't have to. Just stand where everyone can see. Anyone couldn't figure who he was didn't need to talk to him.

It took about an hour. Boy sidled up to him like Tookie might bite a piece out of his arm. "You Tookie? Donte's cuz?"

"Who're you?"

"My name's Nelson."

"You got a last name, Nelson? And it better not be Mandela or I'll take you outside and whip the black off your ass for playing."

Nelson believed him. "Butterfield. People call me Nelse."

"How you know me?"

"Donte point you out one time you up here visiting. Said you a player in B'more and to keep my distance unless I need something heavy done."

"And do you need something heavy done?" Nelson looked like heavy was a relative term to him, like maybe taking a dog bigger than a cocker spaniel out to piss might qualify.

"I-I don't know. I mean, what happened to Donte, that shit ain't right, you know?"

"You sure about that?"

"What you mean?"

"I mean like, you saying what happened to him ain't right, but saying it like a question? You know, like that? Like you ain't sure if shooting my boy in the head right or not."

Sweat beaded on Nelson's upper lip and forehead. He wiped his palms on his suit pants. "No no no, it ain't like that. Whoever done this all the way wrong. I'm just saying, I don't know what to do about it, how heavy to get."

Tookie already thought the heaviest thing about Nelson was the load he was about to drop in his pants. "You do any work with Donte?"

That perked Nelson up. "Absolutely. Donte and me was starting to do some serious weight together."

"So now you're looking to take over?" Tookie knew how much Donte moved. If Nelson thought that was serious weight, Pittsburgh was even more bush league than he'd suspected. No higher than AA.

"Well, I mean, you know, I guess I'd be the reasonable choice, working as close as we did. Thing is, after this, I don't know how deep I want to get. I mean, this some serious shit. I'm looking to make some money, yo, not get my ass killed."

Tookie's disappointment grew every time this sorry-assed excuse for a nigger opened his mouth. "What're you saying, then? You want me to take out the competition so's you can maybe move someplace like Monte fucking Carlo and run things from afar, be a international drug kingpin?"

"No, no, not like that! What I mean is, don't matter what I do here, some-one be after my ass."

"You don't get to the fucking point soon, it'll be me."

"Okay, I'm sorry. Really. Here's how it is. For a long time, Donte got his shipment from some dagoes up the river, bringing it in through this little cracker town called Penns River. I don't know how they was getting it in, but there's no police there worth bothering about, so the exchanges were a lot easier."

Tookie knew this already. He didn't know why it was such a big deal; it wasn't like Donte unloaded freight cars of the shit. The connect might have reasons of his own. No matter now. "So what happened?"

"'Bout a year, year-and-a-half ago, Donte had some issues with the man up there, some greaser name of Mike the Hook." Tookie knew this, too, and let it show. "Donte got the red ass, you know, and went looking for a new sup-ply." Tookie was losing patience. "Took him some time, but he found one."

This was news. Donte had come to Baltimore to see Tookie and ask if his boss would be interested in providing a package, took it hard when Tookie's man passed. Tookie figured Donte would either come back his way or smooth things over with Mike Mannarino. This was the first he'd heard of another possibility. "Who'd he get?"

"Some Russian. Name's Volkov or something. Scary motherfucker."

"He the one did Donte?"

"See? That's my problem. I don't know. I don't think so, but them Russians, they crazy. Donte say the wrong thing, they might do him for sport."

"What about this Mike the Hook? You don't think he got the ass because Donte switched over?"

"There. Now you getting it." Nelson talking faster, still scared but exited, too, seeing Tookie following his train of thought. "That's who I think done it. He had reason. What's to keep him from doing me, too, if I step up? And I can't switch back, or the Russians will feed me to their pet snakes or some shit."

Tookie didn't say anything. It made sense for Mike the Hook to want Donte dead; not so much the Russians. Still....

"Donte give this Russian cause to want him capped? Piss him off?" Then, realizing Nelson wouldn't likely know, "How was business? Everything cool?"

"Most def. The Russian's price better than the dago's, and the shit was good. He didn't make us jump through no hoops, neither, picking the shit up. Just come to the meet with money and leave with dope. No more running way the fuck out in the boonies to make some blind drops."

Tookie had been thinking again. Nelson retrieved his full attention with "blind drop." "Whoa. Back up. What you mean, 'blind drops?' You saying this Hook motherfucker leave the package somewhere alone, then trusts you to pick it up and leave the money? I know you don't leave the money and hope the dope just show up like no manners from heaven."

"No, not like that. Not like blind blind drops. See, he leave the package where hardly no one goes, but you could see from a distance, dig? Like a parking lot or a park. Not so much a park, 'cause if people not going by there at all, even them cracker police notice something up, people sitting in cars all waiting and shit. Be like late after a movie, or this place they got, used to be a shopping center, now it ain't shit, just empty buildings by the bridge. The Hook's people leave the package in like some camouflage, then lay back. They close enough to see and fuck anybody up who takes it by mistake, but not so close they connected with it. You feel me?"

Tookie gestured for him to go on. "We come by, we don't see them, but we know they see us, because they someplace where they can see everything they need to. We drive by so they know we around, then we wait for a call."

"What's he do, call you on a goddamn cell phone and say 'go pick up your drugs. Don't forget to leave my money?'"

"No no no no no. See, we both have burners. This be the only time we ever use them. He—or his boy, prolly—calls and says 'okay' or some such shit and we roll over and make the switch."

"How's he know the number?"

"We leave it with the money the time before. He leaves us his number with the package, case something come up."

"He's not afraid you'll rip him off, leave him a bag of newspapers?"

"Naw, man, he has another car there to follow us away. They get the call the cash not right, we be two dead motherfuckers."

"You ever see the car follow you?"

Nelson had to think. "Yeah, sure, I seen it. Had to be there, right? He wouldn't just trust us with all that dope. No one that stupid."

Well, maybe not *no* one. "Okay, Nelson, follow me. You say business was good with the Russians, and this Hook character had cause to be pissed with Donte. Right?"

Nelson nodded and Tookie continued. "So the Russians have no rea-son—that you know of—to do Donte like this." He nodded toward the cas-ket.

"Like I said, not that I know."

"Now these Russians crazy motherfuckers, right? Not like the Eye-talians at all. Russians do someone, they be all into indulging their darker impulses and shit."

"Absolutely."

"Okay. Had to be the Hook. See, these Mafia motherfuckers, they want you dead and it's nothing personal, like you ratted on them or fucked their daughter or something, they just put two in your head, like Donte has. Rus-sians, they fuck you up, leave you around in pieces and shit." He paused to think if he forgot anything. "No. Had to be the Hook."

"What you want to do?"

"Me? If it's nice tomorrow, I'm going to the zoo. You're going to get me a meet with this Mike the Hook. Tell him Donte made a big mistake and we want to do right by him. You think you can handle that?"

"What about the Russians?"

"You just get the meet set. Let me worry about all that periphial shit."

[7]

"Hey! Benny! Benny Dougherty! Wait up!"

Three people could call Doc Benny and not piss him off: his mother, his father, and Stush Napierkowski. This didn't sound like any of them. He looked around the parking lot, almost to Community Market from PNC Bank, saw who was waving, and replied with the one name Doc knew this person disliked as much as Doc hated Benny.

"Nico!"

Doc held his ground and let Nick Forte come to him. Home field advantage and all. Nick put up a hand to stop a car and jogged over. They looked enough alike to be brothers and each had a brother he resembled not at all. They hugged like cousins who hadn't seen each other in years, which was what they were.

Nick asked first. "Jesus Christ, how long's it been?"

Doc stepped back to check his cousin out, the lopsided smile stuck on his face. "I don't know. Three years? Four? How old's Caroline?"

"She was twelve last month."

"Twelve? Shit, it's been five years? I remember you brought her around to see my parents and the old man gave her a dollar for every year old she was. Made a big deal about how it cost him seven bucks. How's she doing? You bring her with you?"

Nick shook his head. "Not this time. School. Things are slow at work and my mother's having surgery, so I decided to come home for a week."

"What's up with—this is stupid. You have time for a beer?"

"I do, yeah. Aren't you on duty?"

Doc checked his watch. "I won't be by the time we get to the Legion." He nodded toward a building across the street.

"If you don't mind, how about if we went to your aunt's old restaurant? I haven't been there since—shit, probably since we were in high school."

"We can, but it's not the same since she sold it. New owners wanted to keep her name on it and she said no. It cost her money, but she's glad. It's not the same at all."

"I'm not hungry. I thought just for a beer."

"You'll still be disappointed. Seemed like a cool place when we were kids and she owned it. Now we're grown and she's gone and you'll see it for the dump it probably always was."

"I'm a dump kind of guy. Let's go."

Doc knew Nick realized his mistake before they sat down. Tried to hide it as they ordered two drafts from a bartender who was still messing his diapers when they used to hang here.

"This place seemed huge to me." Nick nodded toward the doorway. "I had to duck my head to get in."

"You didn't have anything nice to compare it to then."

Nick tasted his beer, made a face. "What *is* this?" Leaned over to read the taps. "Iron City. It figures. IC Lite's not bad, but they really ought to clean the high-test vats once in a while. Fermenting yeast is one thing, but this tastes like a hypodermic full could cure clap."

Doc laughed. No one he knew expressed himself quite like his cousin Nick. A bit lurked behind every conversation.

"How's business?" Doc said.

"The usual sex, thugs, and rock and roll for a big-time Chicago PI. Caroline stays over one evening a week and every other weekend. Lots of background checks and following insurance cheats. It pays, but the glamour's gone. I can't remember the last time I busted a head or paid a maid for a cum-stained hotel sheet." Sipped his beer and stared at the glass as if he'd expected this taste to be better. "I should've stayed a cop. At least there'd be a pension. Work in a small enough town and I could be on national TV."

Here it came. Last year's Widmer case made national news, *Dateline*, *20/20*, *48 Hours*, and two or three true crime cable shows. A book had been in the works, but the failure of Penns River to get a conviction left open the threat of multi-million lawsuits that had publishers quivering in their brie.

"That Widmer woman really that good looking, or did they work their TV magic?"

"I'll run you by, you want to meet her. I tell her you're an investigator, she'll even put on a show for you. Excuse herself to go to the bathroom, come back wearing a man's shirt with no bra and jeans no one within fifteen years of her should wear, but she manages to get away with."

"Gee, Ben, you're not bitter, are you?" "Ben" was okay. For family. He preferred Doc, but it seemed stupid to make family call him by his surname.

"Me? Bitter? Never. I'll tell you one thing, though. She had two people killed and never chipped a nail. Now she thinks she got away with it. I still open the file, show the pictures around. However long it takes, I swear to Christ I'll get that cunt." A word Doc *never* used.

Nick looked like he might continue, took a drink. "So, you still Penns River's most eligible bachelor?"

"Did my mother send you?"

"Is there no subject you're not touchy about? I ask about work and I get misogynistic rants. I ask about your personal life and I get my head bit off. Do you think the Pens will go deep in the playoffs, or is that off-limits, too?"

"If it'll make you happy, I'm sort of between relationships now." Getting together three times in two years didn't even qualify Anita Robinson as a fuck buddy. More like two ships that pass in the night, but operate in the same shipping lanes. "What about you?"

"Same. I tell my father the women of Chicago have banded together to ensure I never get a sexually transmitted disease." The bartender came by. Nick
asked what was available in bottles and ordered another draft. "What's up
with this casino bullshit? Are they serious?"

"Oh, yeah. Not only will it make the owners rich, everyone in town is going to get well. Be the new Atlantic City."

"AC's a dump."

"Then we have a head start."

Nick thanked the bartender for his fresh beer. "Seriously. That casino in
Pittsburgh is supposed to be really nice."

"You ever hear of a casino that wasn't supposed to be really nice?"

"Point taken, but it's no grind joint, not with the kind of money they put
into it and who's behind it. I drove by this place yesterday. It looks like an
old Sears."

"Uh-uh. Monkey Ward's and Penney's."

"Even better. I'm not knocking Sears. I buy a lot of stuff there. It's not
my first choice of venue for an upscale entertainment experience."

"That's where your big city uppity-ness loses touch with the real world.
They're not looking for an upscale experience. This is a grind joint, pure and
simple."

"A casino for the working man."

Doc flashed to Kenny Czarniak, getting up at four AM to turn on the heat
for people who actually did things. "Just what the working man needs."

[8]

Daniel Rollison wasn't sure he hadn't made a mistake, giving up his investigations business to run security for Allegheny Casino. The job was a constant irritant. Someone always had a problem and the help was unreliable. The next time Kenny Czarniak came in late would be the last. He always had things ready for the work crews at 6:00, but Czarniak's job wasn't just to get things ready; he was to be here at five. Not 5:05. Five. Double-digit unemployment in this town, and the people who were working couldn't be bothered to show up on time.

Then there was George Grayson. Daniel Hecker's name was on the casino's paperwork, as it was with half of Penns River. Rollison knew all about Hecker, how he started as a real estate hustler, then confused timing with genius because he made a fortune in the boom and got out before the bubble burst. He'd spent the past few years bottom feeding, grabbing distressed properties cheap, a foreclosure agent's wet dream.

Now Hecker transcended his humble speculator origins. He was a tycoon, which meant he had people who dealt with people like Rollison. In Hecker's world, there were two kinds of employees: revenue producing and overhead. Overhead was a necessary evil, keeping the lights on so the people he paid to take the bettors' money could see to count it. Rollison was there to ensure no one stole it. Catering kept the suckers from considering going elsewhere for a meal as well as well-lubricated for as long as they stayed. Anyone who didn't actually receive cash from a customer was overhead, and overhead was to be squeezed relentlessly.

Enter George Grayson.

Grayson reminded Rollison of Francis Wolcott, George Hearst's right hand on the *Deadwood* TV show. No observable conscience, probably a sociopath, at least his tastes didn't run to violence, not as far as Rollison knew. What Grayson did was expand the definition of overhead and squeeze it so hard Rollison thought the next step would be to abandon all pretense, hit the chumps over the head, take their money, and dump them in the river. But that would be wrong.

Grayson stood in Rollison's office—he never sat—demanding to know what was being done to minimize the damage caused by the dead body found at the door.

"It's a police matter. I asked for twenty-four hour guards. You refused. I'm not sure what else you want me to do."

"You know what something like that does to our image."

"I do security, not PR. I make sure no one gets hurt on the grounds, and that all the money gets to where it's supposed to go. I have no control over people who are killed elsewhere and dropped here. Not unless you want to provide coverage twenty-four by seven."

"Mr. Rollison. You were hired because we were assured you were a capable man." Grayson left time for that to sink in. Rollison didn't get mad, filed the insult away to recall when it suited him. "Have you done anything at all since this happened? Anything productive, I mean."

"I debriefed the guard who found the body after the police were through with him."

"And?"

"He found a body and called it in. That's all he knows."

"How long was he gone?"

"They brought him back in time to punch out. I had to pay overtime to talk to him while his memory was still fresh."

"What could they have asked him that took so long?"

"The detective in charge and I have history. He was sticking it to me."

"What's his name?"

"Dougherty."

"Is Detective Dougherty going to be a problem?"

"How do you mean?"

"Well, if he dragged his feet the way you described, do you think he'll let the investigation linger? We want it off the front pages."

"Dougherty's a good cop who doesn't like me. He'll run a competent investigation and do what he can to irritate me if he gets a chance. I don't think he'd let it interfere with the case."

Grayson paced with abrupt changes of direction and disconnected hand gestures. "What do you know about their investigation?"

"What I told you. I could guess and say Mike Mannarino had it done, if I felt like guessing."

"Who's Mannarino?"

"He's the boss of what's left of the Italian Mafia in Pittsburgh. We're about to take a bite out of his gambling income. He might have been showing his ass."

"Why kill the drug dealer?"

"Rumor is Mannarino was the supplier for this Broaddus character. Something could have gone wrong. Like I said, I'm guessing."

Grayson continued to pace. He gave Rollison the impression he had more to say but wouldn't. Rollison was neither disappointed nor angered. "How sure are you it was Mannarino?"

"I told you, not sure at all. His name naturally comes up in a situation like this."

"Can you find out?"

"Possibly. I have a source inside the police."

"Do that. Then see what you can do to aid the investigation. If they're looking at Mannarino, give them something to look at. We want the casino to be seen as a good citizen, though we can't appear to be self-serving about it. Can you handle that?"

"I think I'm capable."

[9]

Earl's was nicer than Doc's aunt's old place only because the room was bigger, the ceilings were higher, and Earl had accepted the twenty-first century. Three high-definition televisions hung from the walls, the sixty-incher placed in Earl's most comfortable line of sight. Doc ordered a beer and a dozen wings and asked Jefferson West what he'd been up to.

"I'm retired, Detective. I'm not up to nothing."

"Right. And I'm Elliott Ness."

"A pleasure, Mr. Ness. I've heard a lot about you."

"Ball breaker." West did a thing with his lips and eyes that passed for laughter. They had met during Doc's infamous Widmer case, when they sheltered two homeless boys under the radar of Family Services. It went bad—such arrangements always do—and the kids were pulled out absent ceremony. It was a testimony to Jeff West's integrity that they were allowed to return to him after a suitable background search. Now they lived with their mother for as long as she could stay out of jail or rehab. Doc and West got together at Earl's once a month to eat chicken wings and trade Army stories. West retired Vietnam-era; Doc did nine years, including two tours in Iraq.

Doc picked up a wing, dropped it back into the basket, flapping his fingers. "Hot. Damn. You see the boys lately, Mr. West?"

"They come by most weeks for dinner. Thursday, usually. I think their mama has meetings Thursday nights. They both fine. Wilver about grown now."

"They staying out of trouble?"

"Far as I know, and I think I'd know. Neither of them's a good enough liar to look me in the eye and fool me. Wilver talked about wanting to be a vet. I hope to hell he meant veterinarian."

"Why a vet?" The wing now cool enough to eat. Doc took a bite, talked as he chewed. "It's a good profession and I'm proud of him if that's what he wants to do, but I'd bet no one ever grew up in the Allegheny Estates and became a vet. Medical doctor, maybe. Lawyer, well, smart kid would see that as a recession-proof industry where they grew up. But a vet?"

"Maybe that's why." West blew on a wing. The calluses on his fingers didn't seem bothered by the heat. "He wants something completely different from what he's seen here. He's heard us talking, knows we're Army, maybe he did mean our kind of vet. Be a way out for him."

Doc didn't mention that neither he nor West had used their military service as a way out. Both had come back to the town they grew up in, even after years away. Their choice. Neither had lacked options.

"What about David?" Wilver's younger brother.

"David's still at the age he wants to be LeBron James on the days he's not Dwayne Wade."

Doc grunted. "They're not even Pittsburgh guys. Couldn't he want to be James Harrison? Andrew McCutchen, maybe?" Doc's loyalty to the Pirates was undaunted, eighteen losing seasons and counting.

"Look around next time you're over my way. See a lot of room for ball fields? You grew up in the country and had room for baseball and football. These boys play a lot of basketball, and I mean a *lot* of basketball. Wilver says David can ball, too, and I don't think it's just brother talk."

"Well, I hope he's not good enough to hold the dream for an unreasonable amount of time. Good enough to have some fun, go to college and actually get an education, not drop out and become another goddamn playground legend."

They drank their beers, dividing attention between hockey, basketball, and baseball on the televisions. West bought a round. Doc bought a round. Tossed words around casually as bowling balls. West referred to Doc as Detective; Doc replied to Mr. West. West knew things about Doc his parents didn't and Doc knew things about West his sons didn't care about. The "In Case of Emergency" card in Jefferson West's wallet had Benjamin Dougherty's name and cell on it. And it was still "Mr. West" and "Detective."

Doc covered his glass with a coaster and West said, "One more." Doc removed the coaster and waited for what West had to say.

"You remember telling me about that guy who ran organized crime around here? Mannarillo? Marratino?"

"Mannarino," Doc said. "I remember. What about him?"

"He still around?"

"Yeah, he's around. Why do you ask?"

West tasted his beer. "You told me the only benefit to having the Godfather living here in town was how he kept the crime down. Never let anyone shit where he ate."

"Right." No point pushing West any more. He'd say what was on his mind when he was ready.

West tried more beer. Liked it so much he drank again before putting the glass down. "I think they're selling drugs in the Estates." Allegheny Estates was built to be affordable working-class housing, close to the mill. Now it was Penns River's version of a ghetto.

Doc's glass paused halfway to his lips. He took his swallow and set the glass down before he said, "Have you seen it yourself?"

"I think so. Mind, they still kind of shy about it. It's not like *The Wire*, hollering out brand names on the corner. Everything on the down low, but the signs are there. I maybe can't see to read without glasses, but I can see from my stoop to that parking lot by the tracks clear as a bell. I walked down that way a couple times and they scattered."

"Don't do that anymore." Doc said it faster than he meant to. "If they are selling, you don't want to walk up on them at the wrong time."

"These aren't hard cases. I think they're just boys playing at drug dealer like we used to play cops and robbers or cowboys and Indians."

"You're probably right, but you never know who's looking to make a reputation, or who decides you might be about to put him in for a felony. Call us next time you see anything. You want, I'll hook you up for a ride along. Now that you got me thinking about it, I wouldn't mind an evening in a squad car. 'Interfacing with the citizenry,' I think they called it."

West did his visual laugh thing. Doc finished his beer, made sure West saw him put the coaster on his glass. West nodded. Doc stood and zippered his windbreaker.

"Mr. West."

"Detective."

[10]

Pot roast. Mashed potatoes. Peas in creamy white sauce. Tossed salad. Homemade Syrian bread. Ellen Dougherty still cooked as though she had two large and growing boys at home. Now it was just her and Tom, Doc on Sundays. The leftovers would feed him for half the week and keep him on the treadmill the other half.

Tom Dougherty had been Doc for as long as anyone alive had known him. One day a high-school-aged Ben stopped into the Legion for a ride home and someone noticed the resemblance. Father and son almost exactly the same size then, Ben a dead ringer for his father at that age. Thus was born Little Doc, so Tom had to be Big Doc. Ben's peers called him Doc now, but his father's friends stuck with Big and Little, though Little Doc had three inches and thirty pounds on his father.

They sat watching the news while Ellen finished the dishes. They'd offered to help, like they always did. She scooted them into the living room, like she always did. It was as much a part of the routine as an eastern sunrise.

"Pretty big meal for a weeknight," Doc said when they were situated.

"We're going up to Saxonburg for that farm tour on Sunday."

"So she makes a roast on Tuesday?"

"For your leftovers. She doesn't want you to starve."

"You're shitting me." Tom looked away from the television for the first time, until he caught Ben's eye. "Okay, you're not shitting me. I can cook, you know. It's not like I live on frozen dinners when I don't have leftovers."

"I know. Tell her."

"I have."

"Make any difference?"

A bank robbery in Point Breeze nets $5,000. Shots fired in the Hill District leave one dead and one man clinging to life at UPMC Presbyterian Hospital. WQED wins a grant from the MacArthur Foundation.

Next commercial, Tom said, "I hear your cousin Nick's in town. How's he doing?"

"Seems fine. We had a beer in Mary's old place the other day."

"Lordy, I haven't been in there since she sold it."

"You're not missing anything."

They watched a Geico ad in silence. Tom said, "I wonder about him sometimes."

"Who? Nick?"

"Yeah. His little boy getting killed like he did. What was he? Five?"

"That was a long time ago. He seems okay."

"I hope so. Talked to his dad last week. He say's Nick's different now. He notices it more every time they see him."

"How often's that? Everyone changes, but you see someone every day, it's not as noticeable."

"I guess. Maybe I'll have the three of them over. We'll shoot some pool and your mother can watch old movies with Shirley."

"I thought Shirley was sick. Nick says he's home for her operation."

"I'll call over, anyway. See how she's doing. If she's in the hospital, maybe Bill and Nick will want to come. I know you can cook—so you say—but Bill sure as hell can't."

New trees on the river walk outside PNC Park. Two-alarm fire in Sewickley leaves two families homeless. Accident in North Versailles has residents angry over a dangerous corner they've been asking the town to do something about for years.

A march for prostate cancer awareness didn't interest Tom, who'd been without his for three years. "How's your Uncle Stush?"

"How come you ask about Stush just as this prostate cancer thing comes on? You know something I don't?"

"Don't you know your Uncle Stush is the biggest asshole around?" Ball busting *in absentia* was reasonable behavior in the Dougherty family. No disrespect intended. "No, really. How is he? I haven't heard about anything wrong with him. I'm wondering more about how things are at work."

"The casino isn't doing him any favors, then this murder comes in. He's catching it from both sides."

"You guys need to solve that case. The quicker the better."

Doc digested that, turned toward his father. "What have you heard?"

"You know, I'm not part of the in crowd up there," meaning the City-County Building, "not a lowly member of the Zoning Board like me, but I go in for meetings and do a little research on laws and policies and legitimate exceptions. I hear things. You know how it is. If you're not one of the politicals, it's like talking in front of the hired help. Who cares what they hear?"

"So what do you hear?"

"They want Stush out bad. Funny thing is, from what I can gather, they wanted him out before because they didn't think he was up to the job, not the way the town's changed. Now they want him out because they can't walk all over him. He had a fighting chance before. You and the rest of the cops did well enough to cover him. Now that might work against him."

"Jack Harriger's been trying to get that job since he got here. Stush can hold him off."

"That worked so long as it was just Harriger and a couple of council members he palled around with. Now I hear Harriger is sucking around Danny Hecker. Hecker decides Stush has to go, he's gone."

Jeopardy started. The returning champion had $35,300. Doc said, "Why does Hecker care about Stush?"

"I don't think he cares half as much about Stush as he cares about doing what he wants. There's not a meeting goes by one of his people isn't in front of us asking for an exception for a home or a business. New construction, easements, you name it. He doesn't get it, council passes a new ordinance their next meeting, or the one after. Town don't look much different, but he owns half the businesses on Leechburg Road, leases them back to the old owners. They kiss his ass because they think he singlehandedly kept the town from going under. Wait till prices come back up and he can make some money off the real estate."

"That doesn't tell me why he wants rid of Stush."

"Because Stush is a hard-headed old Polack who doesn't do a whole lot sometimes, but no one can tell him how to do it when he does. I think they already tried to buy him out once and he told them to go shit in their hats. Maybe he can sandbag them until he's sixty-five, but then he's gone, no matter what. Mandatory retirement for all non-elected city employees."

Three more years. "I guess I better start thinking about what I want to do. I sure don't want to work for Jack Harriger."

"Then you might want to work on your resume. Couple years ago, you had a chance for Stush to hand the job off to you, what with your Army and other experience. Now they want someone who'll do as he's told, and you're not him. At least I hope not. You never did what I told you. I'd hate to see you start now, for strangers."

[11]

Allegheny Casino opened at ten; the parking lot started filling at nine. Cops directed traffic at each of the three entrances. Leechburg Road backed up eastbound all the way to the City-County Building, cars with nowhere to go because the lot was full, overflowing nearby businesses' lots and residential streets. At ten in the morning.

Rollison called at 9:30 to ask for police to help keep traffic flowing in the lot's aisles. Stush told him the police were responsible for city thoroughfares, the casino could hire private security for their own property. He knew several guys who were off-duty today and could probably use the cash. Rollison hung up.

Doc stayed as far away as he could. While Willie Grabek ran down unpromising leads in Pittsburgh, Doc worked on their backlog of other cases. The Broaddus investigation was on life support. A bigger city, where it wasn't such a big deal, it might have died a natural death.

Doc spent much of his morning in the Flats section of town, where social climbing white trash aspired to be rednecks. Closed a bad check case and told a young man who probably should have been in school what would happen the next time he cherry bombed mailboxes. He was only a mile away when the call came in, officer needs backup. He told Janine Schoepf at dispatch he'd take it and drove over to Hill Street.

The Flats only deserved the name within fifty yards of the highway. Hill Street was a ten percent grade with a ninety-degree bend, so tricky to navigate only Harry Waugamann would plow it.

Doc stopped in front of a brick two-story with a brick porch and three wooden stairs. Satellite dish, a pickup truck that probably wouldn't pass its next inspection, and a mailbox with Steelers logos on it. Barb Smith stood on the porch explaining contemporary concepts of interpersonal relationships to a raw-boned guy about Doc's height. Dirty blond hair hung in his face, too thin to obstruct his vision. A woman in jeans and a Penns River High sweatshirt stood behind Barb, emphasizing points she thought Barb hadn't drawn enough attention to.

Doc stayed at the frontier of the pavement; no curbs on Hill Street. Barb had asked for backup, not assistance; he was thirty feet away. He reached into the car for the dark sunglasses he only wore when he needed to look menacing. Couldn't make out many words, mostly inflections and body language. Near as he could tell, the woman had been on the rag for over a week, which ain't natural. She said he was a goddamn liar, it hadn't been a week, and she couldn't help it she had bad cramps, which he hadn't made any better by pushing her around. Of course, he didn't lay a fucking hand on her, she called the cops every time they disagreed, which appeared to be a regular occurrence, as Barb was on a first name basis with both of them.

Doc and Barb had a falling out a year earlier, collateral damage of Marian Widmer's reign of terror. Doc tended to fall all the way out with people when that happened, so they'd exchanged no more than civil greetings when work or coincidence put them together. The wisdom of this policy became less certain to Doc as time passed. Now, watching how well Barb handled herself with the modern family, he reconsidered whether he should maintain such a self-imposed distance. She'd made it clear she was willing to let bygones be, and had a presence about her that demanded his respect. Her crooked nose was as endearing as her dimple, and her ass....

"Bitch!" Then a slap, and Barb was falling off the porch.

Doc cleared the stairs in one step, catching and balancing Barb as he went by. Gripped the redneck's collar and the back of his jeans and rode him straight through the screen door. The wooden slats snapped and the screen gave way and the solid door slammed back, knob embedded in the drywall. He slammed the neck's face into the kitchen table once, then stood him up. The cuffs were in his hand while little cartoon birds still circled the guy's head.

"You're under arrest." The bracelets were on before his new prisoner could run his tongue over his lips to check for blood.

"Who the fuck are you? Open these bastards up and I'll show you who's under arrest. What the fuck did I do?"

"Assault on a police officer." The redneck's breath was stale; alcohol seeped through his pores. "I'm advising you to shut the fuck up before I add Resisting Arrest."

"Doc!" Barb yelled and he turned in time to deflect the wife's nails from his face before Barb pulled her away.

"You son of a bitch! You let him be!"

Barb controlled the woman by pressing her against the refrigerator. Doc cinched the cuffs with his hand to force hubby onto his toes. Looked to the wife, then to Barb. "Who called you into this mess?"

Barb didn't turn her head to answer. "She did."

"Did you?"

"Fuck you!" She tried to spit, managed to drool on Barb's shirt. "Let him go, goddammit! Younz can't come in here like this. This is *our* fucking house!"

Doc left the hand holding the cuffs where it was, leaned toward the woman. Said, "You. Shut your fucking mouth!" and she did, cowed by the surprise of being spoken to like that by a stranger, and by the size and expression of said stranger. "You don't get free calls to put your old man in his place and send us home when you've had enough. You can't handle your own family situations, you can't bitch when things don't come out your way. Now shut the fuck up and stay in that corner or I'll take you in for interfering with a police officer in the pursuit of his lawful duties."

He was pretty sure that wasn't how the law read. He figured her for someone intimidated by formal terminology and saw he was right when Barb let
her go and the woman did as she'd been told. Not exactly meek about it, but
Doc wasn't interested in style points.

She opened her mouth like she might say something. "I don't want to hear
it. Officer Smith gave you both plenty of time to explain who was right and
who was wrong. You wasted it. I don't want to know who said what or did
what to who. I don't care who's a drunk bastard or who's a frigid bitch. All
I know is I got a misdemeanor in handcuffs who's about to get at least one
meal on the city. You want to join him, talk dirty to each other through the
bars, then go ahead, run your mouth. We got two cars, plenty of room for the
whole family. Now, what's it gonna be?"

He let Barb have the collar and made it to Fat Jimmy's before the lunchtime
chili ran out.

[12]

Irish Alzheimer's is when all you can remember are the grudges. Doc was as Irish as anyone in Penns River, but there's a time and a place for every-thing. He made sure to be back at the station when Barb Smith came off shift.

Halfway through a bottle of Bass—Denny Sluciak stocked it just for him—when Barb walked into the Edgecliff with damp hair and no makeup. It agreed with her. Barb didn't dress up well, looked like a farm girl in the big city, uncomfortable outside her element. She was what she was, not Four Seasons elegant but small town cute, a little awkward, someone with an open, friendly face who didn't try to be anything she wasn't. Few heads would be turned by Barb Smith, least of all her own.

He bought her an MGD and they found a table away from the entry, not too secluded. They each took a swallow before Barb cut to the chase.

"That was quite a show today. Have you worked with those two before?"

"First time I ever laid eyes on them. The three of you seemed pretty fa-miliar."

"I see them almost every week. It's not their drinking that's the problem. It's the next day, when one of them has a hangover and remembers something the other one said or did and can't help bringing it up. Depending on how hung over the other one is, it might get loud. Stuff might get broken. I don't think either of them has ever laid a hand on the other in anger."

"Until today."

"It wasn't her he hit."

"He still hit a woman."

"He hit a cop. He might've been showing off for you. Sometimes I think they save their best material until I get there, but I'd never seen him do any-thing like that. It's not only her that calls, you know. Every fifth or sixth time he'll hit us up on the speed dial and hold the phone so the 911 operator can hear what a goofy bitch he's married to."

"Kids?"

"Grown and gone. Thank God, but I have to wonder how they turned out."

"Grown and gone? I didn't figure either of them to be past forty, and they have to look older than they are, hard as they live."

"Thirty-six, thirty-seven. Something like that. About your age."

"And they have kids—plural—grown and gone? Are we *that* close to West Virginia?"

Barb snorted into her beer, wiped foam from her lip. Looked into her glass when she spoke. "Not that I don't appreciate the help, but I could've han-dled him."

"I know. I almost let you, but I needed the exercise. The look on his face when he realized I wasn't going to open the screen door before we went through it made everything worthwhile."

"You had him off the porch so fast I don't think Louise—the wife—knew where he'd gone. You didn't have to arrest him, though. They would've worked it out."

"He put his hands on a cop. You let one alcoholic jagov get away with that, pretty soon we have to go to every domestic in pairs. The city can't afford that."

Barb looked like she might say something, reconsidered. Re-reconsidered, then settled for a sip of beer.

Doc turned over possibilities in his mind, how to finesse his way into the next topic. Settled for, "I was wrong to come down so hard on you after that Family Services thing with Jeff West and the boys. You meant well, and you did the right thing. I still think you made a mistake with how you did it, but I can't fault you for it."

"You're right. It was a mistake." She played with the simple cross that hung around her neck. "I'd do it again, and you know why." He nodded. "What I can't get over is how I could've thought Jack Harriger was the person to ask for advice. I've watched him since that happened. He lives for petty things he can use to control people, and I handed him a big one. I've been meaning to tell you I was sorry for a year now."

"You did, that night on the bypass. I didn't want to hear it. How about we just say we both could've handled the whole situation better and leave it at that?" He tried to think fast about what came next, so she wouldn't notice a pause. "I had fun when we used to get together after work. I'd do it again, if you're okay with it."

"Friends?"

"Friends."

Barb extended her hand and he shook it, couldn't decide if they maintained contact long enough for it to be significant. Larry sent two more beers their way, gave them both excuses to disengage. Doc asked if she was hungry, hoped she'd say yes because he was ready for a fish sandwich and didn't want to eat in front of her. She declined and he settled for a swallow of beer. He could lay back and get the sandwich when she left.

He waited until he supposed a suitable interval had passed since their almost personal moment. "You spend much time down the Estates lately?"

"I spend every day in the Estates, there and the old downtown, over to the Flats once in a while. Not much to do out this way."

"You have any reason to believe drugs are being sold there? I don't mean people hooking up their friends. I'm talking about right on the corners."

Barb didn't answer right away. "Why do you ask?"

"I saw Jefferson West the other night. He says he's seen signs, down by the tracks. Walked down there himself a couple of times and disrupted them."

"He shouldn't do that."

"That's what I told him. Said he should call us, watch from his window if he wants. Maybe I'll drive around with him some time in my own car so I don't look too cop, let him point out some candidates. Could be he's just an old man who's seen too much television. That's why I asked if you've noticed anything."

"Maybe, now that you mention it. I didn't think much of it at first, because it looked pretty random and disorganized, and I know Mike Mannarino does-n't allow it here in town. But if we want to think of it as just getting ramped up, yeah, maybe. You think Mannarino's changing his policy?"

"I think it's more likely that's why that kid got iced and dumped in front of the casino. What I can't figure is, why dump the body there?"

"It's going to cost him a lot of money, isn't it? It would be in his interest to put some stink on their image."

"I guess." Doc laced his fingers behind his head, leaned back as far as the chair would allow. Something about how that opened up his chest seemed to make him think better. "Here's the thing: it won't cost him *that* much money. I mean, it's all slot machines. I can see where it would hurt him if he was making a living on numbers or had a policy racket going, but I don't think he does. His gambling income is from the sports book, and they're not touch-ing him there. Besides, this dump is small potatoes to what they have in Pitts-burgh."

"This is in his hometown, though. Adding insult to injury, you know?"

Doc blew air out from puffed cheeks, leaned back until the chair's front legs lost contact with the floor. "It *could* just be Mike showing his ass. Thing is, everything points his way, and we'll never touch him for it. Too well done. I want to close this. Stush needs it."

"You've been around. You know they don't all get closed."

"No. They don't." Marian Widmer flashed through his mind, an almost daily occurrence. Her case was closed—they knew she was guilty—yet Marian breathed free air. Any reasonable person who read the file would say she was guilty of arranging two homicides and was working on a third before Doc intervened. She beat one case and Sally Gwynn, the DA, wouldn't pros-ecute the other. Said each defendant only got to make a fool of her once. That's how it went; cases were closed without a successful prosecution all the time. They could close this one if they wanted to, say Mannarino had it done and declare victory. Doc knew of places that worked that way, where the brass had to show statistics and middle management had damn well better deliver them. Penns River wasn't like that. Saying "We know which asshole had it done" wasn't good enough here.

He let the chair come forward, finished his beer. "Do me a favor. Now that you're aware, look at things down there differently. Downtown, too. You know what drug traffic looks like. Watch with that mindset. Drive by and disrupt them, see if they scatter or hold their ground and eye fuck you. I don't want to holler fire over some barbecue smoke, but it would be a plus for Stush if he could get out in front of a problem no one else knew we had."

Doc paid for their drinks and walked Barb to her car. Thanked her for accepting his apology—such as it was—told her not to be bashful about putting him in his place the next time he got his ass up on his shoulders. He meant it, though if it ever happened again he wouldn't remember he'd told her until after the fact.

He closed her door and waited for her to clear the lot before going back for his fish sandwich. He'd gone as far as the door when his cell rang. Stush's number.

"What's up, Boss?"

"Benny, it's Helen." Stush's wife. "Stan had a heart attack. We're over at Allegheny Valley. He asked for you."

[13]

Stush didn't look all that bad to Doc by the time he got into Coronary Intensive Care to see him. Not if he discounted the needles in his arms and tube up his nose. The wires attached under the gown that almost reached around him, connected to monitors for his heart, blood pressure, and respiration. The clip on one index finger that measured... something. Temperature, maybe.

To Doc, seeing his Uncle Stush in any state other than embalmed was a relief after three hours of Bill O'Reilly, Sean Hannity, and Greta van Susteren in the waiting area. Stush was allowed one visitor for five minutes each hour, and Helen got the time. His kids lived out of town and were on the way. Helen was told Stush was out of danger during her ten o'clock visit, go home and get some rest. Doc drove her and was back by eleven.

"Sorry to keep you out so late." Stush's voice not weak so much as it lacked its usual resonance. "I know you're an early riser."

"I wouldn't mind if there was anything wrong with you. You're no pastier than usual. What the hell?"

"Sleep apnea."

"Huh?"

"You know. Like snoring."

"I know what sleep apnea is. This," Doc gestured around the room, "don't look like sleep apnea. Helen said you had a heart attack. If this is just snoring, I'm going home."

"I'm telling you. I dozed off in my chair, like I always do. I guess I was snoring, and you know, stopped breathing. So my heart stopped. Must of figured, no air's getting in, why bother? I'll tell you something, your heart stops, it wakes your ass up in a hurry. I sat up, stopped snoring, breathed, and my heart started. I feel fine. They're making way too much of this."

"Humor them. You don't look too bad to me, but my grandfather told me a minor heart attack is when it happens to someone else. Said it right after he had a heart attack."

"What I said. To you, this happened to someone else. So it's not that bad. I'll be at work Monday."

"You don't trust me to bring in doughnuts twice a week?"

Stush paused, made an effort to maintain his smile. "Benny, there's nothing I wouldn't trust you with. I just don't know how long Jack Harriger will let my chair sit empty."

"That little prick tries to take over your office while you're out sick and I'll run his ass into the street myself."

"I appreciate that, I do, but it's not up to you. You could probably shame him into standing down while I still have the job officially. I'm afraid this will be their excuse to get rid of me."

"They can't fire you for having a heart attack."

"They could retire me."

"They can't force you to retire, either."

Stush made small side-to-side figure eight motions with his head. "There's ways."

"What? Buy you out? The city barely had enough money to plow the streets last winter. There's money to buy a lifetime employee out of three years of service?"

"When someone like Danny Hecker wants you gone, money can always be found. Here's how they'd spin it: valued city employee, thirty-eight years of service, sacrificed his health to keep the city safe, a benefactor has stepped up to allow the city to grant him early retirement. Maybe a disability can be trumped up."

Doc looked at Stush in bed, wired up like an astronaut, thought maybe a disability wouldn't have to be trumped up. "You'd still have to accept."

"I'm stubborn, not stupid. They make the deal sweet enough, damn right I'll retire. Move away, too, they make it worth my while. Just not to one of those redneck states. Montana, maybe. I could live in Montana."

"Awful cold in Montana in the winter time."

"You ever spent a winter in Montana?"

"No, but I can read."

"So can I. Sure it gets cold, but it's a dry cold. Clear up my sinuses, get rid of this fucking sleep apnea."

"You want dry, move to Arizona."

"Awful hot in Arizona in the summer."

"You ever spent a summer in Arizona?"

"No, but I can read. A hundred and ten degrees is a hundred and ten degrees, I don't care how dry it is. Go out to get the paper, come back and you're a raisin."

"You're even harder to get along with sick than you are the rest of the time." Doc fought back a smile; it would ruin the effect. He'd turned down opportunities with the Feds, state police, and half a dozen major cities to come back to Penns River. Much of it was to be close to his parents, but he'd always liked the idea of working for Stush. Never a day went by the old man didn't make him smile. The idea of Stush retiring had become less of an abstraction as his hair grayed and stomach grew, but Doc figured they'd still get together once a week or so to bullshit. He hadn't thought of Stush moving away, and never thought of him dying until Helen's phone call that evening.

A nurse touched her watch outside the glass wall of the ICU. Doc nodded, raised his eyebrows, held up one finger. She let him wait long enough to know she was doing him a favor before she nodded.

"Stush, they're about to throw me out of here. What do you want me to do?"

"Do? Hell, you know what to do at work. I'd appreciate you keeping an eye on Helen until the kids get here."

"Come on, Stush. You didn't ask for me from the emergency room just so we could shoot the shit for five minutes. What's on your mind?"

Stush looked through the glass to the nurses' station, saw the one who'd hurried Doc about to come in, waved her off. She held up one finger with emphasis, turned away.

"Where are we on this Broaddus file?"

"The truth? I don't think it's gonna close. We're pretty sure Mike Mannarino had it done, but we don't know why, and I doubt we'll ever be able to prove it."

"That's fine. I don't like it, but we both know some cases don't close. I'm afraid Harriger is going to try to dress Mannarino up for it. There's plenty of things the Hook deserves time for, and this is probably one of them. If it's done right. You with me on this?"

"Absolutely. I want Mannarino as bad as you do, but I want to see the look on his face when I put the cuffs on him fair and square."

The door opened. Stush lifted his hand and Doc took it. "You're a good boy, Benny. I love my three girls, but the only thing I was ever jealous of your old man about was how you turned out. Your brother's a hell of a man, too, no disrespect, but I couldn't love you more if you were blood. My time's coming. The way things have been, I'm about ready for it. Until then, I need you to make sure the department doesn't embarrass us while my name's still attached to it. Can you do that for me?"

Doc didn't want Stush to see him cry. It wouldn't make him seem weak or soft; he just didn't want to listen to Stush bust his balls about it a year from now. They squeezed hands and Doc nodded. The nurse shushed him out and he drove home wondering if his life had changed forever while he wasn't paying attention.

[14]

Buddy Elba drove while Mike Mannarino sat next to him thinking how this whole thing of theirs had turned to shit. If he'd asked for a meeting a few years ago, he'd drive to New York, they'd sit down, then he'd either go home or hang around for a few days. See a show, let Liz do some shopping. Hell, he'd fly if he felt like it, let the Feds find out his itinerary. Sure I was in New York those days. I took my wife to see *Cats* and went to Spark's Steakhouse for the Paul Castellano Special, six free shots, skip the steak. So what? If the big bosses were in the mood, sometimes they'd meet in AC or Miami, get some sun, talk some business, some food, some booze, some pussy. A working vacation.

Today, Mike and Buddy drove Buddy's wife's car way the fuck up in the Poconos to Hawley, which Mike never heard of until Sal Lucatorre told him that was where the meet was. Hawley's a resort town, you'll like it, Sal said. Call us when you get there and we'll tell you where the meet is.

Ehrhardt's Waterfront Resort was a nice place, and Mike would have liked it if the reasons for being there weren't so chickenshit. Listening to Sal tell Buddy about the trip from New York didn't improve his mood. *Analyze This* shit, meeting up with two identical cars that went their separate ways coming out the parking garage. How they didn't call for a reservation until they were in town, had someone back home book it with an untraceable credit card. Real Mickey Mouse stuff.

Took them forever to get down to business. Tino DeFelice bitched about how his favorite place for *gabbagool* closed, now he couldn't get the good stuff. Mike knew three places on The Strip in Pittsburgh with capicola as good as anything in New York. He also didn't care about Jimmy Valente's daughter's wedding, Sal's gout, how Dominic Castellabre was fucking up everything the Lucchese family had built in the garment district, or the double-jointed broad Freddy Boca picked up at a strip joint in Lauderdale. Especially not the broad.

"Gentlemen, all due respect, but me and Buddy got a long drive ahead of us. Can we get down to business, please?"

"Take your time," Sal said. "Spend the night. We got some broads coming over later."

Mike looked at him like he'd ordered a turnip juice and dishwater cocktail. April in the Poconos. Too late to ski, too early for anything else but staying inside. Patches of snow clung to shady spots. "What the hell kind of broad is around here this time of year?"

"Don't be so small time, Mikey. We got half a dozen thousand-dollar girls coming in later. We figured, we got to go out of town, let's go to town. Bring it with us. Whatever."

These were the guys he'd come to for help. Jimmy Breslin and Martin

Scorsese together couldn't make these *strunzes* look like gangsters. Mike had his faults; self-delusion wasn't among them. This "man of honor" bullshit was exactly that, a front for criminals to get respectable people to stand up for them. No one played that game better than Mike the Hook Mannarino, with his "no crime in Penns River" edict. But this was business; be adults. These guys were like a bunch of high school kids with the parents away and the keys to the liquor cabinet.

"We'll think about it." Buddy shot him a look and Mike gave it right back. "But first, I really need to talk about the problem I got with these Russians."

Tino got things on track. "You're right, Mike. I'm sorry. It's nice to combine business and pleasure, but it's business first and what Mike has is serious. Go ahead, and be blunt. We're all friends here."

Mike laid it all out. The issues he'd had with Donte Broaddus. How the Russians came in without a word to undercut his business. He moved less than half as much heroin last month as he had a year ago. And that little porch monkey bragged about it, blew off meets, practically dared him to do something. Everyone there knew him, he was old school, and there was no way some twenty-year-old *melanzana* was going to cost him money and rub his nose in it. The kid had to go. Everyone agreed. One less boon was nothing to get worked up about.

Then that Russian came to him—at his legitimate business—with his "wop cocksucker" this and "big fish and shark" that and did everything but tell Mike to tongue his ass. The casinos were squeezing him, his heroin business was drying up, what was he supposed to do?

"Casinos are always a problem. You know that." Tino dipped his cigar in brandy and let Mike wait while he got it burning how he wanted it. "Those fucking Indians in Connecticut cost us big. Sal has some names, guys you can call down in AC. How they adjusted their operations, found ways to use the casinos to create spin-off business for them. I know a guy you can talk to— he's in Florida now—worked Vegas when the locals grew a conscience and threw the families out. They still make a good living. They just had to adapt. It's the way of the world, Mikey. You have to adapt. We all have."

"I understand that, and I have. Found new businesses. What you gotta understand is, Pittsburgh ain't New York or Vegas. There aren't as many opportunities. I'm not complaining. I can live with the casinos. I need to do something about these fucking Russians."

About the time the pause became uncomfortable, Tino said, "What do you have in mind?"

"Way I see it, guy comes into my place and tells me he's taking over, I can have what he don't want, the only way I see to deal with that is he's a dead man."

"You do what you gotta do, Mike," Tino said. "We understand that."

Mike locked his glare on Tino. "I got three made guys, Tino. Including me.

Maybe a couple others who'd pitch in if they thought they could move up, but the books are closed. I reach out to Youngstown or Detroit, it costs."

"It's all coloreds in Detroit now," Sal said. "Unreliable." Which showed how much Sal knew.

"I need help," Mike said. "That's why I'm here. I'm asking for help."

Those last four words let the air out of the room faster than if the girls had shown up with sores on their lips. Not a sound for almost a minute. Mike scanned every face. Everyone had something else that demanded his attention.

"It's not like we don't want to help," Sal said. "But, you know, we all got problems, Mikey. Sometimes you just gotta make do."

Mike glared at Sal, slid his line of sight over to Tino, who didn't say anything. At least he didn't look away.

"How long have I been kicking up to New York? To all of you? I don't just mean since I took over. I know every dollar I kicked up to John Bazzano and Mike Genovese, hell, even before that when I worked for Lennie Strollo, a piece of that wound up in New York. That's over twenty years, I don't know how much money. Millions, maybe. I never asked for a fucking thing.

"I got three made guys and you closed the books. I don't complain, it helps me stay under the radar. FBI says there's nothing left in the Pittsburgh region resembling an organized crime syndicate and I laugh my ass off. No pressure. Life is good so long as I don't get greedy. I'm not getting rich—not like some I know—but I get by.

"Now this Boris Badanov cocksucker wants to tell me how I can and can't earn. He'll put me out of business if he wants, and he got resources I can't imagine. So where's the service I been paying for all these years? Now that I need it?"

Tino DeFelice was the oldest, most experienced, richest, toughest boss in New York. Shot four times by Carlo Rizzo's crew after Tino was promoted captain ahead of Carlo. Lost his spleen and a kidney. Made Richie Campise, family boss at the time, swear on his children he wouldn't do anything. Took Tino a year to regain his strength and two more to kill Carlo's whole crew, one at a time, even the guys who weren't in on it. Saved Carlo for last, found him in North Carolina, hiding like some bimbo.

"You're right, Mike. I mean, when you're right, you're right. You're a good earner, always have been. And we like working with you. You're reliable, no drama, every month the money comes in. If you'd asked anything else, we'd just say 'What do you need, are you sure that's enough?' But this—this Russian thing. This is different. What was the guy's name, come to see you?"

"He didn't feel the need to tell me. I found out later it's Volkov. Yuri Volkov."

Nods around the room. "That's what I thought you'd say. We have some experience with Mr. Volkov, heard he was getting his own operation out of town somewhere. I didn't know it was Pittsburgh."

"You know this guy?"

"Know of him."

"You run him out of New York and he landed on me?"

"It's not like that. Something you got to understand, Mike, we all make arrangements. The Russians, they have their niches carved out and we don't fuck with them. Live and let live. There's plenty to go around."

Mike didn't like the direction this was going. "Arrangements? Deals for profit, right? You're not telling me these guys come in and take what they want."

Tino fiddled with his drink. Took a sip, farted around with the stirrer while he spoke. "This is a business, Mike. First and always. A business. Business requires cost-benefit analysis. Something isn't worth doing, doesn't bring in more money than it costs, you don't fuck with it. Cut your losses."

Tino waited like he expected Mike to say something. Mike had said all he wanted until he heard something worth commenting on. Tino took another sip and went on.

"These Russians aren't businessmen, not the way we mean it. A Russian wants something, he takes it, no negotiation. It's you or him. They got no concept of perspective. All offenses are capital offenses, and they are some easily offended motherfuckers."

Volkov was Mike's first direct exposure to Russians; that didn't mean he was ignorant. He had a year of college, read on his own, and knew people who were afraid often built what they were afraid of into invincible foes. Men who were afraid of their wives painted them as psycho bitches. Those afraid of dogs told stories of pit bull attacks and Dobermans fighting in a ring. Tino DeFelice, a man Mike believed until half an hour ago would tell the devil to fuck himself, was afraid of Russians. It dripped off every word like curdled milk.

Tino was still talking. "It's not worth it, fighting these cocksuckers. Did you know Pete Calcagno?"

"Heard of him."

"Petey Cans. Good earner. Real tough guy. Had a lot of union activity on the docks, moved some good dope. The Russians wanted in. Pete told them, they wanted to provide some service, he'd see what kind of a split could be worked out. They made a move and Pete's crew stood them off. Then Pete—he was a pistol, that one—he decided to threw some fear at them. Picked up one of their guys at a club like they wanted to bury the hatchet, took him to a warehouse, strung him up like a piñata and took batting practice. Dropped him off with a note said this wasn't like sneaking broads into the country. Call when they were ready for some man's work."

Tino finished his drink, jiggled the ice left in the glass. Sal Lucatorre jumped off the couch to refill it.

"Petey didn't show up at his club one day. We called his house, all the usual places. Nothing. That night, about eleven o'clock, a bunch of us were having drinks at this joint Pete owned, thinking he might come in, and this van pulls up, some guy with four bags of dog food. Says he's making a delivery. We tell him this is a fucking strip joint, no dogs here, but the guy shrugs. Says someone paid him a grand for the delivery.

All the bags have numbers on them. One, two, three, four. We cut open Number One and there's about fifty pound of some shit inside with Pete's clothes all folded up on top. Next one was shoes. The fourth bag had Pete's head in it. He had a note in his mouth. 'Go to my house.'"

Sal handed Tino his fresh drink. Tino tasted it before he finished. "So we did. Basement had blood everywhere. His wife and kids were tied up in the living room, hysterical. They all had to go to the hospital. Those mother—fuckers shaved pieces off Petey while he was still alive. Made ground meat of him in his own house. And those bastards made his wife and kids listen.

"You want to fight 'em, Mike? Good luck. You can get help in Youngstown and Detroit? God bless you. You win, I'll kiss your ass on the pitcher's mound at Yankee Stadium. But I want no part of it. I worked too hard to end up in some fucking dog food bag."

[15]

"You got the meet set up yet?"

Tookie wondered how Donte lasted as long as he did, no account niggers like Nelson Butterfield working for him. Nelson still hadn't put Tookie together with Mike Mannarino, and Tookie could tell from the look on Nelson's face it wasn't on the horizon.

"I'm trying, I mean it. Ain't like I can walk up in the man's place of business and ax him do he want to step outside with me. They's protocols and shit."

Tookie understood protocol; it was the shit that bothered him. He knew Mannarino worked in some cheap car lot up out of town. No reason not to walk in and spray his head all over the leather chair Tookie imagined he sat in. Walk out and disappear back to Baltimore. No one would recognize him, and he'd be home before what passed for police up that way finished stringing their yellow crime scene tape. Almost mad enough to do it, too, but it was a chump move.

"You get what you needed in Baltimore?" Nelson said.

"Don't worry about what I got in Baltimore. You got plenty to do just getting me an appointment with a man got every reason to want to see me."

He didn't get what he wanted in Baltimore. That was none of this Bama's business. Went back to his boss, man who owed him already, helping get Donte killed like he did. Boy come to him with a proposition last year, not begging or nothing, wanted to get his deliveries from Baltimore. Cut Mike the Hook all the way out, tired of always being disrespected. Got nothing for his trouble but a lot of weak bullshit about not offending some big shooter in New York. What choice did the boy have except go to the Russians? Got his ass killed, too. Donte was family. Tookie figured he was owed.

Other hand, didn't take but a few hours with Nelson for Tookie to know he could *run* this motherfucker if this was how they played the game in Pittsburgh. He couldn't do it on the down low from Baltimore, so Mannarino still breathed air instead of dirt. For now.

"See, the thing with the Hook, I don't think he's even around," Nelson said. "It's like he's gone away or something."

"What, like on a vacation?"

"No no no no no, not like a vacation. He go away on bidness sometimes, just for a while. He be back in a day or two."

Tookie's mind wandered while Nelson made his excuses. His man in B'-more gave Tookie the same song he gave Donte: do all the work, take out the competition. Come back alive and we can talk. All Tookie asked for was a couple guys—three tops—in case Mannarino's crew came back on him after their boss got capped. They weren't critical to the plan—Tookie didn't have much regard for Italians' staying power—but it would be nice to have someone watch his back while he consolidated.

Nelson said, "Be a lot easier, you know, if I knew what it is you want to see the man for. Like do you want to see about getting a package from him."

"What the fuck else would you tell him? My boy Tookie wants to talk at you about how you did his cuz? Damn, nigger, how dumb are you? First, he don't expect you to know why I wants to talk, and he best not find out Donte was family or we both dead, you dig? You find whoever Donte used to talk to, tell him you got a man want to talk to Mr. Hook, or whatever the fuck you call him. He push you, tell him you know Donte was out of line, you never thought switching was a good idea, and now you with someone got a better understanding of the situation. You think you can do that?"

Nelson looked more confused than usual. "Yeah, sure, I can do that, but, I mean, you really looking to do business with the man just capped your cousin?"

Tookie wanted to slap Nelson like the stupid bitch he was, maybe knock some sense loose. He didn't, and he didn't say the first thing that came to mind. If Nelson was too stupid to figure out what Tookie was up to, there was no way he could play dumb. He had to be left dumb.

"Nelson, I'm sorry. I been short with you. Here's the lay: Donte was my boy. We used to hang, talk shit, like we was brothers. The way this mother-fucker did him ain't right. We both know that. But we got to get past it. This is bidness, and bidnesses got this thing they call cost-benefit analysis. Means you cut the best deal you can. You don't forget what come before—only a fool make the same mistakes twice—but it don't matter. We work with this Hook character, we have to watch him like a motherfucking hawk, every day. But it don't do no one no good to kill this cracker if all it do is cost us money, just so we feel good for a couple days.

"Set up the meet. We'll build this up the way Donte wanted to, then I promise we'll take care of his moms and his brother. And Mr. Mike the Hook. You feel me?"

[16]

"Where are we on the Mannarino case?"

No one looked at Jack Harriger. Doc and Neuschwander contemplated each other's shoes. Grabek gazed past him with a thousand-yard stare hard enough to make the wall glow.

Harriger gave it an uneasy thirty seconds. "You *are* working on the Mannarino case, correct?"

Grabek's voice was flat. "We're working the Broaddus case, Jack. It's poor form to call a case by a suspect's name. Makes it sound like your mind's made up."

Harriger glared at Grabek. Grabek's eyes never flickered. Doc willed himself to be still.

"Fine," Harriger said. "The Broaddus case. Where are we?" The silence lingered. "Dougherty? You're the primary."

Doc focused on a spot near enough to Harriger to keep from being accused of not looking at him. "We're working it. We don't have much."

"What *do* you have?"

Doc took a second to modulate his response. "We have a body. We have an ID. We know what he did for a living, and we have a reasonable idea of how he spent his last day, up to a point. We're still missing a few things."

"Such as?"

"A crime scene would be nice."

"What did you get from the casino?"

"The body. Period."

"And that's all we're going to get," Grabek said. Harriger arched an eyebrow. "He wasn't killed there. We got no worthwhile fibers from the body. No usable trace evidence that might tell us where he was killed. Dead end."

"Work with the body."

"Well, he was in good health." Grabek opened a folder he'd held on his lap. "Blood showed traces of alcohol and THC. We know he ate a steak around seven, so he died somewhere between ten and midnight. His cholesterol was a little high, but not something a twenty-year-old would have to worry about. His right arm had an old break that had healed well." Flipped a page. "Internal organs were unremarkable."

Harriger's ears were red. "Something relevant."

Doc stepped in before Grabek pushed too far. "A pair of .22s in his head. Too badly damaged for any tests."

"Which is fine," Grabek said, "because we won't find a gun to compare them to."

The redness spread down Harriger's neck. "You're a professional, Detective Grabek. You're paid to get a job done. Being defeatist won't do it."

"Being unrealistic won't either. This was a professional job. Two in the head from close range with a .22. Not enough power for exit wounds, so they just rattle around inside chewing up brain and ruining the slugs. Guy falls dead, doesn't even bleed all that much. Wrap him in a sheet of plastic or a tarp, throw him in the trunk. Drive to the casino in the middle of the night. Pop the trunk, roll him out of whatever he was wrapped in, drive away. I don't know. Maybe you learned some cool tests when you were with the Staties up at Emporium this worn out old homicide cop from the Burgh isn't aware of."

Harriger now red from his hairline to his collar. Cords stood out in his neck. Visible effort was required to keep his voice as even as he did. "Have you found his car?"

"Yeah." Grabek. "In Garfield. Tires and sound system gone. Key in the ignition. Someone either ripped it off or the killers made it look like someone ripped it off."

"Or they left it somewhere it would get ripped off," Doc said.

"Or that."

"Who saw him last?" Harriger said.

Grabek flipped pages. "Nelson Butterfield, friend and probable business associate. Said they ate dinner—steaks—and Broaddus left him about eight-thirty. Said he had something he needed to do. Didn't say where, didn't say when, didn't say who with. Butterfield thought he might have had a date with some woman he wasn't supposed to be sniffing around."

"Did you lean on Butterfield?"

"With what? He's not suspected of anything in this jurisdiction."

"Maybe he's holding out on you. He was close to the victim. Maybe Mannarino used him to get close to Broaddus."

"Nelson Butterfield is a zero. A good day for him is when his shoes don't come untied. He's not sharp enough to play both sides of the street."

"All right. Forget Butterfield. You said yourself it was a professional job. Two in the head, close range, small caliber weapon. Who else, if not Mannarino?"

"Don't get us wrong, Jack. It probably was Mannarino." Doc knew Harriger hated being called "Jack" by subordinates even more than Doc hated "Benny." Treading a line, wanting to seem cooperative enough to deny insubordination without either cooperating or acting subordinate. "All the things Willie mentioned, the things we're missing, make it look like a mob hit, and Mike Mannarino has the local concession. Problem is, we can't make a case by showing what we don't have and telling a jury it had to be him because someone else would've left more clues."

Then Grabek said what Doc wanted to say, but didn't dare. "You want a conviction, Jack, or do you just want the file closed? We can probably close it now. We know enough to satisfy each other and a reasonable observer that Mannarino and Broaddus were moving drugs together and Mike decided the kid had to go. I would've suggested that three days ago, but I thought we didn't work that way in Penns River." Doc could have kissed him on the mouth.

Harriger stood behind his desk, palms pressed onto the surface, head down when he spoke. "I thought we couldn't prove the drug connection."

"We can't," Doc said. "We've been trying for three years now. We know he's doing it, but we can't put our hands on anything even close to proof. Whatever they're doing spans jurisdictions, and the Feds are too busy looking under their beds for terrorists to care. Not enough weight moves through here to rate a decent headline for them."

Harriger held his position, staring holes through the desk. "Unless someone here has a better suspect, I want Mannarino for this, and I want a case even Ms. Gwynn can win. Any questions? Now get busy. I don't want to see anyone hanging around the office drinking coffee until that son of a bitch is in the basement behind bars."

[17]

The morning rush at Donut Connection had slowed by 8:45. Neuschwander fixed his cream and sugar while Doc and Grabek found one of the quieter tables and arranged their coffee and doughnuts.

Neuschwander came to the table, coffee in one hand, bag of doughnuts in the other. "Guys? I don't want to be the old maid, but I thought we were just picking up stuff to go. Jack's really pissed."

"Sit down, Ricky." Grabek emptied two packets of sugar into his cup, stirred. "Harriger said he didn't want to see us around the office drinking coffee. He didn't say dick about drinking it here."

Neuschwander was a good cop, the department straight arrow. Grabek didn't need the job, two years retired from Pittsburgh, punching in to help pay for a daughter's college. Not who Neuschwander would trust for a ruling. He looked to Doc, who swallowed some coffee and thought about it, decided it was suitable, and pushed away the sugar packets.

"Relax, Noosh. No point in us going off in three different directions. We have to sit down sometime and decide what to do next, and this is as good a place as any. Look around. Coffee and doughnuts. How cop can you get?"

Neuschwander sat, didn't look comfortable. Sipped his coffee through the hole in the lid. Left the bag intact but open, laying the doughnut on the edge as though he might need to snatch the bag and leave on a second's notice. Doc and Grabek tore open their bags for easy access, drank from open containers. Their body language told anyone coming by they'd be there a while.

"You worked a mob hit before, Ricky," Grabek said, crumbs falling from his lips. "That guy we found on the steps of the Bachelors Club. What's his name? Orszulak."

Neuschwander knew Grabek didn't need input from him to continue.

"That's still an open file, but we're not working it, and we know Mannarino had that one done, too. A properly executed mob hit—sorry, no pun intended—they don't get solved, not on their own. One of three things happens: someone talks, someone fucks up, or something horribly unlucky happens. I remember, must've been twenty years ago, some guy in Buffalo got whacked. They had him in the trunk of his own car to take him to long-term parking at the airport and a drunk driver hit them. Explaining why you don't have the registration and insurance card is easy. The dead body in the trunk is a bitch."

"Remember that time last year, year before, we went down to PNC Park early to watch batting practice?" Doc swallowed, washed it down with a generous gulp. "Saw where some of the balls went, and the throws they made from the outfield, just warming up and jacking around? How good they were?

And the Pirates stink. They didn't have five players a good team would want. But they're pros. They do it for a living. We talked about how when people are really good at something, how the average guy can't realize it. I mean, what they were doing looked like the same baseball we played when we were kids, but it's a whole different game.

"That's what these guys do. They're criminals. Period. It's how they earn their living. They don't do anything else, and they've been passing down the tricks of the trade for a hundred years. The FBI says Pittsburgh doesn't have an organized crime presence anymore. Okay, they're Feds, they're smarter than me. I guess what I see going on around here sometimes is just—I don't know what it is, but they say it's not organized crime. Fine. To me, what it means is Mannarino can't afford to carry any dead weight. He wants heavy work done, the guy he gives it to is very, very good." Another swallow. "We'll never prove dick here, unless someone involved gets jammed up and wants to make a deal."

Rick Neuschwander knew this was all true, but had never internalized it. He knew it the way people "knew" about hurricanes and earthquakes, things no one *knows* about until they've been through one in person. Crime worth mentioning didn't go unsolved very often in Penns River. Part of that was good police work. Part, admitted under duress, was Mike Mannarino's prohibition on serious crime not committed by him. Donte Broaddus was the fourth homicide in less than two years, and it became clearer every day that no one would do time for three of them.

Grabek saw the frustration and, for once, took pity. "No offense, Rick, you never worked in a big city. House or business gets broken into, the victim does the police report online. Cops don't even come out unless the dollar value's over a certain amount, or someone got hurt, or the vic has some juice. No one has time. Call the insurance company, replace your stuff, get better locks, move on with your life. We get spoiled in a town like this. Bad things—really bad, I mean—they don't happen very often. That might be changing. I hope not. I didn't come here to put up with the same bullshit I had downtown. You just have to understand, sending someone to jail for a crime isn't always the most likely outcome."

Grabek saw the look on Neuschwander's face. "It's not all bad. Sometimes you catch a guy—a burglar, let's say—and you close forty or fifty cases, because he did them all."

Doc finished his coffee, crammed his empty bag into the cup. "Mike Mannarino is a disease. Has been for as long as I've been around. The thing is, our immediate problem is Jack Harriger. He wants an arrest and doesn't care how we get it. I'm not playing that game."

Grabek shoveled the last of his doughnut into his mouth. "I'm not saying I never played that game, but I won't do it this time. Not for Harriger, and not for a case we can't win, anyway. Fuck him."

They sat for a couple of minutes, waiting to see if Neuschwander wanted to debate. He looked like someone who just learned he does, in fact, have the serious illness he's worried about but never went to see the doctor for until it was too late. Doc felt for him. He wanted the job to be what Rick thought it was, helping people when things got out of hand, nothing too serious allowed to go unpunished. His illusions fell away one by one in the army until a stint at Abu Ghraib purged him once and for all. He came back to a small town where things like that didn't happen, only to find what he'd hoped to escape had followed him home.

His cell danced across the table as it vibrated. "Dougherty."

"Doc? It's Janine Schoepf." The dispatcher. "Kenny Czarniak's here. He says he wasn't completely honest with you the other day."

[18]

Doc sat a large container of coffee on the table in the interview room with enough sugar and creamer to make ice cream. "How you doing, Mr. Czarniak? I don't remember exactly how you like it, so I figured I'd cover you either way." He cracked open his own coffee, took a sip. "No hurry. I got to run to the can real quick. Be right back."

He spent enough time for Kenny not to feel rushed, then knocked as he came back in. "All set? Officer Schoepf says you have something for me."

Kenny pulled the coffee away from his mouth like he'd been caught jacking off. "Yeah, I do. Look, I feel kind of bad about this, not telling you before. It's not like I was holding back, but I just didn't think much of it, not with everything going on that day. I guess it slipped my mind."

"But something made you remember."

"It's not like I forgot in the first place. Just, you know, like, how much stuff do you remember to say about anything? Someone asks 'How was your day,' you tell them the highlights, but later you think of one more thing that kind of got lost in the shuffle that should've been in there. You know what I mean?"

"See it all the time. What happened to you, finding a body like that, it's very traumatic. It's rare we get everything from witnesses on the first try."

They sat for a minute, drinking coffee. Kenny's must have been a color he'd never seen before.

"So," Doc said, "why don't you tell me what it is you just remembered?"

"It's about the cars."

"The cars."

"Remember, you asked me about the cars in the parking lot, and I said it would be unusual if there wasn't a few there overnight?"

"Yeah. And?"

"There was this one car. I didn't think much of it that night. Maybe it looked a little out of place, is all. Nicer car than you'd usually see there overnight, not something someone on the work crew would drive."

"What was special about this car?"

"Like I said, nothing. Not really. It's just, later, while I was waiting to talk to you, I looked over that way, and it was gone."

"So you came in to tell me about a car that wasn't there."

"Yeah, but it should've been. Who parks their car in a lot like that overnight, then picks it up between five, five-thirty in the morning?"

"Someone who needs to be at work by six. Or someone whose ride back to get his car had to be on the road early. I can think of half a dozen other legitimate reasons if I take a minute. So can you. Now what was it about that car that made you notice?"

Doc gave Kenny all the time he wanted. Kenny drank coffee. Doc thought how funny it would be if Harriger came by and caught them drinking coffee after the morning's tantrum, watch him get wrapped around the axle jumping to conclusions before he realized Kenny was a witness. After three minutes he decided they'd both suffered enough.

"Something drew your attention to it. Or I should say, something drew your attention to the lack of it." The pump remained unprimed. "Did you see another car pull up next to it? Someone get out?"

"No. I told you, all I seen was it wasn't there anymore."

"No one walking across the lot in that general area."

"No."

"Could someone have been in the car all along? Just sitting there?"

"In the car? I didn't look all that close, but, now you got me thinking about it, I don't know that I could swear there *wasn't* anyone in it when I drove by."

"That makes sense. You didn't think to look for anyone sitting in a car because, hell, who'd sit in a car, middle of the night like that?"

"Well, yeah. It was cold, too."

"Frosty?"

"What do you mean, frosty?"

"What time do you leave for work?"

"Quarter to five, twenty to five."

"You scrape your car windows that morning?"

"I got a garage. I never scrape."

"Okay, you don't scrape. What about the other cars in the lot? They have ice on the windows?"

Kenny getting into it now, leaning on the table, helping Doc recover the memory. "Ahhh, no. I don't think so. No ice on the cars."

"Still pretty cold, though. I was there with you an hour later, the sun was coming up, and we froze. Had to be uncomfortable to sit there, even out of the wind. I'm thinking they ran the heater. Cold as it was, the exhaust made a cloud. That might be what stuck in your mind. No reason to think twice about it then—we been watching exhaust clouds all winter—so it didn't register until later."

"Uhh, yeah. Could be."

"So what we got is, two guys running the heater in their car."

"Two guys?"

"Has to be two. You ever lift a dead body? One guy can't wrap him up, get him into the trunk, and roll him out again without making a mess and probably some noise. There's houses right behind that part of the parking lot. Couple of those families have dogs. No one heard a thing. Has to be two guys."

"Okay. If you say so."

"Two guys sitting in a car on a cold night running the heater. Why would they do that?"

"I really don't know. I'm only telling you what I seen."

Doc paid no attention, riffing on his own thoughts now. "They were waiting for you."

"For me?"

"Not you personally. They were waiting for whoever opened up in the morning."

"Why?"

"Think about it. They kill this guy, they could've left the body anywhere. They went out of their way to take it to the casino. Why? To leave a message. For that to happen, it has to be found there. They were waiting to be sure someone found the body."

"If you say so. You're the cop. You'd know about these things."

Doc curled his upper body into a thinking posture, elbow on the table, thumb under his chin, pointer rubbing his upper lip. "I don't suppose you remember anything about this car? The color?"

"It was dark."

"You mean dark because it was night, or the car was dark?"

"Well, yeah, dark as in night, but the car was dark, too. Couldn't say for sure if it was black or dark blue or what."

Doc remained thinking, shifted his eyes toward Kenny. "This is probably too much to ask, but do you have any idea what kind of car it was?"

"You mean like the model?" Kenny thought hard. "It was a four-door. I'm sure of that."

"Big or small? You know, like a full-sized car? Or mid-size or economy?"

"It was pretty big, I guess. Not a boat or anything, but a full-sized car."

"American or foreign?"

The tiniest smile creased Kenny's lips. "I don't know. I told you I wasn't paying much attention when I saw it."

"You know about cars. Was it one of those foreign luxury deals, like a Lexus or a Mercedes? Or an American car? A Caddy? Lincoln?"

"Not American. Something German-looking."

Doc took his time, looked at Kenny so he'd understand the import of what he was about to ask. "I don't suppose it could've been a black E-350 Mercedes, could it?"

Kenny took just as much time answering. "Now that you got me thinking about it, yeah. It could've been. You got any pictures I could look at? Help jog my memory again?"

"You don't think your memory's been jogged enough?"

"You keep asking questions and stuff keeps coming back. What do you think?"

"I think you're a lying sack of shit." Kenny's head jerked back as though he'd been slapped. "Did Rollison pay you to sell me that horseshit story? Or did he just threaten your job?"

"No, it's not like that. Like I told you, I was thinking—"

"What you were thinking was you might need that new transmission after all." Kenny's face confessed for him. "You mentioned it the other day. How much is he paying you?"

Kenny said, "No, I swear. It's not like that."

"Don't swear to me, Kenny. It insults my intelligence. Mike Mannarino drives a Mercedes E-350. You were sent here to make me think it was in the lot that morning. The next logical conclusion would be that he was in it. How fucking stupid does Rollison think we are? First, Mike Mannarino was nowhere near this hit. He wouldn't be—it's common sense—but we checked just the same. He was at the Benedum Center for a concert with his wife and another couple—a straight couple—and they stopped for drinks after. He didn't get home until almost one, by which time we can prove Donte Broaddus was dead.

"Even if he did kill him personally, why would he freeze his ass off sitting in the car to make sure someone found the body? I know Rollison thinks I'm just a small town cop, but I learned enough forensics to know dead bodies don't move around all that much. Unless a bear or a pack of wolves came out of the woods, Donte wasn't going anywhere.

"Plus, just because I'm in a bad mood and don't mind hurting your feelings, you're a shitty liar. You said yourself you weren't sure if the body was a white guy or a black guy until you realized he had frost on him. Dead body's freezing, and the cars sitting in the lot don't have frost on them? You have to have your facts straight if you want to be a convincing liar."

"Two grand," Kenny said. He looked half his normal size, shoulders slumped, elbows bent in on his thighs. "For the transmission. He told me what kind of car, to say I hadn't thought of it before. He didn't tell me much else, just to make you have to pull it out of me. Said if he told me too much about how to do it the whole thing would look staged."

"I could lock you up for this." Something Kenny hadn't thought of, by his reaction. "I won't, but I don't know why not."

Doc let him stew a minute while he thought of how to play it. "This your day off?"

"He gave me the day so I could come over here."

Doc rubbed his eyes. "All right. First thing is to get you paid. Next time you see him, tell him I bought it. Tell him you ran me around but it was me who asked if it was a black Mercedes. I'll stop by tomorrow or the next day and make you look good. He tries to stiff you, let me know."

Kenny's previous look of confusion was placid compared to how he looked now. "You're giving me a break? How come?"

"Beats me. I guess I figure, if anyone's going to get screwed over this, it might as well be Rollison. Now pay attention. I don't want to see you in here again, even if you remember something legitimate. You can't be trusted. If I hear of you floating rumors about this case, I'll make your life miserable. You owe me, Kenny. Don't make me collect. Now get the fuck out."

[19]

Doc cut the five ball too fine and knew he was beat. His cousin Nick had a bunny for the six to close out Tom, then the eleven, fifteen, and twelve to ice Doc. Four ball runs are nothing to assume, but Nick was *good*, and the balls laid out well. Two minutes later Doc was racking.

Bill and Shirley Forte hadn't been able to make it after all, Shirley house-bound two days out of the hospital after gall bladder surgery. Bill stayed with her, insisted Nick get out and get a little entertainment after two days more or less full-time at the hospital. Three-man cutthroat not as much fun as team eight ball, but still a good game.

Nick called time out. Opened a beer and made himself another of Ellen's spicy sausage poor boys. "Damn, these are good. Not too hot to eat, but they make my nose run."

"I noticed," Tom said. "I hope I'm not going to have to replace this felt after tonight." Made Nick wait a second before he arched an eyebrow to let him in on the joke. Tom's pool table was legendary. A hundred-year-old Brunswick he found in pieces in the storage room of an old fire hall when Doc was a kid. Brought the frame home, had new bumpers and pockets made, put the whole thing together himself. Doc remembered the day his father and un-cles showed up with the slate bed, three pieces at three hundred pounds each. No garage then, so no side door. They brought it in through the basement window. Handled each piece like glass because slate chips if a fly lands on it at the wrong angle and they'd never get it level then.

Ellen fussed around, making sure everyone had everything he needed or might need, even if he didn't know it yet himself. She went upstairs to read and Tom asked Doc if he'd been to see Stush lately.

"Not since they let him out of the hospital." Doc finished a poor boy, caught himself in time to keep from wiping his eye with sauce still on his fin-ger. "I meant to go by today but got busy."

"I was over this afternoon," Tom said. "He looks good. Tired, but good, considering." He drank some beer. "I look at him and I'm glad I'm getting old. I don't think I want to see too much of what this town turns into, the way it's going."

"What do you mean, Uncle Tom?" Nick said.

"It used to be nice here. Never had a lot of money in it, but everyone got by. Pittsburgh and the South Hills got turned around, and up north there, along 79 to the Turnpike, that was all trees thirty years ago. None of that came up the river. The Monkey Wards and Penney's where that casino opened the other day been empty for ten, twelve years. Then that Hecker jagov started buying up the whole town."

"Won't it bring in a lot of money?"

"To the owners, maybe. Hard to imagine how a casino could lose money. It's just slot machines and a bar, shitty little restaurant. Can't be that much overhead. I have no idea if any of that money will trickle down to the people that live here." Finished a beer, dropped the can in the recycling bin. "Don't get me wrong, I got nothing against someone making money, and how he spends it is his business. This guy, though, he won't work with anyone. He wants what he wants, how he wants it, and where he wants it."

Doc made a sandwich. Looked at the homemade potato salad, thought better of it, then put a serving spoon's worth on his plate. Sometimes his weakness disgusted him. "The casino, right?"

"You see the mess up on the hill the past couple days?" Tom said. "Goddamn dumb place to put something that generates that much traffic. He came to the zoning board for the easements on the property and we told him no. The infrastructure there couldn't handle it, and there was another parcel of land he could get even cheaper, down by the Ninth Street Bridge where Ames used to be. You can see Old 28 across the river from there, and it can be widened. The bridge would be a mess, but that's only for the width of the river. Changing the traffic pattern on this side would be easy.

"He didn't want it. Said he didn't like the surrounding area. Acted like he was putting in a playground instead of a casino. Promised he'd bring in other—what he call them?—ancillary businesses if we let him build it out here at the old drive-in lot." Tom grew up in Penns River, remembered what Doc thought of as Wards from when it was a drive-in theater. "Said the bypass could handle the traffic. Maybe it can. Wild Life Lodge Road can't, and that's the only way from the bypass to the casino. People coming from Pittsburgh will come up 28 through Tarentum, cross the bridge, then straight up Leechburg Road, and it can't manage the extra traffic, either. Too many downsides for the town for him to put it where he wanted."

"Isn't it already zoned commercial?" Nick said. He'd lived in Chicago over ten years. The level of corruption Tom implied sounded like business as usual to him.

Tom cracked half a smile. "Well, there's commercial, and there's commercial. That property is—was—zoned commercial, retail. He needed either an exception, or for it to be rezoned commercial, entertainment."

"Didn't you say it used to be a drive-in?" Nick said. Tom nodded. "Then didn't it used to be zoned commercial, entertainment, anyway?"

"Yeah, but it's not now. Come to think of it, maybe it never was. Back then, it might've been some kind of unimproved land, so long as they got an easement for the concession stand and the screen. I wasn't on the committee then—I'm not *that* old—but I know things were a lot more lenient."

Doc knew all this and wanted to shoot pool, so he tried to move the conversation along. "Didn't you tell him how easy it would be to put the ancil-

lary businesses in the old downtown? Vacant properties out the ass there."
"You know I did. He gave me some mush mouthed answer about how it
wouldn't be him putting those businesses in. They'd have to be attracted,
and no one would be attracted to that shithole. He didn't say shithole, but
that's what he meant. I asked wouldn't his beautiful new casino be enough
of an improvement right there to start turning that area around, maybe even
use some of the old mill buildings like they used that warehouse for the ball
park in Baltimore. That's beautiful, what they did there."
"What did he say?" Nick said.
Tom popped open another beer. "Nothing. Nothing memorable, anyway.
Pretty much he said if we didn't want to work with him there were plenty
of towns who did want their standard of living improved, and he left. Three
weeks later the city solicitor hand carried copies of a new ordinance to everyone on the zoning board in time for our next meeting. Council had rezoned
the property commercial, entertainment, and built easements into the ordinance that fit exactly with everything he wanted to do. Like he wrote it up
himself."
"Which is it you don't like, Dad?" Doc said. "The casino itself, or having
it rammed down your throat the way it was?"
Tom gave him a look. "You're right. I don't like how it was done. But it's
wrong, too. People's houses butt right up against that parking lot in back. The
loading doors for deliveries aren't fifty feet from a couple of their fences.
What's the dirt and noise going to be like? What'll it do to property values?
The other location, downtown, that's all business. Mostly vacant now, but
no one to keep up all hours of the night listening to drunks argue or get sick."
No anger in his voice. Tom didn't gesture or get red in the face. He seemed
to Doc an aging man who didn't kid himself. Events had passed him and there
was nothing he could do about it. He'd spend his whole life in Penns River,
but the town he'd die in wouldn't be anything like the one he'd lived in. A
man who'd come to understand not only can you not go home again, you
can't even stay there.
"I have a feeling they're not going to do as well as they hope. In a year or
so we'll find out their business plan was overoptimistic and the tax revenues
they promised aren't going to be there, at least not at the levels that got everyone all excited. Then what? The casino will make enough money to justify
keeping it open, but we'll only see the downside. Hecker will milk what he
can out of it and move on to the next town. The best we can hope for is a few
amenities, though we already know who gets to say where they go."
He set down his beer, took a bun from the package. "Come on, Nicky.
Break 'em. I'm tired of being a bitter old man tonight."

[20]

Barb Smith drove with the windows down, heard the shouts of "Five-O!" turning off 13th Street. Kids' voices, lookouts too young for the law to touch in any real way. "Hopper Juniors" what they called them when she worked in Harrisburg. By the time she turned onto Third Avenue the only signs of human life were asses and elbows, running away. In Penns River a year-and-a-half now, today the first time that had happened.

She parked the cruiser in front of Jefferson West's townhouse. Got out, adjusted her hat, slid her baton through the ring with authority. Maintained her best cop look as she came up the walk, rocked on her heels and scanned the street waiting for the door to open, hands resting on her utility belt. The picture of a put-upon cop answering a call.

West smiled when he recognized her. Barb cut him off. "Don't act happy to see me. I think we're being watched. It's better if we don't seem too friendly."

The smile left his lips, stayed in his eyes as he stepped aside to let her in. "Iced tea?"

"Please." The door closed and they discussed a home improvement project and how Wilver and David Faison were getting on. Barb didn't see West as much as she'd like. No excuse for it. She drove past a dozen times a week, sometimes more. Just never seemed right to make a social call in uniform. Of course, she lived not three miles away and never came over off-duty, either. Didn't mean she didn't enjoy Jeff West's company. Everyone has friends like that, people you wonder why you don't spend more time with every time you see them. West was hers.

Barb set down her glass, declined a refill. "Doc tells me you think drugs are being sold up by the tracks."

"I know drugs are being sold up there."

"After what just happened, I agree with you. What bothers me is how I missed it. How all of us have been missing it."

"They're not out there much, not all day and all night like in the city. No more than an hour or so at a time, two or three times a day. The word's out, though, so their customers know when to come."

Barb checked her watch. "And two o'clock is one of their times."

"Every day. Ten to eleven, two to three, and six to seven. Not like they get there and leave on the minute, but I seen some pretty sad-looking characters who got there fifteen minutes late."

"Still. How do forty cops in a town this size miss that kind of thing?"

"Like I said, this ain't the big city. These kids not all brazen like on TV. They skulk in doorways and around corners till someone come by looking for them. Police car—hell, *any* car—come up on them, they melt away. You must have come in a strange way, or maybe they getting careless."

"No one hassles them?"

"I know what you're thinking. I asked Detective Doc the same thing. Re-member him saying about that Mafia guy—Mannarito or something—taking a dim view of such goings on. I seen none of it."

"Maybe that's why they've been so careful." Barb twisted in her seat, find out could she see that corner from here. "More afraid of him than they are of us. You know, Mr. West, Doc's worried about you getting too close to this crew. I can't even see that corner from here, let alone what's going on. You don't go out to check on them, do you? Kids or not, that's a bad idea, even if they're paranoid. Especially if they're paranoid."

West showed ivory teeth. "Come take a look at my perch."

He led her upstairs to the room he used as an office and library. She'd been here before, with Doc and the Faison boys, watching Wilver and David build a car online like the one they'd seen leaving a murder next door. That had been at night. What she saw in daylight surprised her.

"I had no idea you could see the tracks from here. I thought the other houses in the row were in the way."

"Ah, but you see, they don't lay out in a straight line. I have to hold my head just so—" he showed her—"but I can see good long's I hold that posi-tion. Red Hat down there now."

"Red Hat?"

"See him? There with the red ball cap on? He wears it every day, so I call him Red Hat. He usually down there with his boys Tore Hoodie and Zippy."

"Zippy?"

West pointed him out. "On the right. If that ain't a pinhead, I don't know what is."

Barb stared hard. "You can tell them apart that well from here? It has to be seventy-five, a hundred yards."

"Here." West handed her a pair of binoculars from a folding television tray under the window. "After a while I recognize them without the help."

Barb watched and pouted. Her crime radar needed work. "They are get-ting brazen. The unit's parked right outside, and they're working again al-ready."

"That's another reason I'm glad you're here, aside from pleasant com-pany." West picked up a black-and-white school composition book and made a note. "They don't know you can see them from here. I wondered about that before. Now I'm sure."

"What's in the notebook?"

West continued writing. "Notes."

"About...."

"The boys on that corner." West closed the book, put it and the pencil on the television tray. "I keep tabs on who's there, and when. Who they with, who they talking to, is it happy or mad or just boys busting on each other. Every day or two I type it all in the computer. Makes it easier to sort and find stuff than flipping through a book trying to read my writing from weeks ago."

"Can I see it?"

West sat at the desk and booted up. "Took me a while to find the best way to do it. I still make changes—refinements—every so often, but it's working good now." Some mouse clicks. "Here you go. What I've seen there over the past few weeks."

Barb looked over West's shoulder at a spreadsheet with a column for dates, several for names, even one for the weather and lighting conditions. The last was labeled "Activities," with entries in code. West tapped a four-by-six note card on the desk. "Here's the key for that last column."

"How long is this? How many rows?"

"Let's see." West hit Control-End, went straight to the bottom. Man knew his way around a spreadsheet. "Three hundred and sixty-eight."

Barb turned away from the screen to stare at West in disbelief. "*Three sixty-eight?* I thought you said there wasn't that much going on."

"It's not like there's three hundred and sixty-eight separate hoppers down there. Everybody I recognize has a line for every time he's there, and I cross-reference them."

"Cross-reference? How?"

"See, right now Red Hat's there with Tore Hoodie and Zippy. Red Hat gets a line, and they go in the column next to him. Tore Hoodie gets his own row, with Red Hat and Zippy mentioned, and Zippy gets one. Makes it easier to sort."

Barb couldn't help smiling. Her father was younger than West, thought of computers as conspiracies. "How much time does this take?"

"I'm a old man. Been retired twenty years now. There's a lot of handyman jobs I won't do anymore. Fix a faucet? Sure. But I ain't putting in no bathtub. Still twenty-four hours in a day, though, and I ain't ready to spend it all watching television. Hope I never am. Not all day, anyway."

Barb wanted Jefferson West to have a long time to not watch too much television. "Do you mind if I send Doc over to take a look at this?"

"He's the one I been keeping it for."

[21]

Willie Grabek was already behind his desk when Doc walked in, first time he'd got there earlier in the year-and-a-half they'd worked together. Reading a file, spoke while Doc was still setting down his coffee. "I hear that Polack guard was in here feeding you a story yesterday."

Doc cocked his head, pulled his brows together. "Aren't you Polish?"

"That's why I can call him that without offense. Like two black guys calling each other nigger."

Doc didn't think the similarity was as close as Willie did, but he'd never seen him so enthusiastic and didn't want to kill the buzz. "He came in here with a cock and bull story about how Mike Mannarino's car might've been in the lot when he got there that morning. Rollison paid him two gees to make me goad it out of him."

"That prick. He got over on us one time—not that he had much to do with it—and now he thinks we're complete hicks. You might be—you grew up here—but I'm no more than twenty percent hick. Twenty-five, tops. Fuck him."

Grabek was in such a good mood Doc wondered if he got laid last night. Or his ex-wife had an accident. "You're awful cheery today. What's up?"

"Let's go outside and talk. Napoleon doesn't want us sitting around drinking coffee in the office, remember?"

They went out the back, stood facing south. A single line of trees separated the city parking lot from a small apartment complex. Light traffic along Tarentum Bridge Road going north toward the river and 28. The eight o'clock breeze no warmer than yesterday's, but today's carried spring.

"Beautiful day," Grabek said. "Almost makes me wish I still smoked. Anyway, while you were getting jacked off yesterday, I did real police work, beating the bushes down Homewood and over on the North Side."

"Was it good for you?"

"It'll be good for you, too, when you hear what I got. Took me all day, but I found out Donte Broaddus dumped Mike Mannarino as his connect a few months ago."

"We've never been able to prove Mannarino was the connect in the first place. How can we prove he was dumped?"

"We don't have to yet. It's just another string to pull. This Nelson what his name? Butterfield? Maybe I sweat him a little more with what I got yesterday."

"I thought he didn't know where Donte went after dinner."

"That's what he said. Doesn't matter. It's not like some broad or jealous boyfriend put two in Broaddus's head and drove the carcass all the way out here. I have business questions for Nelson. We trip him up—which doesn't look that hard to do—maybe we get a handle on the Mannarino-Broaddus connection. I heard Nelson and Broaddus worked together. Maybe he was actually there when a package changed hands."

"So you're back to Mannarino."

"I never left him. We never left him. You know that. We just want to close it to our satisfaction, not Harriger's. This piece of evidence leads that way. I'm following it. You coming with me?"

"Yeah. Yeah, I am. Sorry, Willie. I got too much peripheral bullshit going on to make sense of what that means. You're right. Mannarino almost certainly did this. Had it done, anyway. Be nice to squeeze him for a change."

"I asked around about cooperation from Pittsburgh, but he doesn't bother them enough, especially if he's not the primary drug supplier anymore. Everything else is nickels and dimes to them."

"Still enough to keep Mike and his couple of made guys living well," Doc said.

Grabek popped a stick of gum into his mouth. "Everybody's happy. The cops and Feds can say they eradicated organized crime in Pittsburgh, and Mike and Buddy Elba and that Dolewicz asshole—what do they call him? Stretch?—still make out. I always thought the secret to being a successful criminal was don't get greedy. Enough falls through the cracks for someone who pays attention to make a lot of money. Mannarino's a lot of things, but he ain't stupid."

"We're not stupid, either, Willie, but I'll be damned if I know what to do next."

"I don't know about you. I'm going downtown and wake up Nelson Butterfield. Get him to direct me to someone. Anyone. Tap a few old contacts. Shake some trees. See what fruits and nuts fall out."

[22]

Doc was not home ten minutes before the doorbell rang. The man on the top step was around fifty. Salt and pepper hair cut short. Blue suit, white shirt, red tie. Black oxfords. Doc saw the gun on his right hip, even though the suit was cut to hide it. The man's right hand rested on the door frame, far enough from the gun not to be a threat.

"My God," Doc said. "A federal officer, come right to my house. What can I do for you?"

"You could invite me in," the man said.

"You could show me some identification," Doc said. "It's not just Feds who dress unimaginatively."

Special Agent Raymond Keaton didn't sit until invited. Doc asked why he was here and Keaton said, "I was wondering if you were tired of fucking up the Mannarino investigation yet."

"I'm just a small town cop, Special Agent Keaton. We're nowhere near running out of ways to fuck this up. If you're here to teach me some of the cool things Feds know to fuck up investigations, I pass. We'll call you when we need you."

"Come on, Dougherty. You think I picked you at random? I checked. You're slumming in a town like this."

"Your research should've told you I don't think of it that way. Why are you here, at my house, talking to me? You're supposed to go through my chief."

"Stan Napierkowski's on sick leave."

"Jack Harriger's acting."

"I'd rather Harriger didn't know I'm here."

Doc didn't feel like guessing what Keaton meant by that. He waited for the Fed to go next.

"Word is you're good, and you're trustworthy," Keaton said. "You know when to talk and when to listen. That's why I came to you."

"Is this on or off the record?"

"What difference does it make?"

"If it's off the record I can plead innocence and ignorance when you fuck me."

Keaton smiled. Not one of those tight, superior, federal agents tolerating abuse from his lessers' smiles. He looked like he was having fun. "How do you like it? You want me to come back with flowers, or should I just bend you over the couch?"

Doc smiled in spite of himself. "Looking at you, you might want to come back with booze. A couple of trips worth. Okay, you're probably still a backstabbing, glory-hogging prick, but at least you have a sense of humor. What can I do for you?"

Keaton shook his head. "No, really, it's what I can do for you." Doc gave nothing away. "Maybe later, if you're so inclined, I might ask for something in return, but even then it will be in your best interest to do it. Not a threat." He held up a finger. "Our needs may coincide here."

Doc tilted his head and opened his hands in Keaton's direction.

"You know who Daniel Hecker is?" Keaton said.

"Owns the new casino and half the town."

"You're close about the town. He doesn't own as much of the casino as you think."

"Hecker's the only name you hear."

"He has a silent partner."

Doc waited for Keaton to continue until the pause grew meaningful. What it meant, he had no idea. "I have a feeling you're about to tell me a story, and that can be thirsty work. You want a beer?"

Keaton surprised Doc, still seated when he delivered the drinks. Most Feds would have examined everything in the living room, asked to go to the bathroom and opened the medicine cabinet. Keaton sat and waited for his host like a normal person.

He thanked Doc for the beer and gestured around the room. "You see this little row of condos from the outside, they seem bland. You have to get inside and look around to see how boring they really are."

Doc dipped his head. "I went to school with a girl named Kathryn Whitlock. She was, well, slow, and that's being charitable. We used to call her Special Kay behind her back." He took a swallow. "I just assumed Special Agent had the same origin."

"Not bad," Keaton said. Took his time with the drink, straightened the cuff of his pants. "Hecker made money in dot coms, cashed out before the crash. Started flipping houses before it became fashionable. He was smart enough to know the housing bubble wouldn't last and went all in when he saw Pennsylvania was about to allow limited casino gambling."

"Why didn't he get involved in one of the big places downtown?"

"Remember how that went down. Competing ownership groups, only one would get the franchise. Hecker was the odd man. A little sleazy, came across a bit too much like a hustler to suit the squeaky clean image they wanted downtown. So he got frozen out.

"By this time he's believing his press clippings. Someone who made as much money as fast as he did must be a genius, right? And now he has a hard-on because they wouldn't let him play with the big kids. So he picks a town that's on the skids, too far upriver for the downtown money to bother him, but close enough to still draw from the population."

"Penns River."

"Hecker needs friends, both here and in Harrisburg, and the kinds of friends he needs don't come cheap. He also knows an elegant place this far out will become a white elephant, so he builds a grind joint, plain and simple. Quarter slot machines where people without much money can enjoy themselves and not pay for a lot of overhead. Of course, this has the added benefit of costing a lot less to build."

"This is very interesting," Doc said. "What does it have to do with Mike Mannarino and Donte Broaddus?"

"Relax. You're learning something and I don't want to overload your circuits. You have anything to eat around here? I had a shitty lunch."

Doc went into the kitchen, came back with a half-eaten bag of Tostitos and a jar of picante sauce. Tossed them one at a time to Keaton from ten feet.

"Thanks." Keaton opened the jar. Undid the chip clip and looked into the bag. "Good. I like the scoops. So, Hecker greases all the right people, says all the right things, but those are all distractions and he forgets what's most important." Keaton took a second to arrange his meal around him on the chair. "You don't have any cheese, do you? Velveeta's fine."

"I might have some individually wrapped slices of American. Will that do, or should I order out? I realize a top flight education like this doesn't come cheap."

"Is it yellow American, or that white shit? Never mind, the chips will hold me until I can stop on the way home." He scooped what looked like a pint of sauce out of the jar with a Tostito.

"What did Hecker forget?" Doc said.

"Huh?" Keaton loaded up another chip, still chewing the first.

"The most important thing. You said he forgot the most important thing."

"Csh furr." Keaton swallowed. "Cash flow. He was so busy counting how much money he was going to make, he forgot to keep track of how much he was burning. Lost a bundle when the housing market went to hell. He winds up with all his ducks in a row politically, but not enough money to build the place, and no one—no one—is lending." Washed down the bite with the last of his beer.

"Do you know vultures can smell a dead mouse from two hundred feet in the air? Well, human vultures are always looking for guys like Danny Hecker. There are lots of people with money they don't want to account for. They're always circling, looking for more or less legitimate ways to invest cash in relatively untraceable locations. So Hecker gets a call from Sergei Volkov."

Keaton sat like he was waiting for something. Doc said, "You want another beer?"

"That's it? I give you Sergei Volkov—and yes, I do want another beer, thank you—right here in your little town, and all you can do is ask if I want another beer?"

"Gee, Special Agent Keaton, I'm just one of forty cops in a town of thirty thousand people that gets smaller and older every year. Maybe to a big time federal officer Sergei Volkov is like Keyser Söze, but he means dick to me."

"I'll wait until you bring the beer. You're going to want to give me your full attention." Doc brought back two beers, handed one to Keaton, and sat. Keaton opened his, took a drink, wiped his mouth with the back of his hand. "At least you appreciate beer. I met with a guy last week, all he had was Bud Light. Acted like he was doing me a favor giving it to me. I dumped half of each can down the toilet."

"Keaton?" Doc said.

"What?"

"Sergei Volkov."

"Volkov. Right. He passes himself off as an oligarch now, but his nickname in the old country was The Terminator. He's only a silent partner in the paperwork and government sense. When Volkov says jump, Hecker asks 'how high,' and he's already in the air when he does it."

Doc was past impatient with Keaton. Tried everything to show it short of screaming "Get on with it." Tapped his foot, drummed his fingers. Crossed his legs, then reversed them. Looked at his watch. Yawned. Yawned while looking at his watch. Switched to sitting still as a stone and staring right through Keaton until he realized the Fed might be getting off on driving him crazy.

"Sergei's out of the hard core criminal stuff now, wants to be respectable but doesn't know how. No one too savvy will mess with him because they know he's the five hundred pound gorilla. Imagine the look on his face when a schmuck on the make who's not as smart as he thinks he is drops into his lap with a thousand slot machines. So Volkov built the casino in Hecker's name and lets little Danny collect the quarters he hopes will wash the stink off his money. Gives Sergei a chance to enjoy the quieter things in life, like teenage girls and an occasional effeminate boy. But I digress."

"Tell me about it. Look, Keaton, I have to go to work in the morning. Now that I know why the whole town has that funny smell to it lately, you want to get to the good part? It was Broaddus and Mannarino got you in the door."

Doc could have been talking on the phone with someone else for all the more Keaton reacted. Waited until Doc finished, took a healthy swig, suppressed a burp behind his hand and wiped his mouth. "Sergei's easing his way into retirement, but his son, Yuri, is a different story. Yuri wants to follow in the old man's footsteps. He generated a lot of heat in New York, and when Dad opened up shop in Pittsburgh, Yuri saw virgin territory. It was him cut Donte Broaddus's drug business away from Mannarino. That's why Mannarino dumped the kid where he did."

Doc was seething by the time Keaton came up for air. "How long has the FBI known Mannarino was Broaddus's connect?"

"At least five years. Hell, we knew within three months after they started."

Doc stood, walked behind his chair, leaned on the back. "We asked you at least once a year if you had anything on Mannarino selling drugs. You told us no."

"I never even met you before."

"Don't get cute. They lied to our faces every fucking time."

"You didn't have a need to know."

Doc squeezed the chair's back, stared into the seat. "What do you want?"

"I just came here to let you know Mannarino did kill Broaddus. We might even be able to make a case for it."

"You have a source?"

Keaton paused, not sure if he should tell Doc even this much. "Yes. And that's all I can say."

"What do you want from me?"

"I told you. Nothing."

"Bullshit. I never met a Fed in my life who'd give a blind man a quarter without asking him to keep his ears open. I'm thinking you're here this time to prime the pump. Ask me what you want now so I can tell you to go fuck yourself tonight and save you a trip."

Keaton stood, brushed crumbs off his lap. "Don't be hasty. What I want should help everyone. Mike Mannarino is getting squeezed. Yuri Volkov will kill him if he doesn't roll over, and we have a possible conspiracy to commit murder for hire. Thing is, we can't use the murder."

"Why not?"

Keaton looked out a window, the first time he'd looked less than certain about himself. "It's not a federal crime."

"Give me what you have and we'll charge him."

"We don't want him charged with it."

"You're telling me you have a chance to cut off most of the drug trade in western Pennsylvania and eastern Ohio and you won't take it?"

"Grow up, Dougherty. The government's spent years and millions of dollars building a case on the whole operation here, from Pittsburgh past Youngstown to Cleveland. We keep pulling some of these threads, we'll get Buffalo, too."

"We have a problem here now."

"And arresting Mannarino on a case you *might* be able to make won't solve it. You disagree? I'll make you a deal. Go over to his car lot and kill him. Right now. It even slows down the supply of drugs to Pittsburgh, I'll swear you were with me the whole time.

"You won't do it because you know better. You're a smart guy. Money abhors a vacuum. Mannarino goes and within ten minutes a dozen minor league gangsters will start shooting each other to get whatever Yuri Volkov leaves them. It's the way of the world. There's always another one."

Doc was as close to speechless as he ever got. "How the hell can you come to work every day if that's your attitude?"

"Me? I love my job. Love it. They put me on white collar crimes a while ago. I lasted a year and a half and begged them to let me out. You know what I missed most? Waiting outside the courtroom when they brought the guy out for the ceremonial eye fucking. I live for that. Yeah, it's just one guy, and there are five more to replace him, but I got you, asshole, and you're going away, and that's my present for the day.

"You know we'll never win, not completely. There will always be criminals. You have to look at it the way someone who plays for the Pirates looks at it. No one on the team now will ever win a World Series in Pittsburgh. Hell, the guys on that team now probably won't be alive the next time the Pirates win. They have to go out every day to win *this* game, get *this* guy out, drive home *this* run. That's where their victories are. The system won't let them have more than that."

"You think that's enough?"

"It better be, pal. That's all there is."

Doc stared at him a few seconds, realized his mouth was ajar. Closed it and looked away. Keaton hadn't told him anything he didn't already know. All of it no more than the other side of the coin from what he and Grabek had told Rick Neuschwander. "So what do you want?"

"We need one key domino to fall. We think Mannarino might be it. We want to make him a confidential informant."

"Mike Mannarino a CI? Good luck with that."

Keaton nodded. "I know. That's where you come in. We think you might be able to turn him."

"You're delusional. He hates me."

"He respects you, too. He knows you want him put away so bad you can taste it, you can smell it, and he knows you won't cheat to do it. Mike likes to think of himself as an honorable man. He knows you are. You can talk to him, if you do it right."

Keaton was crazy, even by Fed standards. "I'd never pull it off. I won't be able to pretend I can live with the deal."

"You won't have to. Present it as a win-win and make the introduction. Then step aside before you have a chance to rub each other the wrong way."

Doc finished his beer, pitched the can through the doorway toward the recycling bin in the kitchen and missed. "I don't like working like this."

"I know. We'll make it worth your while."

"How?"

Keaton waited for eye contact. "You help us flip Mike, we'll use him to get a case started on the Volkovs. They go down and you have a chance to get ahead of the curve for a change." He half smiled. "Come on, Dougherty. No piece of ass you've ever had is going to feel as good as the eye fucking you'll get from Yuri Volkov on his way to Lewisburg."

[23]

Mike Mannarino didn't impress Tookie much. Reputation he had, people live or die on his say-so, Tookie expected someone more like Tony Soprano, not this salesman-looking motherfucker. Showed like he spent his days talking you into the Impala instead of the Cobalt, or explaining why ventless dryers were the big thing.

"See, what I'm saying here, Mr. Mannarino, sir, is I hear you looking to move product, and I need a supply. We got one of them, you know, spheres of influence things going on, dig?" Tookie laying it on heavy, wanted to come off only as smart as it took to be taken seriously.

Mannarino drank bourbon, rocks, sitting in the Hilton's lounge like it was his living room. "What brings you around now?"

Tookie looked out of place in his hoodie and Timberlands. Part of the act. He could have worn a suit—he had a phat one in the closet at his aunt's, serious O.G.—knew Mannarino needed to feel superior, like Tookie could be had. "There's like a power vacuum now, what with Donte gone. Someone need to step up. Might as well be me."

"No offense, but I dealt with Donte for over five years. I never heard of you. Now you come out of nowhere and say you were close."

"Well, you see, Mr. M, Donte and me was close, but I been, like, away for a while, if you know what I mean. Like in college, dig?"

"Yeah, I dig." Mannarino looked to his right, where Nelson sat with some white dude Mannarino didn't feel the need to introduce. They sat at one of those tables for two, barely big enough for their drinks. Nelson had something with an umbrella in it. White dude was dry. "What I want to know is, if you two were so close, why're you talking to me instead of the guy Donte wound up doing business with?"

Tookie sipped his champagne. Skinny white bitch made him buy the whole bottle for a hundred and seventy five bucks. He'd look small if he argued about wanting just one glass. He'd get a piece back out of her tip. "I always thought Donte was hasty making that move. Them Russian cats, they too—*voluminous* to work with. You know, all unpredictable and temperamental and shit."

"I know what you mean. Russians can be very voluminous."

"See? We on the same page. Now you, you a businessman. Come here, nice place, drinking your drink, we talking like two what you call long-term associates. My boy Nelse over there told me how you used to work the drops. That shit was tight, ain't no one getting over the way you done it. That's how I'd want to do it, you want to get together on something."

Nelson came to him this morning, finally had the meeting set up. Tookie didn't care for the location. He knew Mannarino picked it to make him feel out of place, bunch of traveling businessmen dressed for the office careful to walk around the nigger dressed for the street. Tookie was cool. He hadn't planned to do Mannarino the first time. "Okay—uhm what is it? Tookie? Is that short for something? Too—no, too—fuck. What would it be short for?"

"Not short for nothing," Tookie said with more heat than he intended. "Just a nickname, all."

"Okay, then, Tookie," Mannarino paused like he was listening to a private joke. "We might be able to do something, if you can show me you're serious."

"How I do that?" Mannarino rubbed a thumb and fingers together. "Oh, I see. Money. I like that, you getting right down to it. How serious you need me to be, and how soon do I need to get so serious?"

"Thirty by next Tuesday."

About what he expected. "That's cool. I can do that. Like, where and what time?"

"Like, have your boy Nelson talk to Stretch over there. He'll fill him in."

"No offense, Mr. M, but first time and all, I like to deal with you direct. I don't know your boy Stretch over there, and, tell the truth, I ain't know Nelson all that good, him coming into the picture while I'ze away. You think maybe you and me could do this one, put my mind at ease?"

Mannarino sipped his drink, looked away for a second like the waitress serving another table might have the answer written on her ass. "No offense, Snooky, but Stretch there is the only man you'll see unless I call for you. You don't trust Nelson and want to talk to Stretch yourself, be my guest. I don't know you, either, and I'm not taking a chance of going to prison just so you can feel comfortable." He paused, leaned closer. "You feel me, bro?"

For three seconds Tookie was willing to skip the plan and slap this cracker ofay white bread dago wop honky around like the bitch he was. Kill his cousin Donte—no, not kill him, *have* him killed—not even man enough to do the nigger himself. Had to be his house boy over there, Stretch, done Donte. Well, Tookie was a man, a serious player in the life, muscle for the biggest drug dealer in Bodymore, Murdaland, and he'd look forward to doing this white piece of shit on his own when the time came. And that time was a lot closer than Mr. Mike the Hook Motherfucker Mannarino expected.

[24]

Buddy Elba met Mike and Stretch at the Aspinwall Sportsman's Club. "How'd it go?"

"Amateur hour," Mike said. "Fucking Tootsie Roll wants do to business direct—just me and him—while he gets comfortable. Says we never heard of him because he's been in the joint the last five years. Must've been more than five, if his name never come up the whole time we talked to Donte. I don't know what kind of friends he made in prison, but I can see how he's dumb enough to get sent there."

He asked Stretch for a drink, get one for himself, and did Buddy want another. Stretch brought two glasses of red wine and sat at the bar with a beer.

"You think it's a set-up?" Buddy said.

"If it is—and it probably is—it's either the Russians or the Feds. I don't think it's the Russians. They'd just get me out somewhere and kill everyone in the car. They wouldn't fuck around with this straw man bullshit. They're too voluminous for that." He laughed.

"Voluminous?"

Stretch chuckled. Mike had told him the story in the car on the way from the Hilton. "Yeah, voluminous. That's what this nigger said when he meant 'volatile,' why he wanted to do business with me instead of them. I know, he could've been putting them down so I'd think he didn't come from them—his way of being cute—but I don't think so. Like I said, they would've had that retard Nelson set up the meeting and shot Stretch and me both about fifty-eight times getting out of the car. Along with any pregnant women, old ladies, and kids in strollers who happened by. Maybe a dog if they got lucky."

"So you think Feds?" Buddy said.

Mike held out his glass. "Stretch, dump this out and get another bottle. There's something wrong with it." Buddy looked at his half-finished glass with a puzzled expression, handed it to Stretch.

"The Feds? Maybe. This Tookie or Mookie or Dookie or whatever his name is, you'd think they'd do better than him for a go-between, but The Wire's been over for a few years now. Maybe they don't know what's current."

Stretch delivered two fresh glasses of wine. Mike tasted his and nodded. Buddy waited until Mike signed off, then drank. Said, "So you think it's the Feds."

Mike held up a finger while he swallowed. "One more possibility. This numb nuts could be for real. Maybe he has been away and wants into the game. Maybe he just wants to take over Donte's turf and the rest is bullshit.

Tell you the truth, that's the possibility I like least. The Russians decide to kill me, well, they can only kill you once. The Feds, if this is their idea of a slick operation, we can play them. They been trying to put me inside since I was in college, and I still ain't slept a night in any bed I didn't choose myself. But this Cookie, if he is the real deal, could be just smart enough to be worth doing business with. The deliveries don't worry me, we can keep him safe on our end. I'm worried he might fuck up on his own and someone will roll him back up to us."

"Fuck him, then," Buddy said. "We don't need the aggravation."

"We could use the money, though. We took a hit when Donte dumped us, and now that fucking grind joint is taking away even some of our usual sports action. Most of that will come back when the excitement dies down, but we still got cash flow issues."

"Take him for a spin," Stretch said. Unusual for him to say much in meetings. The Pittsburgh *borgata* was just the three of them now. Mike was boss. Buddy was underboss and *consiglieri*. Stretch did everything else. Capo, soldier, collector, muscle, tax assessor, recruiter, delivery man. Mike and Buddy developed policy. Stretch implemented it. Still, with three guys, Mike didn't enforce the hierarchy like a New York family. He didn't care who had an idea, so long as it made money. "See how you feel about him, how his money spends. You get a bad feeling, think he might have friends we wouldn't get along with, the same thing could happen to him as happened to Donte. It's not like we don't know how to fix problems like that."

"How'd you leave it with him?" Buddy said.

"He's supposed to have thirty large together by Tuesday. Stretch will call and set something up. I ain't decided if he's actually going yet. Maybe we'll let Nookie play with himself for a while, see how he handles it. Meantime, I want you two to find out what you can about this dinge. Buddy, we got friends should be able to tell us if he did time and where. Spend a little money if you have to. Just keep it low profile. No point letting him think we don't trust him until we want him to."

[25]

Doc didn't come to Fat Jimmy's any more than he had to. Once in a while he felt the pull, like a fitness addict who can't resist the occasional McDonald's run.

James Wolfe got the name "Fat Jimmy" in high school, to distinguish him from "Thin Jimmy" Susini and "Regular Jimmy" Truver. He grew into the role, waddling around behind the bar at under six feet and over four hundred pounds. He weighed himself every Sunday on a bathroom scale that topped out at 300. Ask him how much he weighed, he'd say, "More than three hundred."

Doc sat at the bar, his cousin Nick Forte to his right. Most of Fat Jimmy's clientele lived in the Flats. Unbuttoned flannel shirts over heavy metal tees, Steelers or Harley hats, and jeans bought at Wal-Mart were the standard uniform for men and about one in five women. Doc recognized the citizen he'd busted at the domestic—what was his name? Dan Something. Yeah, Connor—at the other end of the bar. Doc kept his distance. His job put him in plenty of confrontations he didn't have the option to avoid. He didn't need one off the clock.

Nick wore a "Chicago Bears, 2006 NFC Champions" hat turned backward so it faced the room. "You wore that hat just to bust my balls, didn't you?" Doc said.

"What hat?"

Doc laughed like someone who'd seen a dog do something dog stupid. "Nicky, you just don't give a shit, do you?"

"Sure I do, cuz, about some things. I just don't give a shit about the same things most people do, or what people expect me to. Keeps 'em guessing."

"Keeps me guessing, that's for sure." Doc took a quick look, saw no one paying attention. "The reason I asked you here, I wanted to talk to you about some of the stuff my dad said the other night."

"And I was hoping you brought me here to get me laid. See the one over there, with the tattoo on her neck, butt hanging on her lip, and two-inch black roots? She's had her eye on me since I walked in."

Dan Connor's voice floated along the bar. "Probably a faggot. Afraid to come in here alone, brought one a his faggot buddies with him."

Doc said, "How's your mom?"

"Good, all things considered. She's not supposed to leave the house or even go upstairs for another week, but she's up and around. Drives Dad crazy, all the stuff she wants to do and can't, makes him do it, and it's never the way she would've done it."

"I've seen how that works. They're sisters, you know."

"Kind of scary at times there, shooting pool, watching your mom and won-dering who let mine out of the house."

Connor's voice louder now, fifteen feet away. "Had a gun and a badge and still had to sucker punch me."

"Is that guy talking to you?" Nick said.

"What makes you think so?"

"Well, he's already used faggot, cop, badge, and sucker punch. I don't see anyone else who might qualify."

"I arrested him last week. How long you planning to stick around?"

"The weekend, I guess. Keep the load off Dad, let him get out of the house some. She has a doctor appointment on Friday. He tells her it's okay to get around, I'll hit the road. Why?"

"Interested in doing a little work while you're in town?"

"What do you need done?"

Dan Connor explained to the bar in general the difference between pussies and faggots, and why what happened to him was the work of a faggot, never using Doc's name. Doc told Nick about Ray Keaton's visit.

Nick finished his beer, waved for two more. "That's all very interesting, but it doesn't answer my question. What do you want me to do?"

"I can't figure out why Keaton went to the trouble of going around Har-riger and I don't have anyone on the force I can ask to help. Harriger knows them all, and their time is accounted for. I hate to ask them to do it off the clock."

"And you're not one hundred percent sure who you can trust."

"And I'm not one hundred percent sure who I can trust. A few, yeah. But I don't want word to get out."

Dan Connor was five feet away, over Doc's left shoulder. "I wonder how he'd do when a man was ready for him, in front a witnesses?"

Nick said, "What do you need?"

"Can you keep an eye on Harriger after work? I'll try to get the couple of cops I trust to keep loose tabs on him during the day when we might have ex-cuses to run into him once in a while."

"Sure," Nick said. "I could use something to get me out of the house. What are you looking for?"

"Where he goes, who he sees, when he's there, how long. Like that. Don't worry about what gets said. It's not worth getting burned over. Right now I only care if that Fed skipped him because he doesn't like him, or if there's a legitimate reason not to trust him."

"I'll get you license numbers and pictures if I can. You can run them, right?"

Connor bumped Doc, spilled beer on his shirt. "Oops," he said. "Don't hit me, police man. It was an accident."

Doc took a deep breath. Ignored the wet spot on his shoulder. "I have a case number I can use. What's your rate?"

"For you? Dick. I know you and your folks look in on my parents. I appreciate it. This is a chance to show it."

"Thanks, but this isn't a personal favor. The city can pay."

"You'd use city resources if it wasn't a personal matter. You want to do something for me? Salve your conscience? Make me a special deputy, get me a carry permit. Give me some cover in case I wind up someplace where it might come in handy."

"You're sure that's all?"

"It's plenty."

Connor poked Nick on the right arm. "What about you? Come in here wearing that goddamn hat for a team that never won shit. Six Super Bowls the Steelers got. What about you? Come in here wearing that stupid goddamn hat. You another faggot here to protect your buddy? Think maybe both of you can handle one man in a straight up fight? Two faggots to one?"

Nick looked straight ahead, watched Connor between the flyspecks in the mirror over the bar. "Check with your mother before you call me a faggot."

"What did you say?"

"Or your sister. Either one. Mom's slowing down, but your sister can still pull a train and ask for seconds."

Connor dropped his right foot, cocked his hand. Nick didn't turn, drove the back of his fist into Connor's nose so hard Doc heard the crunch. Nick reached back for a handful of Connor's hair and pulled his head down to ram into the edge of the bar, and again. Connor slumped to the floor, nose covering half his face.

Nick reached a bar rag, wiped blood off his hand. "We'll get together tomorrow so you can point this Harriger guy out to me."

[26]

Doc stopped after work at Giant Eagle for chipped ham and Isaly's barbecue sauce. Sweet peppers to grill up with sausage his father brought from a butcher in Apollo who made them on site. Drove across the lot to Get Go for gas and went inside for a couple of Slim Jims and a bottle of Gatorade.

His cousin Nick had come by at 2:30, asked Doc to point out Harriger's car.

"There," Doc said. "The blue Crown Victoria in the space marked 'Deputy Chief,' Master Detective."

"He's a cop and he buys a Crown Vic for his personal vehicle? Christ. Come with me."

They walked past the back door to the police station. Nick paused at Harriger's Ford, looked around, reached under the right rear wheel well. Saw Doc's expression when he stood.

"GPS. One man tails are hard, even in a burgh like this. Gives me a chance not to have to stick too close to him. I'll email you any license plates and pictures to your Gmail account as I get them. Anything else I should know?"

"Raise your right hand." Nick did. "Do you, Nicholas Forte, solemnly swear to uphold the laws of the Commonwealth of Pennsylvania and the City of Penns River, to protect and serve its residents to the best of your ability, placing the lives of the innocent and helpless above your own, so help you God?"

Nick stared at him. "You're shitting me. *That's* the oath for a special deputy?"

"Say 'I do.'"

"First tell me that's the actual oath you have to administer to deputize someone."

"Not just anyone. You."

"That's my oath?"

"Uh-huh."

"Just give me the badge."

"You don't need no stinking badge. It's just an ID card."

"And for that I have to swear to that stupid oath you made up while we're standing here."

"I'll have you know I spent most of the morning thinking of that oath."

Nick shook his head. "Small town cops. Okay. I do."

Doc handed him the credential. "Do what?"

"Swear to what you just said."

"Then swear to it."

"You mean like recite it back to you?"

"Yes."

"I don't remember it all. *You* don't remember it all."

"Sure I do. Come on. I, Nicholas Forte, do solemnly swear...." Nick glared at him. "Do you want the carry permit or not?"

"You got me a carry permit already? Without me even making an appearance?"

"I know the magistrate." Doc held up the permit. "Let's hear it: I, Nicholas Forte, do solemnly swear...."

"I, Nicholas Forte, do solemnly swear to uphold the laws of the Commonwealth of Pennsylvania and to protect and defend the sick, the infirm, and those of limited mental capacity—" he paused to stare Doc down—"to the best of my ability, with liberty and justice for all. Amen. Will that do?"

□   □   □

Doc chuckled over the memory, concentrating on tearing the Slim Jim wrapper with the precision required to extract the sausage without mutilating it so much he walked right past her until the car brought him up short. A two-year-old Monaco Blue BMW 528i sedan Doc would recognize if it had been through a compactor.

Marian Widmer held the nozzle as she gassed up, looking everywhere except where she might be unable to avoid eye contact. Shorter hair, still getting away with wearing jeans designed for women ten years younger. Both her kids were in the back seat. Doc finished his business, pocketed the receipt, and stepped across the island behind her.

"Hello, Mrs. Widmer."

She had to know he might speak, still couldn't keep her shoulders from slumping when he did. Recovered like a pro, turned to look at him like she hadn't seen him. "Hello, Detective Dougherty."

Her voice was flat and cold. Her glance flicked across his face only long enough to show disdain. Not as hot as she thought she was, though still hot enough to have slept her way to getting a man to con her husband into killing her former female lover, then have her accomplice shot twice in the head while she watched. She had a third man teed up when Doc intervened. The hitter she hired was found dead for poaching on Mike Mannarino's turf without a license. Three corpses on her tab in less than a month in a town that had never seen three homicides in a year before she got busy.

"How have you been?" Doc said.

Marian focused on the gas nozzle. Her throat tensed as if she might speak, but she didn't.

"I was just doing my job," he said. "It was nothing personal."

She hung the nozzle and stared with a combination of hatred and confusion. "Why are you telling me this?"

"It's a small town. We're bound to run into each other."

"Ignore me."

"Seriously, Mrs. Widmer. When's the last time a man ignored you?"

He watched the internal struggle play out on her face, the desire to tell him off tempered by her uncontrollable reaction to the flattery, overcome at the end by common sense.

Doc said, "I have something on my mind, and you might be just the person to ask. I have a date coming up, and I want to take her someplace quiet and romantic. You know, make her feel special. I read good things about John Anthony's over in Plum Borough. You've been there, haven't you?"

He knew damn well she'd been there. Read it in the late Carol Cropcho's diary, how she and Marian had eaten there before the first time they made love. Stopped in himself a few times to chat up the staff, show Marian's and Carol's pictures around, try to find someone who could place them together and provide the link the prosecutor insisted on having before she'd bring the case to trial. Time was passing and memories of isolated encounters between wait staff and customers faded every day. People moved on, replaced by others who'd never had a chance to see Marian and Carol together. Over a year now and Doc still stopped somewhere at least once a week, always on his own time.

Marian stared through him with an intensity that would have unnerved someone less confident. Still didn't speak.

"Hello? Mrs. Widmer? Anthony's? Any advice?"

She spat in his face. Her children pointed and stared. Doc watched her get into her car and lay rubber as she drove away. His smile grew in stages from the left until he felt his lips separate.

[27]

Stush Napierkowski had lost weight. It looked good on him. No sunken cheeks or waxy pallor or other signs of the gauntness of infirmity. He projected energy, though all he did was sit in his favorite chair and drink orange juice. Stush looked like he'd lost weight because he wanted to. He didn't sound like it.

"Damn right I look like I lost weight. You would, too, you had to eat the shit she gives me three times a day."

Helen Napierkowski gave as good as she got. "I've been buying the same groceries for years, Benny. He always brought home food or got something out. Now he can't get around, so he has to eat what I buy. It's his own fault."

"I thought you always ate Helen's cooking," Doc said.

Helen beat Stush to the reply. "He does, but he doesn't like to eat what I buy. He comes home with steak and ground meat and sausage and tells me to cook it up. I buy asparagus, I buy broccoli, and he tells me I can eat it. He eats mashed potatoes or French fries. His idea of healthy food is celery with his deep-fried chicken wings."

Doc looked at Stush. Thought of his own diet of bar food and a weekly salad. Made a note to call the doctor for a cholesterol check and to resume his aerobic work. "Whatever you're doing now is working, Helen. He looks great."

"Goddamn it, you encourage her like that I'll send her over to cook for you," Stush said.

"I have laundry to do," Helen said. "Benny, you want a beer before I go downstairs?"

Stush answered before Doc could. "Can I have one?"

Helen gave him a look. "You know you can't. Why do you even ask me?"

"Then he can't either. Goddamned if I'll sit in my own house and let some-one works for me eat or drink anything I can't. He can have a rice cake and a low sodium V-8 or he can go to hell."

Doc didn't bother to stifle all of his laughter. "I'm good, Helen. I'll stop by the Edgecliff for a couple of Basses and a poor boy on the way home."

Stush called him an asshole. Helen laughed and went downstairs.

"You want a beer, get one," Stush said. "I only put on a show for her ben-efit."

"I'm good. Can't stay long, anyway. I just stopped by to keep you in the loop."

Stush reclined the chair. "Let's hear it."

"I think I told you the other day I got my cousin the PI to follow Harriger around."

"After Jack made the big push to pin that homicide on Mannarino."

"Right. I like Mike for it, too, but I don't care for how Harriger wants it done."

"Good for you."

"Anyway, Nick's been on him a few days and all he learns is Harriger leads a pretty boring life. Then last night, he goes down to Smokey Bones at the Mills alone, without his wife. Nick emailed me the license plate of the guy he met with, and a picture." Doc rocked back on his heels, blew out a breath.

"This ain't *Law and Order*, son. Don't make me ask who it was."

"Dan Rollison."

"You're sure."

Doc made a noncommittal gesture. "It's the plate to his Lincoln, and no one could say the picture Nick got on their way out *wasn't* him."

"Your cousin go inside?"

"He went to the bar. They were around the other side, so he couldn't see, but he says they were definitely together."

"How long?"

"Over an hour."

Stush's hands were folded on his somewhat diminished belly. He tapped his thumbs against it as he thought. "Doesn't mean anything. Rollison's Director of Security for one of the biggest employers in town, and they had a homicide dumped in their laps. They have good reason to talk."

"Then why go out of town to do it? Why not call Rollison in, or go over to the casino and see him there?"

"You sure he didn't?"

Doc hesitated. "He's being watched at work, too."

"Your cousin?"

A longer hesitation. "Barb Smith and Eye Chart Zywiciel are helping me out."

"Off the clock?"

Still longer. "On. Eye Chart keeps Barb in the area, calls her to get on Jack's car when he leaves the office."

"No other crime in town, we can keep two cops watching one of our own all the time?"

"If she's needed elsewhere, she goes. We've been lucky so far."

Stush sipped his juice, tapped his FOP ring against the glass. "You'd make me a lot more comfortable if you'd have a beer. So I wouldn't feel guilty about depriving you."

Doc sighed inwardly, got the beer. He rarely drank beer at Stush's house because Stush drank Budweiser and Doc thought Bud tasted like it had been strained through a used sock. Great commercials, lousy beer.

Back in the living room, he popped open the can, made a show of taking a drink. "Better?"

"Yes, it is better, mainly because I know you don't like it. Every time you come in here since I got sick you have bad news. Why should I be the only one that suffers?"

"You don't think Helen suffers, you around the house all day?"

"Trust me, my young friend, Helen does not need your sympathy." Tapped the ring against the glass again. "We need to talk about this."

"That's why I came."

"We're not just bullshitting around here. Harriger will make your life miserable if he finds out what you're up to. I don't know how I feel about it myself, and not just because a lot of the shit will stick to me if it goes bad. How sure are you about him?"

"Not very. I was thinking about calling it off until Nick saw him with Rollison last night. You're right. They have every reason to speak openly, homicide or no homicide. So why sneak around?"

Stush waited a beat, said, "I know you've thought about it. Tell me."

Doc took his time to decide how to phrase it. It occurred to him this conversation had more thoughtful pauses than a Lifetime movie. "Rollison's a spook. He might not be able to help himself with this cloak-and-dagger shit. And Harriger—I think Harriger's out of his depth. He sees the big payoff, but it didn't occur to him until now he'd have to run with some big dogs to collect. Events are coming together faster than he can keep track of them, which forces him to trust Rollison more than he wants to and it scares him."

"You really think he's scared."

"I think he hasn't had a normal bowel movement since your heart attack. Not once he saw how many moving parts there were, and who was involved." Doc swallowed the bottom half of the can in one long swig, get it over with. "I can't argue with him. I'd be scared, too, in his situation."

"Except you wouldn't be in his situation."

"Sure as hell not by the route he took. Look, Stush, I'm good with keeping you out of it, but you're the one guy here with the authority to conduct an internal investigation and get away with it. Everyone reports to you."

"Normally, but these aren't normal times, at least for me. People with a lot of suction are looking for an excuse to put Harriger in my chair. This comes out the wrong way, it might give them exactly what they're looking for." Stush finished his juice, set the empty glass on an end table. Doc pointed to the empty, then toward the kitchen. Stush waved him off. "You couldn't get more from that Fed—what's his name? Keaton?—about why he wouldn't talk to Harriger?"

"Nothing specific."

"I'm more than a little curious why he didn't come to me direct. It's not like I'd tell Harriger about it."

"As well as he knew me, he had to assume I'd tell you. Want me to feel him out about it?"

"Do more than feel him out. He wants you to extend yourself to help his investigation. Experience says, you work a *quid pro quo* with a Fed, get your *quo* up front."

[28]

Barb Smith said she had an errand to run, could they meet at the Edgecliff at six, instead of right after work. No problem for Doc. He lived two hundred yards away as the crow flew, he'd be there whenever. He sat at the bar and discussed drywall with Denny Sluciak until she walked in and he saw her errand had been to get her hair cut, add a little makeup, and change clothes from the polo shirts she wore to work into a well-chosen pullover sweater. She looked nervous, too, which surprised him. He'd seen her upset, angry, scared, flustered, and uncertain. Not like this, fingering the silver heart that hung from a thin chain around her neck like it was a rosary.

He ordered and paid for two beers and steered her to a table away from the flow of traffic. Business picking up now as families came in for dinner on spaghetti night, $8.99 buys all you can eat, or two adults pay and kids eat free. Your choice.

"You hungry?" he said when they were seated. "The spaghetti's great, and they throw in two extra meatballs for a buck. I'd come just for the meatballs if they'd let me."

She wasn't hungry yet, maybe in a little while if that was okay. They each took a drink and Doc asked how her day had gone.

"Jack only left the office for lunch at Clementine's with his brother. I recognized him from—"

"Whoa. I didn't ask how Jack Harriger's day was. How was yours?"

This answer required more thought. "All right. Nothing special happened. Wrote a ticket, handled an accident. Don't you want to hear about Harriger?"

"I thought I already did. Is there more?"

"No. Just lunch. Sarge kept an eye on him in the office the rest of the day."

"Then we're done with him. Don't get the idea I'm like that *Les Miserables* guy, lay awake nights thinking of how to put Jack away. He didn't do anything interesting today. Fine. Let's drink a couple of beers and discuss something else. We're off the clock."

"Okay." Wary. He waited to let her choose a topic. She sat. He knew this was when he should comment on her hair, any vague compliment would do, what mattered was showing enough interest to notice. It didn't feel right. She could be nervous about "dressing up" for him and if he said something about it she might think she'd been too obvious. Problem was, it did look good, and he did like it, would probably have made a comment if she'd walked into work like that. He liked how it looked enough that nothing else came to mind to ask her, which let the silence ripen, every second making it harder for someone to break it.

Ben Dougherty sure was a slick one with the women.

They talked about the weather, segued into a recap of Doc's drywall dis-
cussion with Denny. Barb had bought a house in Valley Heights—"Oxy-
moron Hill," Doc called it, where the terrain rose straight out of the Allegheny to give a great view of the river shimmering in the sunlight, when
there was any. The basement was semi-finished and she was thinking of finishing the job, had no idea how. Doc felt platonic gaining momentum like a
marble bouncing down a set of concrete stairs and was glad when she excused
herself to go to the bathroom. He needed to think about how to turn the conversation, or whether it should be turned at all, if it was a good idea to maybe
get involved with someone at work.

His train of thought derailed when Anita Robinson kissed the top of his
head, bit his ear, and plopped herself into the chair next to him. "Wow," she
said. "Talk about one of those cosmic confluences. Ben Dougherty, out
alone—again—and my kids staying with their dad tonight. Don't you owe
me a rain check from the last time I stayed over? I remember you were right
in the middle of something when you got a phone call and had to go."

"Hi, Anita." Shit. Doc liked Anita, and picking up where he'd left off
when the call came in for Donte Broaddus was an appealing idea. Except for
right that minute, which was when Anita happened to be suggesting it. Almost insisting on it, in fact, sliding her hand along his leg and leaning one of
those resilient breasts into his arm. Anita was no slut, had an appealing earth-
iness about her that was erotic in an unrefined way. "I—I'm kind of here with
someone right now, if you know what I mean."

Anita didn't know, not right away. The confusion showed on her face,
then her eyes flicked to the unattended glass. Her horror at what she'd done
showed when she saw the look on Barb's face, approaching the table.

Doc tried. "Barb Smith, this is Anita Robinson. Anita, Barb and I work
together. She's a cop." He would have pushed his teeth out of his mouth if
they could have gathered the words back, realizing his mistake in the split second between articulation and sound.

Barb looked like a kid who'd had her eye on a bike for months watching
someone else take it out of the store. Anita was mortified. "Hi, Barb. It's nice
to meet you. Doc and I are old friends. I like to tease him sometimes. Don't
think anything of us."

The embarrassment on Anita's face gave the lie to any harmless explanation she tried. Infants in strollers would have seen her posture and the redness flowing into her cheeks and known she'd been seducing Doc, not teas-
ing him. Barb was a cop. Good luck with that.

Doc's turn. He was as out of his depth as Harriger was with Rollison, tried
to act as though what just happened was the most natural thing in the
world. He'd done nothing wrong, no apology was needed—at least not
from him—let's all have a drink and ignore the elephant shitting on the table-
cloth. "Anita came by to say hi. Her kids are spending the night with their

dad." The effect wasn't quite the same as if he'd slapped Barb, but he'd saved himself the effort of having to stand.

Barb said she needed to be going, she had an early day tomorrow. Anita said she saw the girlfriend she'd come to meet and everyone couldn't help but look toward the door where no one was standing. Doc said it was always nice to see her and couldn't Barb stay for one more while Anita backed away from the table.

Barb sat and it was left to Doc's social graces to salvage the situation.

She spoke before he could. "Do you want me to stick with Harriger tomorrow?"

Good. Talk about work. Defuse the situation. Get her concentrating on something other than what just happened. "You think he's worth the time? Rollison's probably the key player here. Whatever's going on, he's likely the broker."

"Okay, then. I'll follow Rollison." Barb stood, slid her coat off the chair back.

"Wait. How are you going to do that? You won't know when he comes or goes."

"Haven't they been complaining about wanting increased security in the parking lot? I can be a presence. Ask Sarge to keep me close." She shinnied the coat over the shoulders. "I don't know how I'll do it. All I know right now is I want to go home and not talk about this anymore. Is that all right with you?"

Not really. But it wasn't like he had a choice.

[29]

Dwight David Wierzbicki didn't think he was named after the president, but after a general. Thought it was "some Civil War dude." No straight job skills to speak of and too bad a criminal to make a living at that. He'd been the man who could put Marian Widmer together with the hit man she hired. Got cold feet at the line-up and Marian walked.

Doc remembered that, and the day he'd spent at the food court in Pittsburgh Mills hoping Wierzbicki could identify Marian. How Wierzbicki had alternated complaining about his lot in life and commenting on women less than half his age.

Even fresher was the memory of last night at the Edgecliff. Doc spent the morning trying to think of ways he could have handled that worse, couldn't come up with any. Having to wait for lunch until he'd talked to this jagov didn't bode well.

He made a point of ignoring Wierzbicki, spoke to Rick Neuschwander, the other cop in the room. "Before we start, before he says a fucking word, will he testify if we need him?"

"He says yeah, Doc. Bick told me he knows he was wrong on that Widmer thing. He knows he owes us."

"That's what he says now. What's he going to say when the trial gets close, or we ask him to point someone out for the record? My ass still hurts from the last time our ace snitch did me a service."

Wierzbicki's chair rasped across the floor. "This is bad, even for cops. Hello? You're talking about me like I'm not even in the room. I'm right here, boys."

Doc turned on him with a glare that had cowed Iraqi insurgents. "No. You're not. Not until I say so, and I'm not saying shit until I hear something good. A woman with three corpses on her sheet is walking around loose because you didn't come through. I don't even owe you simple courtesy. You owe *me*, shithead."

Wierzbicki held the glare for a second, dropped his eyes. "I know. I was wrong about that. I know I can't fix it now, not with that hitter getting clipped the way he did. Maybe what I have here can make it up."

Doc asked Neuschwander, "What's he trying to get out from under this time?"

Neuschwander said the Bick had nothing pending. He'd come in on his own, claiming he had information that would be of interest to the cops working the Donte Broaddus case. "He's done that a few times over the past year or so. Giving us tips, I mean."

"Any of them pan out?"

"Yeah, actually. He's pretty good."

Doc looked at Wierzbicki, who looked away. "What's your motivation?"

"My what?"

"Why are you doing this? Volunteering to—come to think of it, what the hell are you volunteering to do?"

"You're working this black drug dealer got dropped in front of the casino a couple weeks ago, right?"

"Yeah."

"I seen him that night. Well, the night before. You know, the night he got clipped."

No one spoke until Doc lost patience. "Where?"

"Down Aspinwall, in the alley off Brilliant. The Sportsman's Club, or something like that. Dumpy cinderblock-looking joint."

Doc knew it well. Mike Mannarino's place of business for things he didn't want to taint the legitimate atmosphere of Bypass Motors. The question was, did Wierzbicki know?

"How'd you know it was Broaddus?"

"There's a streetlight there, just off the corner. I seen him when he come through it, before he went into the alley."

"I mean how did you recognize him? You ever meet him before?"

"I seen him around."

"Where?"

"You know, places."

"What places?"

"Different places. Not around here so much. Down the North Side, mostly. He used to do business with a guy I know."

Doc raised an eyebrow. "You into drugs now, Bick?"

Wierzbicki couldn't help it, smiled when Doc used his preferred name. "No, nothing like that. We're friends, is all. Me and this guy."

"This guy who does business with the biggest drug dealer on the North Side, now deceased."

"I didn't say they did drug business together."

"Guy does business with a drug dealer, what kind of business does he do?"

"Dealers do more than just sell drugs."

"Like?"

Wierzbicki looked to Neuschwander. "You know, like food and shit. Even drug dealers got to eat."

"So your friend runs a restaurant."

"No. It was just an example—"

"A supermarket."

"Don't jump ahead like that. Listen—"

"Convenience store."

"All right, he's a fence, goddamnit."

"Which explains his acquaintance with you."

"Not recently, but you know... do I, like, have immunity here?"

"No."

"I got to have some protection."

"You want a lawyer? You worried about incriminating yourself?"

"I didn't do nothing wrong. It's you, trying to twist everything I say into me being bent on this, and I'm here trying to help."

"Let me give you some food for thought. I'm looking into a murder. You hook me up with the killer and I'm not going to worry about a few under the table purchases." Doc raised his hand when Wierzbicki opened his mouth. "But come up short on me again, and I'll bury you."

Wierzbicki picked at a loose veneer edge on the table. "Everything you say, you always say it both ways. Like, you'll look the other way if I help, then you'll bury me if I don't. I don't know if I can trust you."

Doc's voice was low. "Have I ever made a deal with you I didn't keep?" No answer. "We both know you've broken a deal with me. That was your free one. It doesn't matter if you trust me or not. You want something from me, I need to trust you, and I don't. You want to fix that, come across."

Wierzbicki stopped playing with the table. Looked into a high corner of the room, the effort of his forbearance etched into his face. "What do you want to know?"

"What time did you see Broaddus in Aspinwall?"

"Must have been around ten. No later than ten-thirty."

"What were you doing there?"

"I was meeting a guy at a bar down there."

"What's the name of the bar?"

"Ain't no name on it." Doc gave him The Look. "Really. There's a sign out front, says 'Bar.' I knew to go there by the address."

"Who were you meeting?"

"It don't matter. He didn't show."

"What's his name?"

Wierzbicki thought. "Name's Rick Butler. Lives in Blawnox. I don't know the address, since I know you're gonna ask. I know it's Blawnox, though."

"Anybody in this anonymous bar see you?"

"Sure. Bartender. Another guy asked me for a light."

"Think they'll remember you?"

Wierzbicki sat up straight, like the proceedings had only then become interesting. "Whoa. You're making me build an alibi here, like I'm a fucking suspect. Think what you want about if I'm trustworthy, I don't do heavy work. I don't need to prove I was there."

Doc looked at Neuschwander. "Is he always this thick? If I thought of him as a suspect, I'd be making him prove he *wasn't* there." Back to Wierzbicki.

"You're not a suspect, douche bag. I'm trying to see whether you're actually a witness, or if you have something big hanging over you we don't know about and you came in to trade a horseshit story for an umbrella."

Wierzbicki turned his head at "hanging over you," and Doc wondered how big it was. "The bartender might remember. I only been in there once before, and he wasn't there the other time. I only stayed about a half hour."

"Did you see him leave? Broaddus?"

"No. I just saw him as I was going by."

"You see anyone else there?"

"No."

"How did Broaddus get in?"

"What do you mean, 'How'd he get in?' Someone opened the door."

"Did he knock or ring a bell?"

Wierzbicki paused and Doc watched his eyes to try to guess if he was thinking or remembering. "Pushed a button. Must of been a bell."

Doc crossed his arms, leaned against the door frame. Let Wierzbicki wait. "Anything else?" Wierzbicki shook his head.

"So... you saw Donte Broaddus ring the bell and be let into the Aspinwall Sportsman's Club around ten or ten-thirty on the night before he was found in the parking lot of the Allegheny Casino. That about it?"

"That's it. All I know."

Doc waited until Wierzbicki looked toward him. "We'll check the parts of that story that can be checked. It holds up, I'll talk to the prosecutor. It doesn't, I'll talk to you. Last chance for amendments."

"No, man. That's the straight shit. I'll swear to it."

Doc snorted. "You'll swear to it? Right. Just like the check's in the mail and I won't come in your mouth." He left the door ajar when he went out.

[30]

"No. Not this one again." Willie Grabek pitched his empty coffee cup in the direction of the trash can. Just back from court, still in his testifying suit, and Doc's retelling of Dwight Wierzbicki's story killed his post-conviction buzz. "You know the old saying. Fool me once, shame on you. Fool me twice, fuck you and the horse you rode in on. Lincoln, I think."

"No argument here." Doc's hair still wet from spending the afternoon canvassing Aspinwall in the rain. "Don't forget, he got me, too. I wanted him to tell his story walking so I could go to lunch, but I had to at least check it out. There *is* a bar a block or so away from Mannarino's place, just says 'Bar' outside. No one there remembers him, but they don't not remember him, either. You know, the usual. 'Maybe. What night was that? Christ, that was three weeks ago, I don't even remember if I was working that night. You'll have to talk to Lou.' I'm going back after I eat to talk to Lou."

"So that's worthless."

"Ah, but..." Doc held up a finger. "Mannarino's place, the Aspinwall Sportsman's Club, does have a button for a buzzer. There is a street light where he said it was, and he should've been able to see Broaddus if they were both where he says they were. I'll look at that, too, when I go back tonight. See how bright it is."

"What about the guy he was supposed to meet?"

"I couldn't find him. Not surprising, considering all the more time I had if I wanted to get back to see you. I left word with the Blawnox cops we're looking for him. Wierzbicki was accurate about one thing. Butler is a fence, nothing heavy, just the kind of guy a stooge like him would use. He's also rumored to move the occasional eight-ball, so it makes sense he'd know Broaddus."

Grabek took his time to answer, like he had to be prodded. "Okay. I been asking around. Broaddus was mostly heroin, but he wouldn't walk away from a coke deal if one fell in his lap."

No one spoke. Doc knew better than to rush Grabek's judgment. Wouldn't want to, anyway. Willie was smart and experienced and an egotistical prick who preferred clues he found to anything else that turned up. Wierzbicki's story was enough to move on, even with his history. They'd need corroboration—that history couldn't be ignored—in case The Bick got cold feet again.

Neuschwander wasn't used to being lead dog with evidence. "He's been reliable since that Widmer business, Willie. I've closed half a dozen cases with him."

"How big?" Grabek's tone showed he'd been looking for an excuse to use it. "Parking meters? Snatch and grab at the Dollar Store? He's going to have to sit in court, Mike Mannarino not thirty feet away, and say the last place anyone saw Donte Broaddus alive was walking into Mannarino's club. I don't see it, and he's not worth a shit to us if he doesn't come through."

Doc said, "Not necessarily. Wierzbicki's a leaky witness to put on the stand, but if his story checks out, he's pointed us in the right direction. Today I checked whether he was there. I'll look again tonight and take Broaddus's picture with me, see if anyone recognizes him. Probably too much to ask for someone to have seen him that night, or going into Mike's club, but we're due some luck on this case. We don't know of anyone else who saw him after that half-wit—what's his name?—Butterfield had dinner with him. Now we at least know where to look."

"You really going to work this off the clock?" Grabek said. He worked on his own time only when Halley's Comet was visible.

"You don't think Jack will approve overtime if I say I have a lead might put Mannarino on the spot? He wants this to go down so bad, I might as well let him pay for my trip to Yellowstone this summer."

[31]

"You can see all the way to the bakery from here."

Doc invested the time before he could return to Aspinwall by making his overdue visit to Jefferson West's townhouse. Viewing the local bakery from an upstairs window was not as expansive a vista as the mountains of Yellowstone, or even downtown Pittsburgh from the top of the Incline. Still, Doc hadn't expected to see as far as the railroad tracks, and Scarpetta's bakery was twice that far.

"Me, either, till I lived here a while," West said. "The way the ground lays, you don't notice how it slopes away. Logan's house sits lower than mine, and beyond that's the flattest stretch of ground around here. I can see the old PPG plant with the field glasses."

Doc held out a hand. West gave him the binoculars. "Son of a bitch. I never imagined."

"Neither do them boys. I can watch all day from here, no one the wiser."

"Except you."

"And you, if you care to take advantage of what I learned."

"Show me."

West moved the mouse to clear the screensaver. "There you go. Everything I have so far, going on six weeks." He tapped an index card near the monitor. "That's the key to the Activity column."

Doc scanned the screen, scrolled up and down. Saw a pattern and ran a sort to group things, then another. West hovered over his shoulder like a child who didn't want to feel too proud of a project until his father had passed judgment.

"I see you have nicknames for all these guys. Are they based on obvious and consistent physical characteristics?"

"Best I can, yes."

Doc pointed to the screen, careful not to touch it. "These rows here. Name 'Wilver' on all of them. How come he gets a name and no one else does?"

West didn't answer. Doc stared at the screen like if he looked hard enough it would change. "I don't suppose it's because he just reminds you of Wilver Faison, is it?"

"No," West said.

Doc withdrew his hand, rubbed his chin. "He only started showing up last week, and he's not very regular. When's the last time you talked to him?"

"'Bout three weeks." West paused, looked out the window, away from Doc. "I meant to check up on him, see where he been, but I got busy playing like I was on The Wire or something. Even shopped for cameras one day. Too busy thinking of ways to get those boys who already bent to worry about keeping one straight."

"Seen David lately?" Wilver's younger brother.

"He stops by couple times a week after school."

"By himself?"

"Lately he does. Their schedules different now. Wilver gets out almost an hour before, don't hang around waiting for him now that David old enough to walk home by hisself."

"David's still in elementary school, and Wilver's, what? A sophomore?"

"First year in high school. Wouldn't that be a freshman?"

"Usually, but the ninth graders still go to junior high, at least until the board makes up their minds about that middle school. Let's see. Wilver catches the bus, by the time he gets here and walks over to David's school, he's not waiting long to walk the kid home."

"That's not how it works. Wilver's in high school, he's a young man now. David's still a boy, but he's grown enough not to worry about all the time. He probably don't want Wilver walking him home every day like he's a baby. You know how boys are."

Doc leaned back in the chair, joined his hands and reached above him to stretch. "I know. It's just, they used to be inseparable."

"Part of growing up. Remember, too, they were pretty much on their own then, and they had that one's in the ground now harassing them." Donte Broaddus.

"I hear their mother's been clean since that last rehab at County," Doc said. "Be a shame if Wilver went bad just as things showed promise." Tapped a finger on the desk. "This isn't my place, and I'll shut up if you want me to, but have you—"

"Have I thought about going over and talking to him?" Doc lowered his eyes, nodded. "You know I did. First time I saw him, I figured he just passing by, maybe see someone he knows, say hello. Second time I wanted to tell him not to do it no more, there's nothing but trouble there for him. This last time I know it needs to be done."

Doc gave him time to explain why he knew it needed to be done, but hadn't, shirking not being something associated with Jefferson West.

"The thing is, it can't be me does it. One, word gets out to the hoppers down there I can see them's good as I can, they'll move someplace where it's harder to watch them. Or they decide not to move, and make trouble for me instead.

"The other thing is, best I can do if he don't want to listen is threaten him with what can happen. Ain't nothing I can actually do. That's not how it is with him and me. I'm not his grandpa, but I'm like one, caring for him, wanting the best. Kids don't take to scoldings from their grandfolks.

"But you. You a cop. His friend, yes, but still po-lice. You could tell him how it is, and how it might be you has to take him in when the time comes. Besides, it's your business to know. Me, he'll know I'm an old man looking out the window. You? Who knows how you found out?"

This was how it started before, Doc going outside channels to keep the boys safer than they were, but not as safe as they could be. He should call Family Services, knew it wouldn't do any good. Sherry Gibson was the Juvie officer, and a good one, but Doc had cut her out of the deal last time. Now she had no prior relationship when Wilver needed someone he knew and trusted. Barb would do it—she loved those boys like an aunt—but boys needed to hear some things from an alpha. Chuckie Faison was a ward of the state of Tennessee for cutting up a Mexican. Not the kind of alpha influence Wilver needed.

Funny how the jobs you don't want are the easiest to get.

[32]

"You didn't come here *directly* after talking to the police, did you?"

"Give me some credit. I was there around noon. It's what? Five-thirty now? I went home, hung out, and then ran around a little. It's not like they followed me."

"It's also not like no one could've seen you come in here."

"I'm in here all the time. What you're paying me for this barely covers what I dropped on the slots since you opened."

Daniel Rollison drummed his fingers on the desk blotter. "Okay, then. Who did you talk to?"

"I went in and asked for Neuschwander. He's the one I know, and he's not the smartest cop in the world, if you see what I'm saying. He listened for about five minutes and went and got that prick Dougherty."

"How did it go with him?"

"He jerked me around. Asked why I was there, how I knew Broaddus, how I saw him. Treated me like a fucking suspect."

"How *do* you know Broaddus?"

"Like we haven't been over this fifty goddamn times already?"

"I want to hear it the way you told Dougherty."

"I told him Broaddus did business with a friend of mine. He worked me over pretty good, you know, how does he know him? Is your friend a drug dealer, too? Am I selling? Shit like that."

"What did you tell him?"

Wierzbicki's hands moved like a spastic juggler. "I told him the friend was a fence."

Rollison closed his eyes. "Did you tell him you were there to meet Butler?"

"Yeah."

"And Butler really is a fence."

"So?"

"So now they might think Butler knows Broaddus, and they'll try to cross-reference your story with his. We're going to have to get that straight, which means I'm going to have to pay him again. I should take it out of your end. It's your fault."

"It's not like what you're paying us will break this joint."

Rollison exhaled through his nose. "Okay, then. We do need to get to him first, assuming the police haven't found him already."

"They didn't find him, even if they looked. His cousin's getting married in Weirton. He went down early to party."

"Did you specify Butler knew Broaddus?"

That required thought. "I don't think so. I said I had a friend who was a fence and that was how I knew Broaddus. I said Butler was who I was there to meet, but I don't think I said he was a fence, and I'm sure I didn't say he was the one who knew Broaddus."

"It's not unreasonable for them to assume Broaddus was there to see Butler before he saw Mannarino, but it's still an assumption. Call Butler. Not on a cell phone. Tell him if they ask, he never heard of Broaddus until he saw his name in the paper. If they press you on it, you can always say it was a different fence who introduced you." He'd have to come up with someone for that role, too. Rollison hated these situations. He'd done plenty of them for the government, with professional help and what seemed to be unlimited funds. Money wasn't an object this time, either. Yet. He still hated having to touch all the moving parts himself. His dues were paid.

[33]

Nick Forte picked a sliver of plastic from his beef chow mein, threw it and the fork into a trash can at Lee Ho Fuk's. Took another from the small pile next to his Styrofoam plate.

"Why do these Chinese fast food joints always have such shitty utensils? It's not enough I could be eating ferret chow mein here. I have to worry about a side order of plastic tine while I'm at it."

Doc slurped a noodle into his mouth. "You eat a lot of Chinese food?"

"Not a lot, but there's this place near my office in Chicago makes kick ass General Tso's chicken. I go in once a week. Bought some good plastic flatware at Costco so I can take it in with me, or I go through two-three forks every time I eat there." Doc opened his mouth. "Don't say it. The chicken's great. Those forks couldn't handle a custard pie."

They passed for brothers, though each had a brother he resembled not at all. Their mothers were sisters, their fathers were cousins—"has to be some form of incest," Big Doc said—the gene pool spinning the cousins out like two cars of the same model, a couple of years apart and with different option packages.

"How are we doing on Rollison?" Doc said.

"Following him's no problem." Nick paused to chew and swallow. "What worries me is who he talks to at his office that we can't account for. He's in there all day, getting phone calls and seeing all kinds of people that could be of interest to us if we knew who they were."

"Nothing we can do about that. We don't have anything close to the evidence we'd need for a tap warrant, and it probably wouldn't matter." Nick looked over at him, chewing, a piece of noodle stuck to the corner of his mouth. "Rollison's a retired spook. Far as anyone can tell, his service to the government is completely off the books. We can't even find out what agency he worked for. He probably takes countermeasures."

"How do you know he's a retired spook?"

Doc pointed to his lip, at the spot where Nick had the noodle. "Pittsburgh checked him out pretty good a few years ago. Apparently they got that far and the door slammed."

Nick brushed the noodle with a finger, inspected it, put it in his mouth. "Seems to me they wouldn't even know that much, if he worked deep and dark enough."

"You saying he's bullshit?"

"I don't know enough about him. All I'm saying now is he has this massive reputation based on assumptions. For all anyone knows, he could be a computer geek who worked in HR and erased himself to look mysterious in his old age."

Doc thought about it, not too hard. Nick was good, but he liked to amuse himself when the world failed to. This led him to say things just to get a reaction. Doc's experience with government personnel systems—especially classified ones—said what Nick proposed was not only unlikely, but illegal. Still, he made you wonder sometimes.

"You said following him wouldn't be a problem. Are you relying on your assumption his street cred is bogus?"

"Not completely." Nick dropped the fork onto the empty plate, blew his nose into the paper napkin. "That was pretty good. Should clear out my sinuses all night. No, good as I am, I wouldn't let something this important hang on an assumption, even one of my own." Folded the plate over the napkin, dropped it into the trash. "I took the tracker off Harriger's car and put it on Rollison's. Now I don't even have to hang around that dumpy casino he works in. I can visit with my folks until he's on the move. They only live about a mile away. I'll be on him before he gets to the bypass."

Doc paused in the middle of wrapping up his trash. "Be careful with this guy. Harriger's bullshit. Rollison's a different story. Whatever he's doing with Harriger wasn't his idea. He's working for someone who's probably working for someone else, which means someone might have his back."

"Hecker?"

"He's top of the food chain for most of the stink around here."

"Top of the stink chain in a town like this doesn't make him Al Capone."

"Don't forget, he's hooked up with Sergei Volkov. Retired or not, he knows how to bring the hurt. It won't take him more than five minutes to put a crew on you if the spirit moves him."

"I forgot about him," Nick said. "You're right. Volkov changes how this has to be handled. Even more reason for the tracker. Lets me keep a lower profile. How long are we going to stay on this guy?"

"Couple of days. If they are doing something with Harriger, they can't let it linger too long. My guess is they want the Broaddus investigation behind them and don't know when Stush will be back. Harriger's a lot less valuable to them as Number Two. Where are you off to?"

"The family estate, try to talk my mother out of making me a second lunch. Rollison usually leaves the casino around six. I'll wander over a half hour or so ahead of time, but I'll be ready to move if he leaves early. You?"

"Mike Mannarino's a leading citizen of this town and we've been investigating him for weeks. It's time I went over and told him. See how he takes it."

[34]

There was a time when the salesmen at Bypass Motors would intercept Doc's semi-annual visit like they would any other customer, see if they could put him in a ride. They'd play their charade until he'd get tired and badge them, then stall until he threatened to make a scene and Mike Mannarino would come out of the office and bring him in. Now Art DeSimone stayed at his desk, waved Doc toward the back.

This week's featured car was a Ferrari F430 Spider. Two years old, 7800 miles, a steal at $189,000. There weren't two dozen people in Penns River who made $189,000 in a year, and one of them had an office in back, could drive the Spider any time he wanted. Doc ran a finger along the finish and read the sticker before walking into Mannarino's office uninvited. The boss remained seated, gestured toward a chair.

"Gee, Mike," Doc said, "your guys used to at least put on a show. This new approach takes all the fun out of it."

"I told them never mind. The sooner you get back here, the sooner you leave. What do you want?"

"You know how it is. You don't see someone for a while, you worry."

"Like you don't know what I'm up to every goddamn day."

Doc said, "Drugs are being sold in the Allegheny Estates and the old downtown."

"Then you should be out arresting the dealers and not here busting my balls."

"We'll get them. I'm here because I'm curious if you know anything about it."

Mannarino sat with his elbows on the desk, shirtsleeves rolled halfway up his forearms. The picture of harried middle management. Or a school principal having his fifth parent conference of the day. "Jesus Christ, Dougherty. Usually you're pissed because you think I get special dispensation for not allowing crime in town. Now I get hell because you think I'm not doing enough. You asking me to go in and clean up your corners for you?"

"I'm not asking you to do anything. I'm just wondering why you haven't."

"Maybe I thought I'd see if my tax dollars bought me any police work. Doesn't look like it."

Doc watched a twenty-something woman whose wardrobe anticipated the coming warm weather enter the showroom. Art DeSimone pulled bits of paper and dust in his wake hurrying to hold the door for her. "Your tax dollars pay for plenty of police work. That's another reason why I'm here. What can you tell me about Donte Broaddus?"

"That the jig they found behind the casino last month? Didn't know him."

"That's odd. I have a witness saw him entering your club in Aspinwall the night he died. Far as we know, that's the last time he was seen alive."

Doc looked for Mannarino to get the red ass. Mike disappointed him. "Your witness lied. Broaddus would have no more business in my club than I'd have at one of those hip-hop gangbanger joints. We don't—didn't—run in the same circles."

"I believe you," Doc lied. "You should know, there are people working overtime to put you in for this one." Mannarino gestured toward Doc. "Not me. Don't get me wrong. I think you had something to do with it. I don't hold with those who'd figure you've done plenty of things you got away with, this one will even the score. I want it done right."

"You're my protector now? Get a real job."

"I don't care one way or the other about you. If we put you away for the one serious crime you didn't commit and call it done, there's still a killer walking around. He's the guy I want."

"You know what, Dougherty? Usually I kind of enjoy it when you come in here and bust stones a couple times a year. We go around a few times and I know you can't touch me or you wouldn't have come in. Today I'm not in the mood. So how about you go do some cop thing and I'll try to make a living?"

Doc stood, didn't leave. "What's wrong, Mike? This isn't like you. You sick? Or just worried about something? You're right to be worried. Someone wants you out, and they might have the juice to do it. I'm not sure why they don't just disappear you, but they must have their reasons." He stepped around the chair to go and Mannarino said something that nailed him to the floor.

"Who do you think it is?"

Doc shifted his head to see Mannarino in his peripheral vision. "The name Sergei Volkov mean anything to you?"

"Sergei? No, I don't know any Sergeis."

Doc turned his body to face Mannarino. "Mike, you have a problem here, and you don't even know his name."

"I know everyone who can hurt me, and I don't know any Sergei Volkov."

Doc thought of how to play it. "Enough dancing. Here's what I know. There are people in town willing and eager to put you away for the Broaddus killing, whether you did it or not. They're connected with Sergei Volkov. The word is he's gone legit, but you and I both know how that works. He gets impatient, he's liable to have a relapse. You're in the middle, Mikey. You need a friend."

"Like you? Get the fuck out."

Doc shook his head. "We both know I can't help you. Think of who can. What do you have now, three made guys, counting yourself? No offense, but your team's bound to be rusty. The occasional hit on some unsuspecting—ahh, what's the word?—*strunz* won't keep you sharp enough for a crew of Russians. There might be a few guys around who'd like to step up, but last I heard the books were closed. Maybe you could ask some other families for help, but they don't like warring with Russians on their own turf, I don't see them extending themselves for you. Who's that leave?"

"You're gonna tell me, anyway. So go ahead."

"Not me," Doc said. "No way am I getting between you and a Russian crew that says you go or there's war. I'll give them a ride to your house, siren and lights. I don't have the resources, I don't have the skills, and, frankly, I don't have the balls."

"So who is it, then?"

"There's only one person with the juice and resources to pull you out of this steaming pile of shit and take you, and your wife, and your kids, and put you someplace clean. We're both related to him. You want me to help you set something up with our uncle, give me a call. We won't even have to sneak around. People are used to us bumping into each other. Hell, with this Broaddus business, the people we're worried about seeing us might like the idea of us spending a lot of time together."

"You're out of your fucking mind."

"Probably. I won't lie to you, your welfare isn't high on my list of priorities. I just don't want to see this town crawl even deeper down the hole it's looking into. If getting you a pass can help keep the Russians away and bodies off the streets, I'm good with it."

Mannarino's head sagged as though too heavy for his neck. "You amaze me. An answer for everything. Tell you what: I'll take it under advisement if you'll go away. Right now." He looked up without moving his head. "Just go. I got problems you don't even know about."

Doc paused to check out the Ferrari and watch DeSimone try to talk the woman into a three-year-old Avalon. Noticed something about the front left quarter panel and took a route out of the showroom so he'd have to pass them. Paused next to her, leaned his lips close to her ear.

"Be sure to run a CARFAX report when you get home. All you'll need is the vehicle identification number, right here." He pointed at the dash through the windshield. "I'm sure there's nothing wrong but you never know. Right, Art?"

He left DeSimone to stammer his way through an explanation of how he was just about to recommend CARFAX and wouldn't think of letting anyone buy a car without it.

[35]

Rollison's car moved at 6:42. Nick Forte left the dinner table, grabbed a Coke from the fridge and a ZipLoc bag of beef jerky from the kitchen counter, kissed his mother and left. He followed Rollison to Smokey Bones at Pittsburgh Mills (again), drank two beers while Rollison ate alone. Next stop was Rollison's home in Shaler Township. The garage door closed at 8:27. Forte parked down the block, close enough to see the front door without looking like it was Rollison he was watching.

Forte ate the jerky and drank the Coke and got out once to pee. He'd decided to stay half an hour past the last light going out. His car was dark enough to blend into the gathering twilight and not draw attention. He listened to an audio of Robert Crais's newest book through an ear bud and waited.

Sitting around until someone else did something they might not do was his least favorite part of the job. This didn't make him special. Few detectives like stake-outs; even fewer like flying solo. No one to talk to made the chance of losing concentration too great. Letting the subject walk away was the least of his concerns. He'd made light of his cousin's lunchtime warning, but knew the probable involvement of someone above Rollison meant he was vulnerable. The fact that whoever wanted Rollison shielded might have access to Russians helped keep him on task.

The last light went out in an upstairs window at 11:14. By 11:30 Forte was ready to go. His legs were cramped, his back hurt, and he needed quiet time seated in a lavatory. He tried to stretch a leg without getting out, thought about how his ex-wife gave him the tedious household tasks because she thought anyone with his patience wouldn't mind them. Things like trips to the DMV, holding their place in the grocery check-out line, returning a gift. Took him years to convince her he didn't like waiting any more than she did. The difference was, he'd do it. It became a test for him, his Zen ritual, stay until you said you'd leave, then five minutes more. Just so he could tell himself he'd done it.

A light went on in the same upstairs window at 11:46.

It heightened Forte's attention, didn't move him. Rollison might have to pee. He could be thirsty, or answering the phone. After eight minutes the light went out, replaced by a dimmer one a second later. A shadow passed through the faint light in a first floor window. Ten seconds later the light went out and the house was dark again. The garage door opened and Rollison's Town Car backed into the street.

Forte let Rollison get out of the neighborhood before he started the car. Stayed out of sight, sometimes not even following on the same street. No easier way to get the drop on someone than to wait in ambush for a tail. Both cars found their own ways to Route 28 north and Forte relaxed a little. An ambush would be harder on the expressway, and every mile Rollison drove toward Penns River made it apparent he was going back to work.

They got off at 366 and crossed the Tarentum Bridge. Forte's attention picked up when Rollison didn't turn left at Leechburg Road—back to the casino—but continued on to take the loop for 56 East. He slowed approaching the light at Wild Life Lodge Road and Forte thought this might be Rollison's preferred route until the Town Car turned right to go past the VFW.

This was tricky. Forte hadn't lived in Penns River in over fifteen years, never had been that familiar with this area. His in-car GPS gave his exact location; the tracker only told him where the transmitter was in relative terms. He could lose Rollison in the woods and spend half the night backtracking and looking up roads so narrow two cars needed both shoulders to pass. The best option was to maintain visual contact, but letting Rollison see the same headlights in his rear-view on these roads at this time of night, he might as well call and ask where to meet him. He turned off his lights.

Clear night, with a quarter moon. Forte could see well enough, his primary concern oncoming drivers who took their half of the road out of the middle around the sharp curves. Not a lot of that going on at this hour, just the occasional flash in the underbrush from the eyes of a coon or a possum.

Curves snaked along the terrain, following the road designers' path of least resistance, twisting like an extension cord dropped on the floor. The tracking transponder wasn't designed for these conditions, made it difficult to tell if Rollison had turned, or the road. Forte didn't know for sure he was overtaking Rollison until he saw on the tracker screen he'd passed him.

He pulled into the next turnout and waited. The target remained stationary. Forte let out his breath. Rollison hadn't gotten behind him; he'd turned off. Forte K-turned to go back the way he'd come. Lights still off, adding the new concern of being overtaken by someone who figured no one would be out this late. That kept him going fast enough to miss Rollison's turn-off again. He caught this mistake quicker.

He'd missed the turnoff because Rollison hadn't taken another road. The Town Car was pulled along the side of a one-pump gas station. The service bay had a fifteen foot square attachment that served as a convenience store. A weathered sign over the door announced, "Cheapest Cigs in PR. Ice cold pop." Forte slowed as much as he dared, saw the Lincoln's doors were closed, Rollison nowhere to be seen. No lights showed in either area of the building. The light above the gas pump was dark.

What sounded like a car door slamming moved him along, back to his original stop. Turned the car around and shut it off, sat in the cool air listening to the engine tick while he waited for the Town Car to move.

Ten minutes later the dot representing Rollison jiggled like an unsteady laser pointer, then went back the way it had come, faster. Forte sparked the ignition, pulled out in time to see a dark Lexus sedan leave the gas station ahead of him. He wanted the license number and he couldn't get it driving without lights. Followed as close as he dared until he passed a side road where he pulled in there and made a quick reverse. Turned on his lights and got behind the Lexus again, hoping he'd be taken for a different car. Drove faster than he liked to get a look at the license plate, stayed there to give whoever was driving a chance to write him off as a tailgating asshole. Turned left on Wildlife Lodge when they bore right for the bypass, then hustled over to Falcon Park Road to catch the highway there. The signal was faint, but in the expected direction. Rollison stopped once, at a service station in Etna, where he gassed up, used the men's room, and bought a bottle of water. Then straight home to Shaler, where the garage door rolled shut as Forte drove past.

[36]

Daniel Rollison couldn't remember a day this bad that didn't involve death. The people who worked for him were unreliable and violated house policy more often than the customers. The people he worked for were imbeciles. Rollison could live with them hiring an inexperienced management crew. He'd never worked a casino himself; security was security. A handful of people with a clue tried to steepen the learning curves of four times as many who were hired because a deal had been reached with the city for favorable treatment if a certain percentage of employees were Penns River residents. Everyone knew ninety percent of them would be gone at the first opportunity. Until then, every day was like a new opening.

Add Dwight Wierzbicki to that mix and Rollison had a headache that throbbed in his mastoid bones, stiffened his neck and shoulders. He thought back to a massage house in Bangkok—not some "Me love you long time" whorehouse, a real Thai massage business—wondered where the closest equivalent was.

He didn't mind framing Mike Mannarino for the Broaddus killing. For one, Mannarino was a virtual lock to be guilty of giving the order, if not the shooting itself. Even if he wasn't, he'd done plenty of other things. No one would lament the raw deal he got. Second, Rollison had made a good life doing what his bosses told him. Done it with the government, with his private security company, and now at Allegheny Casino. He didn't make policy and he didn't question it. His job was to implement, and he was damn good.

He left work earlier than usual and stopped at Smoky Bones because he didn't feel like cooking. He also wanted a drink and hated drinking alone. He didn't count a restaurant as being alone. Lots of people were drinking there; they just weren't sitting at his table. Mostly families and teens there tonight. The only other drinker he saw was a younger man who sat at the bar ten minutes after he came in and left as he asked for the check.

He went home and focused only his eyes on the television. One show seemed to be about making fat people do demeaning things for reasons that weren't clear. Their self-esteem, maybe. He didn't pay enough attention to guess, concluding their self-esteem might improve if they weren't flaunting their extra two hundred pounds on national television. Wierzbicki had better get to Butler before the police did, or there would be hell to pay.

Went to bed a little after eleven, used all the tricks he'd learned over the years to clear his mind and fall asleep. Couldn't have been out five minutes when the phone rang.

"Do you know who this is?" Heavy Russian accent.

"Yes."

"Get pen or pencil to write down." Rollison turned on the nightstand light, pulled a pen and paper from the drawer. The Russian gave him an address in Penns River, told him to go there.

"When?"

"Now."

Christ. He'd worked with many Russians in his career. KGB, GRU, SVR, FSK. Professional, competent men and women. The newspapers were full of stories of how Soviet intelligence operatives who lost their jobs when the Union collapsed had become the backbone of the *Mafiya*, using their skills to make Russian organized crime the scourge of the world. He'd give a week's pay to work with even one of them now.

He dressed in cotton slacks and a light pullover sweater. Stopped in the doorway of the bedroom, went back for a gun in a holster he clipped to his belt at the small of his back. Walked downstairs, drank a glass of water, slipped on his leather car coat and got the car. Took forty minutes to get to the rendezvous, a falling-down service station that sold cheap cigarettes and cold sodas. Turned into the parking lot and Yuri Volkov stepped from the shadows between two cars and directed him around back.

"Thank you for coming out so late, Daniel." Yuri's line of sight went over Rollison's left shoulder, toward the road. He paused as a car went by, continued after it passed the station. "How did your witness do with the police today?"

"It could have gone better, but good enough."

"Did the police verify his story?"

"I don't know. I have to assume they tried, but they haven't had much time."

"I am sure all will be well. I trust you so much I have present for you. Do you know who owns this building?" Rollison did not. "Is belonging to Mister Mike the Hook Mannarino. The cigarettes are contraband, brought in from south. Is also a little bit methamphetamine selling here."

"Are you sure? Mannarino has a reputation for not doing anything illegal in Penns River itself."

"Look around you." Maples and pin oaks and spruces grew higher than fifty feet within ten yards of the buildings. The lot was unpaved, an unidentifiable aggregation of dirt and gravel packed so hard rain wouldn't muddy it. The only visible artificial light at least half a mile away. "Out in middle of boondoggles like this, Mister Mike the Hook don't think of it as his town. More like no one in Moscow or Kiev care if someone fuck up in Siberia." He chuckled and Rollison realized Volkov had made a joke.

"Wasn't even since three hours when Mister Mike was here, with his dumb Polack ass wiper Dolewicz. People saw him, you bet. So here is your present."

Volkov gestured to someone sitting in the car next to them. The trunk popped open, occupied by Dwight Wierzbicki, stripped to his shorts. He was bound and gagged with duct tape, covered with bruises. "Sasha was all day looking for baseballs. We do this because Mister Mike the Hook likes to throw them at people he is upset with. Baseballs are harder than they are looking. Is more dangerous game than I thought."

They stepped closer to the car. Wierzbicki's eyes had the dull look of a concussion. "Here," he pointed, "is man who say Mike Mannarino kill that nigger last month, and he is tortured the way Mike the Hook likes to do, at a place he owns and people saw him just today. Plus this." Volkov pulled a small pistol from his pocket and shot Wierzbicki in the head three times.

He held the gun in his gloved hand while he wrapped it in a towel, handed it to Rollison. "Was taken from Aspinwall Hunting Club early this morning. If does not have Mike the Hook's fingerprints on it, it will have those of someone from his crew, no? Now I give to you to do what you want. If police cannot make case from all of this, then I think they are not really trying."

[37]

Doc, Willie Grabek, and Rick Neuschwander stood looking at Dwight Wierzbicki's remains. A front that moved through overnight dumped the last drizzling remnants of an inch of rain on the three detectives.

"That's cold, leaving him in the trunk of his own car," Neuschwander said.

"That's how it's done, Noosh," Doc said before Grabek could say something snotty. "No one wants to mess up their own car. Get him out somewhere and leave him where he won't be seen for a while."

"Then why here?" Grabek said. "All these woods around, must be a hundred places within a couple of miles where they could've left this piece of shit, wouldn't be found for days. Weeks, even. They leave him right behind a place of business." He spat toward the garage. "Not much of one, but someone was guaranteed to be here first thing in the morning."

"But Broaddus was dumped at the casino—"

"That was a message shooting, someone pissed off at the casino," Grabek said. "That's why we think Mannarino had him done. This one—oh, shit. Look who's here. Like this wasn't enough of a cluster fuck already."

Jack Harriger's door opened before the car finished rocking to a stop. He walked in a straight line to Wierzbicki's open trunk, eyes looking to neither side. He wore his badge on a lanyard around his neck.

Grabek nudged Doc, "Look at that. In case someone here forgets he's a cop."

Harriger walked past the detectives for a closer look at Wierzbicki. Used a pen to push back a forelock to see a bullet hole. Stepped back and looked at the three in turn, decided Doc was the one to talk to.

"You and Mannarino have history. Let these two dot the I's and cross the T's. I want him in custody by the end of the day. Enough foot dragging."

"What would you like me to charge him with?" Even Grabek looked impressed by the insolence in Doc's tone.

Harriger quivered with rage. Stepped to within three inches of Doc, his eyebrows even with Doc's chin. "That dead man came to us yesterday and put Mannarino in for the Broaddus killing. Not twenty-four hours later he's in the trunk of his own car in what even you'll have to admit is a mob-style execution. Look at him. Go on, look at him!"

"I been here awhile, Jack. I looked at him already."

"Bruises all over him! The coroner will dance around it because he can't prove it, but I'll bet my pension he'll testify those bruises are consistent with being struck repeatedly by baseballs. Only Mike Mannarino kills like that. He owns this garage. He was seen here yesterday. What more do you want?"

For once Grabek was the voice of moderation. "That evidence cuts both ways, Jack. Mannarino's famous for not shitting where he eats, so why would he leave a body on his own doorstep. Follow that line of thinking and you could say Danny Hecker killed Broaddus."

"How the hell do you figure that?"

"He was found on a property owned by Hecker, wasn't he?"

"It's not the same thing and you know it."

"What?" Doc said. "The car trunk makes all the difference?"

Grabek raised his hand, backed off. "About the baseballs. You're right, they're Mannarino's trademark, but it's how he deals with slow pays and fuck-ups. It's stupid to leave your trademark on a body you know will be found quickly. Mike Mannarino's a lot of things. He's not stupid."

Doc used the time Grabek bought him to cool down, not off. "This actually sets us back. It has set-up written all over it. Wierzbicki gives evidence against Mannarino and dies this soon? Please."

Harriger looked away from both of them. "Neuschwander, when was he killed?"

"Midnight. Ish." Neuschwander looked like he'd rather crawl into the trunk with Wierzbicki than chat with Harriger. "Based on what little I could check on his temperature and rigor, he's been dead no more than eight hours." Harriger gave him a look. "He's stiff, but not completely cooled down."

"That's all you have?"

"On time of death, yeah. ME can tell better. He should be here any minute. We caught them on the shift change." Or at least that's what they told him. Allegheny County medical examiners notorious for not wanting to make the trip to Penns River, Neshannock County not big enough to afford its own crew.

"I meant, do you have anything else?"

"Well, he was shot."

"Goddamnit, I know that! Twice, with a small caliber handgun."

"Three times, actually. There's another hole above his hairline. It's pretty hard to see."

"All right. Three times. Can we agree it was a small caliber weapon?"

"A .25."

Harriger had found someone he could bully. "This must be how you developed your legendary reputation among small town evidence men. You can look at those holes and tell they're .25s."

"Well, Chief, the thing is—"

"*Deputy* Chief," Doc said.

"The thing is, I found three shell casings, and they're .25s."

"What about the gun?"

"Jesus *Christ!*" Doc had had enough. "You think we're going to find a gun registered to Mike Mannarino with his fingerprints on it that matches these casings and rounds? What the hell did you do for the Staties in Emporium? The gun is gone forever. We might as well look for a videotape, in case he made one and left it for us."

"That's enough, Detective. You got away with a lot of insubordination when Napierkowski ran things. That's over now. You *will* show respect for my rank, or you *will* be looking for a job, and not in law enforcement."

"You think you can fire me and blackball me? Go for it. I wouldn't want a job a piss ant like you can take from me."

Grabek stepped between them before Harriger could step up. He looked as comfortable as a tree surgeon doing a vasectomy. Insubordination was his job. "Come on, you two, that's enough. We've all been under a lot of pressure lately. The casino's got traffic backed up halfway through town and we're up to our assholes with D and Ds. Two hits in less than a month. It's no wonder the chief's laid up with a heart attack. Doc's wound a little tight, Deputy. Give him to me and I'll get him calmed down so proper apologies can be made. We kind of need him right now."

Harriger glared at Doc, spoke to Grabek. "Get him straightened out. Another outburst like that and he's gone. He thinks he can get away with this shit because Napierkowski covers for him. We'll see."

Grabek turned to Doc with a glare that quieted him while Harriger walked to his car. He opened the door, paused before dipping his head to get in. "I want Mannarino in custody tonight."

"Think about it, Jack," Grabek said. "It'll take all day just to log the evidence. Then tomorrow to write the warrant. He's not going anywhere."

Harriger ground his teeth, forced himself to come to grips with reality. "When I sit down to dinner tomorrow, Mike Mannarino will have eaten a jumbo sandwich in a cell. Are we clear?" He stared at each cop in turn, daring disagreement.

Grabek made a show of taking Doc's elbow and walking him around Wierzbicki's car to inspect something before Doc could reply. Harriger tore up gravel backing out, almost rammed Nick Forte's car on its way in, then swerved to avoid the medical examiner. Doc and Grabek met Forte halfway between his car and Wierzbicki's.

"What happened to him?" Forte jerked a thumb toward Harriger's departing car. "He hear about a sale on lifts at Walgreen's?"

Doc laughed in spite of himself. "That son of a bitch." Looked at Forte, then at his watch. "What the hell are you doing out so early? In the rain, no less."

"I heard you had *another* dead body on your hands and thought I might be able to help, since they're piling up faster than you can dispose of them."

Doc wasn't laughing now. "Look, Nico, I'd love to stand around and bust balls with you, but if that's what you came for, this isn't the time. I have work to do."

"Show some respect. You just got here. This is my second trip today already."

This caught the attention of Grabek and Neuschwander, who had been showing the ME around Wierzbicki's trunk. "Second time today?" Doc said.

"Yeah, I was here around midnight, a little later. Before it rained. What's in the trunk?"

"You know goddamn well what's in the trunk," Grabek said. "What were you doing here last night?"

"Following Rollison." He gave them a condensed version of the night's events.

Grabek hawked and spat. "I'll be go to hell."

"So it is a set-up," Neuschwander said.

"We figured that," Doc said. "The question is, whose set-up is it?"

"Rollison met someone here," Forte said. "Whoever it was must've called him to come, so they were here first."

"But who's working for who?"

"I'm thinking Rollison works for whoever called him," Forte said. "Boss wouldn't get out of bed in the middle of the night."

"Unless whoever it was called had been told to let him know as soon as everything was in place, no matter when it was," Grabek said.

"I think Nick's right," Doc said. "Rollison's too smart to think something like this would fool us."

"So you think Rollison's working for someone dumber than he is?" Grabek said. "Doesn't make sense."

Doc pointed a thumb in the direction Harriger had taken. "We do it."

"This might help," Forte said. He held out a piece of 3x5 notebook paper.

"What's that?"

"License number of the car that almost hit me pulling out of here last night. Rollison left and I was tagging along behind when this car I hadn't seen came tear-assing out of the lot. See who this belongs to. Should give you an idea of who's working for who."

[38]

"Your cousin's at the end of the bar, by the restrooms," Fat Jimmy told Doc before he had a chance to ask, or say hello.

"You trying to hurry me along?" Doc said. "What's the matter? He break-ing up the customers again?"

"I know a few he might get a shot at later. Look around you." Not an empty chair, four-thirty on a weekday afternoon. "Unemployment checks hit today. Gonna be at least three arguments and probably one fight. Your cousin stays long, maybe two."

"You don't seem too upset."

"I seen the job he done on Dan Connor. He wants to do it again, I got can-didates for him. I never had a bouncer in here, but I'm getting too old for this shit."

"He was only a year behind you in school. Your problem's not you're too old. You're too fat."

"Keep that fat shit up and I'll put extra spit in your beer next time."

"Jeez, Jimmy. I thought fat people were supposed to be jolly. I mean, the sign over the door says, 'Fat Jimmy's.' Now you're sensitive about it?"

"You want jolly? Har-de-fucking-har-har. That better?"

Doc looked at him, wagged his head. "Could you bring me an MGD, and another of whatever my cousin's drinking? I'll open mine myself."

Jimmy flashed him the finger. "You'll drink whatever I bring you, wise ass."

Doc walked to the end of the bar nearest the men's room, elbowed his way in between Nick and a guy he thought might have conveyed with the place when Jimmy bought it, and he had mileage on him then. The old-timer sprin-kled salt in his beer and stirred with a finger that looked like it had four knuck-les.

"This place is something else," Nick said. He wore the Bears hat, backward on his head again so everyone in the seating area could read it. "Chicago has some dives, but this joint has an atmosphere all its own."

"That's because the windows haven't been open since he bought it." Jimmy waddled over and dropped off their beers. "I need to talk to you."

"I figured. Remember, I'm a detective. For example, when you called a few hours ago and said, 'We need to talk,' I deduced that's what was up. My only question is, how come we never meet anyplace nice? I feel so cheap. I'm not the other detective, am I? You know, the one you sneak around with while the legal detective stays at home and cleans up your reports for you."

"That license plate you got the hit on last night. Car's registered to Yuri Volkov."

"Sergei's boy?"

Doc nodded.

"Now we know who's in charge."

Doc tasted his beer. "Get off Rollison now."

"You want me to take Yuri?"

"No." It came out harder than Doc intended. "Stay away from Yuri. I don't have the full scoop on him yet, but I know enough to know you don't want him finding out you're following him. Or Rollison, for that matter. Get that GPS thing off his car. We can't afford anyone to find it accidentally and you not be aware of it."

"You sure about this? Might be nice to know who Yuri spends his time with."

"The only person that might be higher up in this is Sergei. We might as well think of them as a unit. Lay off. Spend some time with your parents. What you got already, connecting Harriger to Rollison to the Volkovs, that's more than I ever expected. When are you going back, anyway?"

Nick wasn't listening. Doc turned to look at what interested him, saw Dan Connor coming along the bar. He moved like he might have been waiting for Jimmy to open this morning. The bridge of his nose was bruised. Both eyes wore yellowish purple bags.

Nick waited until Connor was close, pushed the stool back to impede his way. "How's the nose, Fluffy? Doesn't look too bad, all things considered. You behave yourself tonight, okay? Don't make me scold you again."

Connor looked at Nick only long enough to recognize him. Eyes flicked down, then toward Doc, down again. He mumbled something and turned his shoulder to avoid any contact with Nick. No comments about sucker punches. Nothing said about the hat.

Doc watched him pass. Nick ignored him. "What is it about you?" Doc said. "I didn't rough him up half as bad as you did, and I got a ration of shit. You really did sucker punch him, and not a word."

"He knows I'd do it again." Nick sipped beer. "He's white trash, kind of guy I wouldn't piss on if he was on fire. He likes to play tough guy, so he's learned a few things over the years in spite of himself. One is that a cop has to put up with a lot of shit before he can get physical. I don't. He also knows a cop has to show proportional response, and that I only stopped because he was out. He doesn't know if I liked putting him down, or just don't give a shit. What he does know is that we both understand the real rules of a fight." More beer.

"Which are?"

"It doesn't matter who started, or when, or why, or how you fight it. All that matters is who wins. Lose a fight to the wrong guy, you may never get to fight another one. He thinks I might be that guy."

Nick finished his beer, waved two fingers in Jimmy's direction. Didn't say whether Connor was right or not, about him being that guy. Doc didn't ask. Five minutes ago he knew the answer. Not anymore.

[39]

Special Agent Ray Keaton set the pizza box on Doc's kitchen table, asked for another of those beers he had last time.

"How come you just show up unannounced at my house all the time?" Doc said, handing him a beer. "I leave a message, why can't you just call back like a regular person?"

"I brought pizza, didn't I?" Keaton rolled a slice New York-style, bit off a large mouthful. "I took a chance on this local joint. Probably should've known better, but it's good."

"Where'd you go?"

"I don't know. Some place at the other end of the bridge. Name's probably on the box." He flipped the lid shut. "There. 'Pizza Fresh From the Oven.' I brought pepperoni, figured everyone likes that. You got any of that shake cheese?"

"You got this from Stamkos's. 'Pizza and Gyros,' right above that Exxon station where 366 comes down to the river. Their pizza's good, but next time you drop in for a visit, bring a couple of gyros. Best around, and we won't need but one each." Doc took a bite. "Still hot. Nice work. What if I'd eaten already?"

"More for me. Besides, I knew you hadn't eaten yet."

"How?"

"I'm a federal agent. We have our ways. Besides, I don't figure you to be the kind to eat in a shithole like Fat Jimmy's."

It irritated Doc to know Keaton kept such close tabs on him. "Thanks. I like Stamkos pizza. Tell me about Yuri Volkov."

"Great host you are. I come running when you call, even bring good food. You hand me a beer and start pumping. Makes me feel cheap."

"You're the second person today to say that about me. I could get a complex."

"Try being as sensitive about the feelings of others as you are about your own. Maybe people won't call you on it so much."

"I'll try. Now, about Yuri."

Keaton wiped sauce from the corner of his mouth. "How come it's always Greeks make the best pizza? You ever notice that? Not that Italians can't make pizza, but think about it. Drive by two hole-in-the-wall storefront dumps and see one Greek name and one Italian, the Greek's where to get your pizza. I wonder why that is."

"I don't know. Could be one of those counter-intuitive ethnic things. Maybe Italians make kick ass *souvlaki*. Hard to say." He wanted to tell this Fed to either talk about Yuri Volkov or he could shove his pizza up his ass, pepperoni and all, but he didn't want to give Keaton the satisfaction.

"So," Keaton said, took a swig. "You want to talk about Yuri Volkov?"

Doc wondered if anyone would believe he shot the guy as an armed intruder, pizza and beer on the table. "Sure, if you can squeeze him into the conversation somewhere."

"I could, but we still have the problem I was explaining before you interrupted me."

"Which problem is that?"

"The problem where I'm running around at your convenience and bring food and everything and all you want is what you want. Don't you have anything for me? Some token of appreciation?"

"I gave you beer. Good beer, too."

"It is good beer, and I thanked you, but it just evens out for the pizza. You want information, I should get some, too."

"Like what?"

"How did it go with Mike Mannarino when you talked to him last week?"

"You know I was there and don't know how it went? Don't you have a wire up on him?"

"Not at Bypass. We drop a bug or two into his club three-four times a year, get what we can until he sweeps them out. Haven't been able to find a judge who'll let us bug the business yet."

"We went around for a while, discussed events of the day," Doc said. "He really doesn't like me at all, you know."

"He still let you say your piece, didn't he?"

"Yeah, he did. I gave him the whole 'rock and a hard place' spiel, told him only his uncle could get him free, and he threw me out."

"That's what I expected. What I want to know is, *how* did he throw you out?"

Doc broke a strand of cheese with his finger. "That was the interesting part. First, he actually asked me who I thought it might be who had it in for him. Then, at the end, it wasn't like he threw me out at all. More like, 'Will you please leave?' Like he couldn't bear to listen anymore."

Keaton drained his bottle, made sure Doc knew it was empty. Spoke only after Doc rose for the refill. "That's very good for a first meeting. Go see him again. This goofy set-up last night made points for you. Tell him as much as you feel comfortable with, just nothing I tell you. We straight on that?"

"No problem, since you haven't told me a goddamn thing yet."

Keaton snapped his fingers. "Almost forgot. You wanted to talk about Yuri Volkov, didn't you?"

"If you have a minute."

"I told you about Sergei last time, right? Big-time gangster, cleaning up his act, Terminator, wants to be respectable now?"

"Yeah." Doc made a rotating motion with his hand.

"Well, Yuri scares the old man." Paused to let that sink in. "Sergei was a bad motherfucker, even by Russian mob standards. Chechens were afraid of him. Yuri is off the tracks completely. At least Sergei had to work his way up, so no matter how ruthless he was, a certain level of trust had to be maintained so he could move without looking over his shoulder all the time. Yuri started at the top, and takes what he wants. Sergei has his back, who else does he need? He mixed it up with one of the New York families over some territorial dispute a few years ago. This goombah decided to threw some fear at him. Yuri ground the poor bastard up in his own house, made his wife and kids listen. Sent him back to his boss in dog food bags."

Doc expected bad, but not this bad. "Assuming it's him who wants Mannarino out of the picture, what do we do?"

"First, if Yuri does want Mannarino out, I'm amazed he's not dead already. Must be Sergei trying to keep the lid on. That might be why Yuri's in Pittsburgh and not running some pork store twenty-four by seven grinding people up in New York. Yuri's too colorful for public consumption, so Sergei's keeping him close. Mannarino has maybe three made guys. Yuri won't need to get too innovative with him."

"To get back to my question, what do *we* do?"

"You? Stay out of his way. He *will* kill a cop if it suits his purposes and he thinks he can get away with it, and he always thinks he can get away with it. Mainly because he always has. Let us handle him."

"The way you've handled him in New York, you mean?"

"Don't get snotty. I'm trying to help you." Keaton leaned his elbows on the table. "Listen, Dougherty, I like you. You're a good cop and I believe you truly want the best for this town. I admire how you've passed up opportunities so you could stay here. I bust your balls, but it says on the back of my G-Man license I have to antagonize the locals at every opportunity. I'm telling you, as a cop and a friendly acquaintance, I can't protect you, or the people close to you, from Yuri Volkov. I might be able to take him down after the fact—*might*, if any evidence surfaces—but I can't prevent it. He disappears people like a fucking magician."

Doc was tired of hearing how many things couldn't be prevented, or even punished. He came back to Penns River to help his parents grow old, but also because he loved it. College was fun, and the army was a trip, but everything that grounded him was in this shithill town eighteen miles outside of Pittsburgh. It killed him every time he drove through the old downtown and saw the empty mills, the closed hospital, the business district without business. He hated Mike Mannarino for moving here and "offering his protection." He'd made peace with the idea that he was becoming less a cop than an urban hospice worker, easing the end of the transition from booming mill town to—to whatever happened to towns like this. And now Yuri Volkov had taken an interest. Who made Mike Mannarino seem like Santa Claus.

Keaton picked up on Doc's quiet. "Mannarino has to make the deal. It's his only out. You don't have to close. I'll do that. Get him so he'll talk to me. Mike pisses Yuri off, maybe gets lucky and takes out one of his guys, Yuri'll make him watch what happens to his wife and kids. I'm not making this up. He's done it."

He finished his beer and stood. Doc walked to the door with him.

"Mannarino knows how you feel about this town. He knows your people live here, too. That's the common ground you have with him that I don't. Get me over the hump so I can show him what the next life looks like before Yuri does."

[40]

Daniel Rollison was proud that he could walk into any courtroom in the world and swear on a Bible he'd never tortured anyone. His interrogations were enthusiastic, never enhanced. He'd seen it done plenty of times, and there were those who suspected it was being done under his stewardship. Just not by him. He'd seen men waterboarded, shocked, beaten, forced to stand without sleep for days at a time. He'd seen teeth and fingernails pulled out, and the soles of feet burned with everything from cigarettes to irons to fireplace pokers. Stood close enough to be splashed with blood from a beheading. All part of the job.

Watching Yuri Volkov eat oysters made him sick to his stomach.

He looked around the room, out the window, into the dining area, anywhere but at Yuri. Nothing he could do to avoid the noise. Listening to Yuri eat oysters was the vilest sound Rollison had ever heard, and he'd heard a few.

Harriger was late. The meeting set for eight-thirty, get a drink then go into Torrance's dining room to eat. Three businessmen enjoying man food and a few belts. Had to be at least half a dozen similar groups in what Torrance's wait staff called the Testosterone Room, full of men eating red meat and drinking hard liquor before they retired to the cigar bar that overlooked Route 22. True, a view of a suburban main drag not as special as looking down on the Point from Mount Washington, but no one knew Rollison, Yuri, or Jack Harriger in Monroeville.

Rollison walked in at 8:25, Yuri several straight vodkas into his evening, sweating them out like a pig in a sauna. At 8:35 he decided he was hungry, fuck waiting on Harriger, bring him a dozen oysters. No, two dozen. Now it was ten to nine and he was going through them like pistachio nuts, reaching for the next before he finished swallowing this one.

Yuri pushed the debris away, inhaled a vodka whole, wiped his mouth and forehead. "This cop, Harriger, he is late."

He might not be as drunk as I suspected, Rollison thought. "He didn't want to come at all. I agree with him. It's not good for the two of you to be seen together."

"Is not good for us to be seen not together, too."

"Okay, then, but why someplace this public? Why not meet somewhere he won't have to worry about being seen?"

"You brought us way the fucking hell out here so we would not be seen, I thought. I do business where I want. I'm not hiding nothing. I think we meet in deep dark woods he worry about not coming home if he is pissing me off. Maybe this is better for him."

"Things are moving," Rollison said. "What are you upset about?"

Yuri gestured for another drink. "He is dragging his hands, I think, Harriger is, on this Mannarino business."

At least Harriger didn't drag his knuckles. "It has to look legitimate. It helped when the old chief had that heart attack, but there are still a couple of cops there who know what they're doing and don't like him. One in particular is a lot smarter than a town like that deserves. I think he and the old chief are related somehow. He hates Harriger with a passion."

"Why are we talking about cops in town like this? Pay this Harriger and be done. Pay them all. How much does he want?"

"It's not money with him. I'm telling you, offer him money and you'll scare him off. He wants to be chief, and he knows we can get it for him. That's more important to him than money."

Yuri accepted his drink, swallowed it, and ordered the next before the bartender could step away. "Then he is stupid. Only ambition is to be chief of police in some shithole, then you live in shithole rest of life. Take the money. Live where you want. Is stupid not to. Harriger? Is that Polack name? Does not sound like, but he is stupid enough to be dumb Polack." Yuri laughed.

Rollison was deciding whether to agree with him when Harriger came in the front door. Rollison moved to meet him. "Where the hell have you been? You're half an hour late."

"There's an accident on Logan's Ferry Road. Backed up a couple of miles. I had to show my badge to get by."

"You're going to be this late, call. There's only so long he can be kept waiting."

Harriger's alarm showed. "I can't call you on a cell phone."

Rollison suppressed a sigh, felt his stomach burn. "Even if our cells were bugged—which they're not—it's fine for you and me to talk, even to get together like this. It's Yuri you have to minimize contact with."

"That's what I'm worried about." Harriger ordered bourbon and water. "Why am I here?"

"He wants to talk to you. I told him you didn't like it, and it was a bad idea."

"What did he say?"

"We're here, aren't we? Come on, let's get this over with."

Yuri spoke before Rollison could introduce them. "Hello to my partner in police department." Said it loud enough to be heard in Turtle Creek. Harriger cringed as if someone had found pictures of his wife in *Hustler*.

The bartender set down Harriger's bourbon, looked at Yuri with raised eyebrows. "*Da*," Yuri said. Then, before the bartender could pour, "Wait. We are all here now. Is time for doing business, not for being drunk. Business is sober doing, so I must sober. Bring Black Russian to table."

Harriger brought his bourbon with him. Rollison switched to ginger ale. They made their way to a table in the far corner of the dining room, Yuri as considerate of the other diners as a man his size and drunkenness could be. He took the seat facing the room. Rollison made do with his second choice, did everything he could to keep the others focused on their menus and ordering until the waiter left and Yuri couldn't be deferred any longer.

"Mr. John Harriger, you are chief of police now. Congratulations."

"Acting chief," Harriger said. His voice sounded like a rusted nut being pried off a bolt. "Until Napierkowski comes back."

"Next month is not of interesting to me. Today, you run police department, no?"

"I guess you could say that."

Yuri spoke to Rollison. His eyes were red and going glassy. "Here is problem. Does this sound like man other men will follow?" Then, to Harriger, "Acting Chief Harriger, are you responsible for law enforcingment in Penns River?"

"Yes." Said it like a ten-year-old caught peeking into a girl's locker room. Rollison's eyes rolled shut in disgust.

"Then why the fuck is wop cocksucker Mike the fucking Hook Mannarino not in jail? Is he not guilty enough for you, killing two men? You need more?"

"He's in jail now," Harriger said, gaining confidence. "I gave orders he was to be in jail before I ate dinner. He was there when I left."

The disdain in Yuri's expression matched his voice. "You should say you wanted him at same time as you eat dinner. Mannarino eats his dinner at home, I think."

Harriger flushed and paled simultaneously. "He can't be. I was at the arraignment. I watched them take him to his cell. His bond's a million dollars."

Rollison's voice carried no farther than their seats. "He made bail an hour ago. One hundred thousand dollars cash."

"Jesus Christ," Harriger said.

"I think Jesus Christ has little to do with this—what do you Americans call it?—cluster fucking. This problem is more in your hands, or I would call priest to fix. What are you plan to do about it?"

Harriger looked for support from Rollison, who buttered a roll. "I can't do anything. He's-he's been arrested." To Rollison: "Does he understand how things work here? All I can do is arrest him. It's up to the judge now."

Rollison chewed his roll. Yuri said, "Talk to me. I am the one is doing favor for you. You are going to be chief permanent soon. Was up to me, I kill Mr. Mike wop cocksucker day after he kill my nigger. What I ask is not much."

Harriger looked again to Rollison, who was focusing his attention on the basket of bread. "Daniel, make him understand. There's only so much the police can do." Rollison found a piece he liked, pointed to Yuri. "Hecker told me this would all be taken care of. All I had to do was keep the lid on."

Yuri slammed a fist on the table. Water spilled and Harriger's spoon fell to the floor. "You think pipstink like Danny Hecker tell me what to do?" Jabbed himself in the chest. "Me? Maybe you think because my father is partners with Danny, it is he telling me what to do? You are mistake. Not even my father—who is great man—*tells* Yuri what to do."

Heads turned at nearby tables. Yuri paused, sipped his drink. His voice resumed softer, might have sounded pleasant coming from anyone else. "My father asks me. Not tell. I sometimes maybe get his—ah, what is word for *konsul' tacija?*—his advice." Another drink. "Now, Mr. Chief of Police for now, this is what I tell *you.*" Yuri paused, mouth open. Rollison couldn't imagine what kept him upright. "Mike the Hook Mannarino will be gone from Penns River in one week." He held up one finger. "*Odna, vy ponimaete?* Understand? You can do it, or I will."

Yuri sat back, knocked off the half inch of Black Russian left in his glass. Waved for the waiter. "You go now, little man John Harriger. I eat in peace with my friend Daniel. Do not let your ass hit on the door when you are leaving."

[41]

The transponder had shown Rollison's car on the move as Forte pulled into the casino lot. Doc had given mixed instructions: stay away from Rollison, and pick up the transponder, which was now driving away, probably to Shaler Township. Forte considered himself conscientious and wanted to do as his cousin asked, but what if the device fell off the car? He'd never find it unless he was close enough for the signal, which didn't kick any ass. No harm could come from following Rollison home one more time. He'd get the gadget in the morning.

Rollison took the usual route: Leechburg Road, Tarentum Bridge, Route 28 south. Forte laid back, listened to the radio. Almost missed the turn when he realized the tone was to his left approaching Harmarville, Rollison having taken the exit for 910.

The Town Car stopped at the light for Old 28. Left led to the Turnpike, but right would take him into Pittsburgh through a series of small towns: Blawnox, Aspinwall, Sharpsburg. Rollison pulled into a lane that could go either way. Forte pulled in three cars behind as the light changed and Rollison went left, then moved right. Turnpike.

Limited access to the Turnpike made tailing easy. Rollison went east, got off at the first exit, PA-22, which brought traffic downtown through Monroeville and Swissvale. It entered Pittsburgh through Oakland, and getting to either was a lot quicker staying on 28, so it made sense when Rollison skipped the ramp for the Parkway and stayed on 22.

The Torrance Steak House and Cigar Bar sat off William Penn Highway opposite Monroeville Mall. A new, trendy place, dark wood and smoked glass, where brokers and MBAs could relax and lie to each other about the widows and orphans they'd screwed that week. A hill fell away from the building to the highway, allowing the enclosed deck on stilts that was the cigar bar to extend from the restaurant. A diner occupied the space when Forte was growing up in Penns River; he hadn't spent enough time in Monroeville to remember it. The twenty-one mile trip was an event when he was a kid, a once-a-year expedition that took the whole day: first the Miracle Mile Shopping Center, then the mall, finally dinner at Johnny Garneau's smorgasbord. He got his first real baseball glove at David Weis, back when they sold more than jewelry, an Andy Van Slyke model that was too big to play infield with and he didn't hit enough to play outfield. He played second base and made do.

Forte went past when Rollison turned into the Torrance parking lot, doubled back at the first available street. Parked as far away as he could. Walked into the bar and saw Rollison on the other leg of the L, talking to a man whose alcohol intake showed in his face. Ordered a beer. Rollison couldn't be heard, but the other man spoke loud enough to be heard by Marlee Matlin. Heavy Russian accent, drank vodka from a fire hose.

Oysters arrived. The Russian sucked them out of the half-shell like something in a science fiction movie eating souls. Forte nursed his beer, checked his watch every couple of minutes to look like he was waiting for someone. Turned his stool to look toward the door and not show his face too much the instant Jack Harriger came through it not ten feet away.

Forte knelt to find keys he hadn't dropped. He'd never been introduced to Harriger. He had been seen around the station with Doc, no telling if he'd be recognized, best not to take the chance. Waited for Harriger to pass.

Rollison saw him at the same time, came over to greet him three feet behind Forte. Bitched about Harriger being late, he should've called. Harriger paranoid about using a cell phone, Rollison reminding him they weren't under surveillance—Forte suppressed a chuckle—and weren't doing anything wrong. Told him it was Yuri he should worry about being seen with and Forte restrained the urge to run out of the building and call his cousin. Waited until they were seated to slide eight dollars across the bar and leave as fast as he could without looking like someone in a hurry.

The phone was in his hand before he cleared the deck. "Benny? You're not gonna believe what I just saw."

[42]

Doc had arrested Mike Mannarino alone. Walked into the dealership like it was one of his semi-annual visits, not even a perfunctory delay from Art DeSimone, busy selling a KIA to some kid who looked about nineteen. Rapped on the frame of Mannarino's door, showed the warrant when Mike looked up and shook his head.

"I wondered what took you so long. It's been two days."

"This isn't my idea, Mike. I'll wait in the hall if you want to call your lawyer."

Mannarino had the phone in his hand. "No need. You're expected." Pushed buttons, waited. "Hi, Kelly. It's Mike Mannarino." Ten seconds passed. "Yeah. He's here now. Meet me there." Hung up and stood up. "Let's get this over with."

"I have to frisk you, but I'm not going to cuff you," Doc said. "You'll have to have them on to go into the station—I can't get around that, whoever's there is there—but we can at least walk out of here like we just happen to be leaving at the same time."

"Whoever's there, huh?"

"I don't see any point in your kids seeing you on the eleven o'clock news, so I didn't tell anybody I was coming. I can't promise no one else has."

Mannarino came around the desk, leaned on it as Doc patted him down. "Why all the consideration? You don't like me any more than I like you."

"I told you before. I think you're getting screwed." Doc finished, stepped back so Mannarino could stand. "You can leave your keys and wallet and belt here if you want. You'll have to give them up at the station, anyway."

Mannarino looked at Doc a second, then stepped back behind the desk to lock his keys and wallet in a drawer. "I better keep the belt. I lost some weight and I don't want to walk in there holding my pants up like a goddamn vagrant."

They walked through the showroom like two guys leaving for a beer. Art DeSimone gave an odd look when his boss told him he'd be late, go ahead and lock up.

Outside, Mannarino spoke to Doc. "You're not worried I'll run."

"I'm arresting you for Wierzbicki, not Broaddus. You'd be stupid to run from this." Held the door so Mannarino could sit in front. "Can I assume you're not answering questions once we get to the station?"

"That's what I've been told."

"Then there's no reason we can't talk in the car. No Miranda yet, so nothing you say can be used against you, and I'm not recording anything."

"How do I know that?"

"Because I've given you every break today, and I have no reason to screw you now. You know what? Forget that. You know I'm not recording because I told you I wasn't, and you know I wouldn't lie about it."

Mannarino stopped looking out the passenger window to give Doc his full attention. "Yeah. Okay."

"I'd still bet a week's pay you had Broaddus killed. I know you didn't do Wierzbicki. So why is that the one I'm arresting you for?"

"You got orders?"

"Why does Jack Harriger have such a hard-on for you?"

"Harriger's kind of a hard-on, period. Does he need a reason?"

"Probably not, but he does have one."

"I don't suppose I could stop you from telling me if I wanted to," Mannarino said.

"Harriger wants to be chief of police. He's spent years trying to angle Stush Napierkowski out of the job. Stush's heart attack makes him that much more vulnerable, so Harriger sees this as his chance to step up."

"By hanging this bullshit arrest on me? How's that gonna look when it falls apart on him? Hey, you missed the turn."

"Scenic route. Give us more time to talk." Doc ignored the look Mannarino shot him. "You're right, he'll look bad when this goes tits up. Doesn't matter. It's not the arrest that'll put him over the top. It's his willingness to follow orders. Things are different here now, and the chief of police is going to have to be someone who follows orders. Stush is old school enough to think he's the chief, he should be *giving* orders. Jack doesn't care. He just wants the job."

A furrow appeared between Mannarino's eyebrows. "I'm with you," Doc said. "It wouldn't make sense to any reasonable person. There's history there. Suffice to say Harriger has personal reasons for not only wanting Stush out, but for being the guy that replaces him."

"And the mayor wants me locked up for this bullshit."

"Locked up, gone, dead. Whatever. The mayor doesn't decide which shoe to tie first until he checks with Danny Hecker. Hecker's partners with Sergei Volkov. Sergei's polishing his halo for the trip to heaven, so Yuri handles his gray areas now. Clipping Wierzbicki was all Yuri. Sergei's way too smart for that."

Mannarino almost pointed when Doc drove past the next logical turn for the station. Sat watching the scenery along the bypass, past the high school, until Doc turned toward the old downtown at Seventh Street.

"Sergei might be willing to live and let live," Doc said. "He's made his money. The casino's mostly a laundry to him. But Yuri, he doesn't want to see any of the ancillary business get siphoned off. The Pittsburgh casinos didn't fuss much when Hecker wanted to build his white elephant up here. They got the green light for table games as part of the deal. It's only a matter of time before tables show up here, too, and that'll bring the kind of gamblers Yuri can make real money off of. Why share it with you?"

Mike looked straight through the windshield. "Why doesn't he just kill me?"

"I don't know. Maybe he doesn't want to make the politicians gun shy, and they might if they think Penns River is turning into Deadwood. Sergei's probably sitting on him some, too. Remember, though, his name's not Job; it's Yuri. His reputation wasn't built on patience."

They drove through the old downtown in silence. Dreary by day, a science fiction set by night, dark buildings lining barely lighted streets populated by a few stragglers who had no good reason to be there.

"Make a deal, Mike. This arrest is horseshit and we'll never hang the Broaddus hit on you. That means Yuri has to kill you to get rid of you, and he does want you gone. You can fight him, but you can't win. All you can do is hold him off long enough to turn this place into Fallujah on the Allegheny and get a lot of innocent people hurt."

Doc didn't speak as they drove past the old glassworks and up the hill on Drey Street to Freeport Road and back to the station. Don't oversell. Mike's smart, he'll see it. Just hope he sees it in time.

Mannarino's lawyer was waiting for them. Along with all four Pittsburgh television stations, both newspapers, and at least half a dozen radio reporters. Jack Harriger stood at the door watching the show. Mannarino was booked and taken to the interview room, where Harriger stood with his sleeves rolled halfway up his forearms, rocking on his feet. Doc read Mannarino his rights and the lawyer told everyone his client had nothing to say. Harriger went to the arraignment—the judge came in special after hours—and Doc went home to dinner.

He ate his chicken and corn and washed the dishes, went outside to sit on the stoop to drink a beer while he listened to an evening breeze rustle the trees until the bugs drove him inside. He hadn't sat in his favorite chair long enough to warm the seat when his cousin Nick called to tell him who was having dinner in Monroeville.

[43]

Google Maps says it takes forty minutes to drive from Doc's house to Torrance's. He pulled into the parking lot twenty-three minutes after hanging up the phone, siren and lights and professional courtesy all the way.

Nick stood in the lot where he'd be seen. "Jesus Christ. I didn't think a helicopter could get here this fast."

"They still in there?"

"No one's come out. I think they're having dinner. What's the plan?"

"I'm going to walk in like I came for dinner, act surprised to see them, and shake the tree a little."

"Let's go."

"Uh-uh. Just me. I don't want to let you out of the bag just yet."

Doc strode off before Nick could answer. Through the main door and badged himself past the hostess station before she had a chance to ask what was going on.

Daniel Rollison saw him first, in his peripheral vision, let his head and shoulders sag an inch without turning for a better look. Harriger had his back to the room and missed him altogether. Yuri Volkov was speaking to Harriger, looked up when Doc entered his field of vision. Doc was close enough to catch the end of what he said.

"—let your ass hit on the door when you are leaving."

Harriger started to rise and Doc said, "Wow. Here's about the last three people I'd expect to see together."

Rollison sat back and took everything in. Yuri seemed confused and irritated over the interruption. Harriger looked back, saw Doc, and looked as if he didn't know whether to shit his pants or order breakfast.

"Who the fuck are you?" Yuri said.

"Detective Dougherty, Penns River police." Doc showed the badge, still in his hand. He spoke loud enough for the surrounding tables to hear without straining. "I understand why the acting chief of police would talk with Mr. Rollison here. He's head of security at our new biggest employer, and they have a murder they'd like cleared as soon as possible. What I don't understand is what you're doing here."

Yuri's smile grew. He said to Rollison, "This is one of policemen you were telling about?"

Rollison spoke to Doc. "Detective, this is Yuri Volkov. He represents one of the interests in the casino. I offered to bring him and the deputy together to get him current on the investigation, now that a suspect has been charged. This is a courtesy meeting, nothing more."

"Mr. Rollison, you're so good I could almost believe you, except my boss looks like he just farted in front of the pope. That leads me to believe he did-n't want to been seen with either of you. Forgive me for being skeptical."

"No offense taken, Detective. It's your job to look for the worst in every-thing. Frankly, that's why I got out of investigations. It was making me cyn-ical."

"No harm done then. I only wanted to tell the deputy chief here that Mike Mannarino made bail. Put up the hundred grand in cash." Harriger mumbled something. "I'm sorry, Deputy. Say again, please?"

"I said 'I heard,'" Harriger said.

"Great. I'll be on my way, then." All conversation had stopped at the neigh-boring tables. Not a scene, but a memorable night out. "Sorry if this has been awkward. I never dreamed I'd see the acting police chief of Penns River, Daniel Rollison, and notorious mob boss Yuri Volkov out to dinner together. I mean, who would've expected that?" Everyone heard him. They wouldn't be hard to find if needed.

Yuri's face reddened. Rollison put a hand on his wrist. "I'm glad we could make your day, Detective. How did you know we were here?"

Doc heard Nick's voice from over his shoulder before he could answer. "I guess it was me. Should I have kept that to myself?" Doc blanched before he could catch himself. Yuri might have noticed. There was no way Rollison missed it.

Yuri ignored Rollison's calming hand this time. "And who the fuck are you?"

"Friend of the family."

"I am not asking *what* you are, I am asking *who* you are."

"And the horse you rode in on, Comrade." Yuri confused for real now. "I give my name when I feel like it, to people I feel like giving it to. You want to know, answer me this: who the fuck are you?"

Now it was a scene. Yuri tried to rise as he threw the table aside, could-n't do either with Rollison and Harriger so close. Nick relaxed into a ready position and Doc realized being stuck in the corner was the only thing keep-ing Yuri out of a hospital. Turned away from the table knowing Nick had his back and took his cousin's elbow. Nick allowed himself to be guided out of the dining area as the manager came past.

Doc waited until they were outside. "What the fuck did you do that for? I told you to wait out here."

"You said you wanted to shake the tree. I'd say it's still shaking. Keep walk-ing. I found a spot where we can watch the door and they'll never see us."

Doc allowed Nick to lead. "Goddamn it, Nick, I told you to stay outside."

"You told me not to come in with you. I didn't. I waited." Nick pulled Doc into some overgrown underbrush at the edge of the parking lot thirty yards from the entrance. "Let's wait here, see how they come out."

Doc started to speak. Nick cut him off. "Ssshhh. Here comes your boss."

Jack Harriger came through the door at a race walk. Made cursory looks to either side. Couldn't help himself and broke into a trot halfway to his car. Doc caught a glimpse as he drove past under a floodlight, pale as a baseball.

"I didn't want you to be associated with this," Doc said. "Now there's no way Harriger's not going to ask me who you are and what you're doing. He'll check the records and find out about the special deputy badge and the carry permit. Listen to me." Grabbed Nick by the shoulders, forced him to make eye contact. "I'm a cop. As much of a freak show as Yuri is, that gives me some protection. You're a citizen, and you're not even from around here. He can disappear you and we might not even hear about it for weeks."

He watched the gravity of the situation settle on his cousin's face. Nick was one of the smartest people Doc knew, he'd appreciate what he'd got himself into. He also thought with his glands sometimes, which was how he'd got here in the first place.

Noise came from the restaurant as the door burst open. Daniel Rollison walked away, purposeful and unhurried. Yuri Volkov boiled out a second later, escorted but untouched by the manager and three waiters. Much of what Yuri shouted was in Russian. Some was English profanities, primarily dealing with incest, sodomy, and homosexual acts. The rest was unintelligible. The restaurant employees stood in the vestibule while Yuri kicked the door, kicked the wall, kicked the pavement, and spat on the window glass. He kicked three cars on the way to his own, one several times, denting the passenger door. A car leaving at the same time locked up its brakes to miss him. Another was rear ended when it stopped short on William Penn Highway to make room for him pulling out.

"I'm sorry, cuz," Nick said. Doc knew from his tone he meant it more for him than for himself. "You called the meeting. I should've let you run it."

"It's okay, Nick. You're right about shaking their tree. I just didn't want to put you on the line. There are things about Volkov you don't know."

Nick still looked to where Yuri's car had gone. Some of the light that shone from his eyes, made him a friend to children and dogs everywhere, had disappeared. Doc couldn't identify what replaced it, and didn't want to.

"It's okay, Benny," Nick said. "There are things about me you don't know."

[44]

Tookie Harris wanted Mike Mannarino in jail even less than Mike wanted to go. Tookie couldn't kill him there. No satisfaction in *having* him killed. Tookie wanted to do the Hook his own self. Maybe gut shoot him so he'd bleed a while, give Tookie time to tell him who he was, how he'd made a sucker of the big-time gangster to conduct his own vendetta. No way to do that with Mike in a cage, armed guards all around him.

Nelson still thought they were in the drug business together.

"Nelson, man, I'm telling you, I got to talk to the man before he go away. What the fuck we supposed to do if he don't make bail?" Word not yet arrived Mike walked the streets a free, if somewhat encumbered, man. "He don't get out, who we deal with? Even he do get out, it gots to be only temporary, what with a trial coming up and shit. We need Plan B working, and we need it now."

"I can ax him," Nelson said. "I don't think he be interested, 'sall I'm saying. We been dealing direct with that Stretch dude. We prolly just keep dealing with him."

"I can see why you think that. Now think a this." Tookie forcing himself to stay patient. "What if his connect, you know, on the other side, what if he only deal direct with the big man? Mike out the picture, no product coming in, what the fuck we do then? I don't want to go looking again so soon after we got things set up. I need the word from Mike hisself that there ain't be no interruption. You feel me?"

Nelson rubbed his hand along his chin, thinking. Tookie could tell he was on the wrong track.

Nelson said, "I feel you, absolutely, but here's the thing. This Stretch guy, he all quiet and distant and shit when we talk. I ax for something, even like the motherfucking time of day, and he all over me. This might be something go better you axed him yourself."

Tookie thinking now this might be something go better he put an ad on a billboard, instead of working with this retard nigger Nelson. Like what that Rumsfeld dude say about Iraq. You go to war with the motherfuckers you got.

"You got a point, Nelse. Thing is, if I go to talk to Stretch, we automatically in what they call a subordinate position, dig? If the Number One man in one crew talk direct to the Number Two man in the other crew, that make them equal, right? If our top man same as their second man, then we really working for their Number One man, 'cause he got no one he need to talk to. He just giving orders."

"Ain't that how it be, though? All we do is ax for the shipment. He tell us how much and when and where."

There was patience, and there was what it took to put up with this shit. "We are *not* his employees. Get that thought out your head right the fuck now. We his partners. And any good partnership need what they call mutual admiration, where both sides give a little so the other side stay happy. No one ever figured Mike to go inside when we cutting this deal, so we never thought about what we'd do if he did. Now we have to, and I—*we*, both of us—can't afford to have word trickling down through this Polack mother-fucker, not knowing if he got it right from Mike or making his own deal."

Nelson wiped his chin again. Tookie would do it himself if he had to, talk to Stretch Dolewicz to set up the meeting. It would be harder, might put Mike on his guard, wondering if Tookie had panicked, maybe sever the rela-tionship. Or be better prepared for trouble when the time came. Tookie still hadn't worked out how he'd get Mike alone, no intention of making this a suicide mission.

"Nelson, you know you my man, or I wouldn't ax you to do this. You bet-ter at talking to Stretch than me. I needs you to convince him we just doing our due dissonance, covering everything we can think of. Tell him we axing with all respect, so ain't no misunderstanding at a bad time." The plan com-ing together in his head now. He had the how, needed time to figure out the where. "Just be the two a us and him and whoever he wants. Could be Stretch, or that other one he run with, that Buddy. Meet someplace no one see us, so the meeting, like, never happen, you dig? Remove any chance peo-ple seeing him and me together, which is I know what he worried about."

Just need to think of a place now. Somewhere they'd both have to drive. Be there first, come up to Mike's car all friendly and shit, bust a cap in Stretch's head while he still getting out the car. Do Nelson with Stretch's gun if the boy couldn't be depended on. Then take his time with Mike the Hook, make sure this cracker know he not dealing with some Bamas here.

[45]

Doc wondered how Harriger would play it at work the next day. Brazen it out, or try to put the best face on it. He didn't have to wonder long. A piece of Harriger's stationery sat on his desk when he arrived. *My office. Now.*

"Who was that with you last night?" This before Doc could ask what he wanted.

"That was my cousin. He's a—"

"He's a private investigator from Chicago. What's he doing here?"

"His mother had surgery. He came in to spend some time with her and his father."

"He needed a special deputy's badge and carry permit to visit his mother? Where's she live?"

"He was helping me with something."

"What?"

Doc thought, no more than three seconds. "He's been following Rollison."

"Why?"

"You know what our experience with Rollison was like on the Widmer case. I wouldn't trust him if he told me water was wet."

"On whose authority was your cousin conducting city business?"

"It was a personal favor, a family thing. There's nothing official about it."

"Then how did he get the badge and permit?"

"Judge Molchan owed me a favor."

"Now he owes me several." Harriger sat back in his chair, the school suck-up placed in charge of the class. Doc looked closer, saw the latent uncertainty that came with trying to face down someone unimpressed with the teacher's pet. "Was I ever under surveillance?"

"No."

"That's your story?"

"Think about it, Deputy. My cousin's pretty good, but how long do you think one man could follow someone with your experience without getting made?"

"Quite a while, with this." Harriger set Nick's GPS on his desk.

The Three Amigos were up early this morning. "I told him Rollison was very, very good. Spook good. I guess he thought he needed an edge."

"Did he think he needed a lawsuit? More to the point, did he think—or care—about the ramifications to Penns River because he illegally affixed this device to Rollison's car?"

Harriger in full media mode vexed Doc no end. "First of all, there's no blowback to the city. He's off the books. If anyone would be liable, it would be me. The arrangement was between him and me as private citizens." So he hoped. A lawyer would go for the deepest pockets available. "Second, the device was not 'affixed' in the legal sense of the word. Look here." He pointed to the back of the case. "It's a magnet. Probably stuck it up under the wheel well. To affix it he'd have to physically connect it, wire it to the battery or something. There's no case here."

"A court would have to decide that. There's certainly a hell of a lot of embarrassment."

"More embarrassing than the acting chief of police having a cozy dinner with one of the most violent Russian gangsters on the east coast?"

"I didn't know that until today. His father has a small interest in the casino. Rollison told me Yuri was there on his behalf. It was a courtesy call, keeping a major employer abreast of a matter that concerned him."

"So the public can choose which is worse: that you had dinner with a major mob figure, or that you didn't know he was one. I'm a good soldier, Jack. I'll help you spin it however you think it should play. You want to come across as bent, or incompetent?"

Harriger's face turned a dangerous—for him—shade of red. "Goddamn you, Dougherty! I've listened to you run your mouth and get away with it long enough! Leave your badge and gun on my desk and get the hell out of here! You're suspended!"

Doc took out both, held them where Harriger could see them. "Let me give you something to think about first. We know Mike Mannarino had Donte Broaddus killed. I can't believe he was dumb enough to do it himself, but he had it done, and I have a pretty good idea why. I doubt we'll ever pin it on him.

"We also know Mannarino had nothing to do with Dwight Wierzbicki. Anyone who's seen more than a couple of episodes of *Law and Order* knows that was a set-up from the second Wierzbicki came looking for me. Mannarino may or may not have an alibi, but I have a witness who can place Rollison and, possibly, Yuri Volkov at the scene at about the time Wierzbicki was clipped."

Harriger still red, growing pale underneath. "Your cousin?"

"I don't know how Danny Hecker was able to sneak Sergei Volkov's history past the Gaming Commission. I also don't know why Yuri's been brought in from New York to play in what must seem like the minor leagues to him. I can look a couple of steps down the road and guess why Yuri wants Mannarino out, and why Mannarino doesn't want to go, but guesses aren't evidence.

"You want my badge and gun? Here they are, but consider this: Lyndon Johnson once had an aide leaking information to the media. Everyone wanted him to fire the guy, but Johnson wouldn't. Said he'd rather have him inside the tent pissing out than on the outside pissing in. I want to clean this up. I can do it as a cop, with the advantages and disadvantages that involves. Or

I can do what I can as a civilian. Thing is, if I'm a civilian, I'm no longer con-
strained by the confidentiality of an investigation. I can say what I want, to
whoever I want."

"You'll still be a cop. I'm just suspending you."

"Uh-uh. Suspend me and the paperwork goes in before I leave the building. I'll be a civilian by the end of the day."

Doc told Neuschwander once never to bluff a suspect. He calls and you're
standing there with your dick in your hand. Harriger had a lot to lose, and
no experience in sitting on that end of such a negotiation. Doc watched him
think, wondered if Busy Beaver was hiring.

Harriger spoke through white lips, staring at his blotter. "I expect you to
conduct these investigations in a professional and thorough manner. I'm not
convinced there's nothing we can do about Mannarino and Broaddus. But—
I'll admit the chances diminish as time goes by. As for this Wierzbicki business, we have an arraigned suspect. That investigation is officially closed. And
unofficially. We're through with it. The DA does what she can now."

He looked up. His gaze went past Doc and probably through the wall. "Is
there anything else?"

Doc clipped the badge back to his belt, holstered his gun. "No, I'm good.
Thanks for the chance to clear the air."

[46]

Doc first met Imelda Faison—she pronounced it "Eye-melda"—in County lockup, after her boys walked away from their foster home and he found them in a vacant townhouse next door to Jefferson West's. Wilver and David were ensconced with West at the time and Doc wanted to assess their potential home life after Mom got out. He'd been unimpressed.

The woman who answered the door didn't remind him much of the one he'd met in County. Still thin as spaghetti, more of a healthy thin now, like someone who'd been sick and was much better, not yet well enough to overdo it.

He introduced himself, knew she lied when she said she remembered him. Appreciated him coming to see her, and for looking after her boys. No malice in the lie. She was in rough shape when he saw her last, wanted to cover the embarrassment as much as ingratiate herself with a cop. He'd heard she was clean, and nothing he saw here made him think otherwise.

"Mrs. Faison, I want you to know up front I'm not here as a policeman. I only showed my badge to help you remember me. I'm looking for Wilver as a friend. There's something I want to talk to him about."

"He in trouble?"

"No, ma'am."

Imelda's eyes flicked around the room. "You ain't ask him to snitch, will you?"

"No, ma'am."

She rubbed her hands along her arms and swayed back and forth in the kitchen chair. "Detective, I know you been good to my boys. You and that man West and that woman cop. You all looked out for them and never axed for nothing. I don't mean to sound ungrateful, I truly don't. It's just—I'm his mama. I have a right to ax what you wants him for."

This was a much different woman than he'd met a year ago. That one went what he called "full martyr" on him, wailing and crying about "her babies" and how she didn't want them to see her in "this place" and would care for them when she got straight. He'd heard the speech before, and not often better.

He took a quick inventory of what he could see without being obvious. The apartment was shabby, but clean. Imelda's jeans and blouse were washed and neatly turned out. The marks on her arms were faint and old, her eyes were clear. She looked as much like an ex-junkie as anyone he'd ever seen.

"You're absolutely right, Mrs. Faison." Pushing his politeness hard to remind her he respected her authority. "I promise you he's in no trouble, and I'm not going to ask him to do anything that will put either of you in an uncomfortable situation. The thing is—what I want to talk to him about, it's a guy thing. Kind of topic a boy doesn't want to talk about with his mother. No disrespect, but I know his father's not around, and I keep an eye and an ear open for both boys. I'd just want to chat him up."

Cops tread the line separating lying and bullshit every day. True, he'd wanted to see what home life looked like for the Faisons; he also didn't want anyone to see a cop come for Wilver, then let him go after a short chat. They might assume he'd stonewalled, or they might think he snitched. Depended on how they felt about Wilver in the first place, something Doc had no way to know. No one would believe the two were friends and the cop came by to talk about Pitt basketball. Even if they did, Wilver would be on the Don't Trust list forever. The last thing Doc wanted was to put a kid on the fence in a position where he'd have to prove he was falling the other way.

Imelda picked at her dress and fretted. Doc knew her record. She and responsibility were recent acquaintances; she wore the burden like a too-heavy coat that didn't fit. She wanted to trust him, though everything she'd known told her never to trust a cop.

"Can I come with you? I promise I won't say nothing to embarrass the boy. It just—it just I feel like I'm his mama for the first time now. I need to know more about him than someone who been a good parent all along. Do that make sense?"

Wilver got Doc off the hook by walking in the door. The kid would starve if he ever tried to make a living on the poker tour. He looked at Doc like six men with shotguns sat in the chair.

"Hey, Wilver," Doc said. "How goes it?"

"Hey, Officer Doc. It's all good, I guess. You talking to my moms?"

"We're having a nice chat, but I'm really here to see you. Think you can spare me ten minutes?" Doc looked at Imelda for approval. She lowered her eyes.

"Sure, I guess so. You mean right here?"

"Let's take a walk." Doc stood before either could object. To Imelda, he said, "I'll have him right back."

He led the boy into the hall, closed the door. "Relax. I don't want anyone to see us together any more than you do. Where can we go that's close by and private?"

"The vacant. You know, the one where you found us last year? They fixing it up now, but I still know how to get in. I go there when nobody's working so's I can be by myself."

"You sure we're covered there?"

"Yeah. Ain't no one go there. It's all locked up. They a window in back, the latch don't catch. I gets in that way."

"All right. Make sure no one sees you, and let me in around back in ten minutes."

[47]

The idea of shinnying his 73 inches and 210 pounds through a basement window didn't excite Doc. Seeing the back door ajar was a pleasant surprise.

"They put regular doors and locks on a couple weeks ago," Wilver said. "They just locked from the outside. Once you in, you can always get out."

"Good thing. I wondered how I'd get my big ass through those little windows." A lot of work had been done; a lot was left. The kitchen still no more than studs, wires, and plumbing. Doc strolled through the main floor in the fading light, saw the living room and dining room needed only finishing touches. Whoever did the work had done it before.

"How have you been?" Doc said.

"I told you. I'm fine."

"That was the answer for in front of your mother. How are you, now that we're alone?"

"Really. I'm good. You know, there always this and that, but it's all good."

Doc let that sit on the floor between them for a while. Said, "You know, Wilver, there's only a handful of detectives in this town. What one of us hears, we pretty much all hear."

"Okay."

"I hear there's drugs being sold by that corner where Third crosses the tracks."

Wilver looked him straight in the eye. "I don't know nothing about that."

"I also hear you've been seen around there a few times the last week or so."

"That's not true."

"Yes, it is."

"I ain't selling no drugs. You know I ain't lying about that."

"I didn't say you were," Doc said. "You did lie to me about hanging around down there."

"But I'm not hanging down there."

"Okay, then tell me what it is you are doing, because I know you've been there when sales go down. Don't tell me you aren't."

"What you need me to talk for, huh? You know I been there, you know who else been there. You don't need me to give nobody up."

"I don't want you to give anyone up."

"Then what you want?"

"I want to make sure you're all right."

"I told you that already."

"You told me you're all right now. It won't stay that way if you keep spending time on that corner."

"That a threat?"

Doc took a mental deep breath. "Let's both calm down. The police know what's going on there. Sooner or later we're going to have to do something about it. How old are you?"

"Sixteen."

"You're not a juvenile anymore. You go away, you'll go in with the big boys. The only currency you can use to keep yourself out is who you can give up, and you're sure as hell not going to want to do that if you might go in, anyway. Walk away now while you can."

Wilver jammed his hands into his pockets. "But I'm trying to tell you, I ain't be doing nothing wrong there."

"Okay. We're friends, I believe you. The thing is, some people are doing something wrong there, and it'll rub off on you if you're not careful. Let's back up a step. What *are* you doing there?"

"Just—just, you know, hanging. Couple a them hangs there my boys, you know? We just goofin' and shit. I gets them cold drinks and Snickers, on account of they can't leave the corner when they working."

"You ever touch the drugs or the money?"

"*No!*"

"Ever act as a lookout? Tell them when someone's coming?"

A pause. "Not like official or nothing."

Doc put his hands on his hips. His sport coat pulled away to show the gun and badge on his belt. "Let's not play word games. Describe to me what an unofficial lookout does that's different from one duly appointed."

Wilver toed the dust on the floor into whorls and Doc knew he had him if he took his time. "I don't like, you know, stand there and *watch* or nothing. I—you know, like if they busy, or they needs to piss or get something, they all like, 'Hey, Faze, tell me you see anybody.' You know, shit like that. They ain't paying me, or nothing. We just friends."

"I believe that. Here's something you need to believe: police come by when you're just being an unofficial, friendly lookout, and you'll go with them. To the law you're an accomplice."

"What? For telling them 'Here come Butchie?'"

"No, for helping them with their drug business." Wilver gave him a look. "Think about it. You keeping an eye open frees them up to refresh the stash, drop some money, a lot of things they couldn't do if you weren't watching their backs."

"But it's just for friends. I told you they ain't paying me."

"Prove it."

Wilver choked back a reply. "Huh?"

"Do they give out pay stubs for official lookouts? Matching 401(k) contributions? How do you plan to prove the others are professionals and you're just a friend? Cop sees you trying to tip these hoppers, he won't care if you're getting paid or not. You're all going in together. It's what the law calls a conspiracy."

Doc knew the look, Wilver recognizing the fact he was being told something he already knew, hadn't wanted to admit. "But, they my friends. We been tight since we was shorties."

"I understand better than you think. I know what it's like when friends do things they shouldn't and you have to decide how far friendship goes." Abu Ghraib taught him that, set him on the road back to Penns River. "I know it's harder when you're younger. But you really need to find new friends."

"How? Walk up to someone I don't know and ax him to be my friend?"

"I know it's not easy. I also know these friends of yours are going down, sooner or later, and they'll take you with them." Doc held up a hand to forestall Wilver's objection. "Not out of malice. They won't go out of their way to fuck up, but it won't be your ass they're worried about when they get jammed. You'll get caught up in the current. I've seen it happen."

Wilver made a frustrated sound, stomped around the unfinished room like the front end of a giraffe. "Awwwwrrgghh! What I supposed to tell my boys? I ain't be they friend no more because what they doing wrong and I'm too goody to hang with them?"

"I don't think that'll work."

"What then, motherfucker?" Wilver near tears, having to fight them off making him even madder. "You all full of good ideas 'bout what I should do. Mind telling me *how* for any of it?"

A fair point. The best advice Doc ever received came from a sergeant major at Fort Leonard Wood, who told him never to present a problem without a potential solution. People resent problems, appreciate solutions. "We have to find other things to keep you busy. Give you a reason not to be available."

"What you mean, we?"

"I'm your friend, Wilver. I'll help you."

"Tell me what to do more like it."

"Help me out. What can I do to make this easier for you?"

Wilver's silence answered for him. It left Doc with nothing to play off of. The conversation couldn't have stalled any quicker if Imelda had walked in.

"Wilver." Doc waited for the boy's attention. "Let's slow down. I know I haven't been around much. Part of that is I didn't want to accidentally hang a snitch rep on you. Another part is—my fault. I accepted some responsibility for you and David the night I dropped you on Mr. West, and I haven't been as good as I could've been. Should've been. What if we spent some time together, so we could talk without it sounding like a confrontation?"

"Like how? You just said we can't hang together. First thing you said all night that's right."

Doc thought a few seconds. "When's the last time you went down to PNC Park for a ballgame?"

A look like shame crossed Wilver's face. "Don't remember. Long time, I guess."

Doc drew his wallet from a hip pocket, took out a laminated schedule. "They're on the road right now, but next weekend St. Louis is in town. You want to go?"

"Yeah, sure—wait." Wilver seemed embarrassed by his initial enthusiasm. "We still got the same problem. What I do when people see me spending the day with a cop?"

"A lot of people know you at the ballpark?"

"Ain't like I can drive my ass down there."

"I'll talk to Mr. West. We'll set it up so you and David go with him and we'll hook up someplace. I'll meet you at the game, if it makes you feel any better."

Doc felt bad for him. The kid wanted to go, suspected there was something uncool about it, and didn't know if wanting to go might make it even worse. Doc let him fight it out for himself until "Aight" crawled out of his mouth.

[48]

Doc worked other cases the rest of the day. Went back to the station only long enough to sign out. He didn't bother to shower, went home to wash away the meeting with Harriger. He still made it to the Edgecliff by 4:30. Proximity is a virtue.

Barb Smith didn't get there until five. The Penns River police station had no locker or shower facilities for women. Three female cops among the forty: Janine Schoepf the dispatcher, Sherry Gibson the juvenile officer, and Barb. They had official access to the same showers the men used. That required either someone to stand guard and keep the men out, or waiting until all the men were done, since the stalls were never empty until then. Janine and Sherry didn't complain; they never did anything sweaty. Barb didn't want to make waves, so she went home to clean up. Then drove back past the station to meet Doc at Edgecliff.

He took his beer to a table away from the flow of bar traffic, still too early for families. Didn't feel like shooting the breeze with Denny Sluciak today. Didn't feel much like hanging out with Barb, but she'd called the meeting and he blamed himself for the last one. He drank his beer and tried to make his mind a blank.

He waved to get her attention when she came in, gestured to Denny to bring the beers he'd ordered for both of them. She hadn't gone to as much trouble this time. No makeup, hair a little damp, wore a cotton jersey outside her jeans instead of the appealing sweater. Still had that wholesome, healthy, pretty look to her. She never lost that, not even after long hot days, with hair in her eyes and exhaustion on her face.

"Rumor has it you threatened to quit this morning," Barb said. "I would've asked sooner, but you weren't in all day. I figured if you weren't around, you didn't want to talk about it." Paused as a trace of a blush appeared. "At least not right away."

"It's okay. You were right, I wasn't in the mood before. I'm fine now."

"Is it true? About threatening to quit?"

"A bluff. I thought I might've been too clever when he made me wait. Scared me a little."

"I also heard you got suspended, and that was why you weren't around."

"That was where the bluff came in. He wanted to suspend me, and I said I'd quit if he did." They each drank two beers while he told her the whole story.

"What now?" she said when the next round had been delivered.

"I really don't know."

She had nothing to say to that, and he had nothing to add. They drank in peace, Doc pacing himself not to drink any faster than she did.

Barb said, "What happens now? I mean, it's an unstable situation, right? Mannarino's out, and I can't believe the DA will prosecute that case we left her. Volkov wants him gone." She breathed and her mouth hung open. Tried to form the words, couldn't get them out.

Doc did it for her. "He has to kill Mannarino now. Or Mike kills him. I'm almost rooting for him. Look at the Broaddus hit, and that job he pulled on Frank Orszulak last year. Neat, no civilians involved. If you have to kill some-one in the course of doing business, that's the way to do it.

"Yuri won't be that way. Well, I guess he could, but he has a hard-on—excuse me, a bug up his ass now, and part of that's my fault for showing him up like I did. I tried to make it public enough for him to think twice. I don't really know if he's that kind of guy."

"You think there'll be a war?"

Barb not drinking fast enough, Doc plowed on ahead. "I don't know what to think. I hope to hell all I did was move the process along, not make any-thing worse. Get it over with."

He didn't really believe that and could tell she didn't, either. This day—week, month—already in the shitter, Doc decided he might as well clear the decks. "About the last time we were here. I owe you an apology."

"No. I owe *you* one. I thought about it later and realized I came back in the middle of something and blamed you for it. I hope I didn't mess anything up."

"That's the point, Barb. There was nothing to mess up. Anita and I went to school together. We were friendly, but not dating or anything. I was kind of a dork then, I guess. Didn't know how to ask her out even if I thought she might've gone." Barb did not seem shocked at this revelation.

"She works at the PNC in the shopping center and we started running into each other when I moved back. She's divorced, couple of kids, threw the old man out because he drank too much. Thing is, he's a great father, dotes on those two, and never drinks when he's responsible for them. So once a month or so, he takes them for a night during the week and Anita gets to go out. She ran into me here one time about a year ago and we went back to my place. Last month it happened again."

"And it would've happened last time if I hadn't butted in."

"No, that's the part you aren't getting. It wouldn't have happened. I was here with you. Anita and I are friends. Once in a while our paths cross in the right phase of the moon or something and we spend a night together. We're not dating."

"You mean you're more like fuck buddies."

"Not even. That implies some kind of regularity. We've never planned to spend a night together. It's just worked out that way a few times. She was interested, and knew I hang out here. That's all."

"If she came looking for you, then she's interested in more than just mess-ing around."

Doc finished his beer, raised his eyebrows to ask Barb if she was ready, her glass still half full. She shook her head and he raised one finger when the wait-ress passed.

"How can I put this without making her sound slutty? She gets those nights once a month. We've been together three times in the year she's been doing it. I don't ask, but I doubt she goes home and takes care of herself while mooning over me the other times."

Barb took a drink, then another. "Aren't you—I mean, what about— damn it, I'm an adult. Why am I having a hard time saying this?"

"If you're worried about, uh, hygiene, she and I are always very careful. I have no reason to believe she's not that way all the time. She's a good, re-sponsible mother—hell, she's a responsible *person*. It's not like she's a cat in heat when she goes out. Dad gets the kids every other weekend. Anita stays home or sees her mother then. Says she doesn't want to go out when people have scoring on their minds. She'd rather go out on a normal night, have some fun, see what happens. All I know is how she handles herself the nights we get together, and that she didn't know we would get together until we did.

"She doesn't need me to defend her because she doesn't need defending. I'm just saying she thought I was alone that night, and she was mortified when you came out of the bathroom. We talked about it since then, and she asked me to apologize to you for her. So, I guess I have."

He couldn't decipher Barb's facial expression. She said, "When was this? When she asked you to apologize?"

"Last week," he said through the glass as he drank.

"And would you have told me if I hadn't asked you to meet here today?"

He mumbled something he meant to sound like, "Eventually."

Barb finished her beer, waved off the waitress. "You know, for all the things I've seen you do, and know about you, you're like a little kid some-times."

"I prefer to think of it as boyish charm."

"How's it working out for you?"

"I don't know. Is it?"

She laughed like she wanted to be mad with him and couldn't pull it off.

He finished his beer, put a coaster on the glass. "I'll admit I lack certain interpersonal skills beyond a superficial level. I grew up with just the one brother, went into the army, became a cop, all guy stuff. That's my nature, and it's probably not going to change much. It can be refined, but it's going to take work, and I'm probably going to need some help. So, I was wonder-ing, if, maybe, next weekend, if you wanted, we could go someplace where dinner for two costs more than twelve dollars, you know, maybe see a movie? If there's anything out you felt like seeing, I mean."

An untrained eye might not have seen her lips move, the smile was so small. Doc caught it in her eyes, the way a kid looks when a difficult concept becomes clear. "Are you asking me out on a date?"

"That depends."

"On what?"

"On whether you want to go. If you're not going, I'm not asking."

"But if I would go—"

"Then I'm asking."

"But how can you tell if I will or won't until you ask?"

"You know already. Just let me in on it so I'll know whether to ask or not."

The smile broke out despite her best efforts. "I guess if you were to ask, I'd go. But only if you ask."

"Okay, then. I'm asking."

"Asking what?"

"If you'll go out on a date with me."

"When?"

"I don't know. I'm usually off on weekends. How do your shifts look?"

"It just so happens I'm off on Friday and Saturday this week. Your choice."

"Let's do Saturday. I'm off, so we can eat a little early and not have to go to the late show."

"Deal."

[49]

Doc dropped his keys, wallet, badge, and gun on the night stand and was headed for the bathroom when the bell rang. Ray Keaton didn't waste time coming in before giving Doc his opinion of the events at Torrance's Steak House.

"What the fuck were you thinking, showing your hand like that? Do you have any idea how long it takes to pull someone like Yuri Volkov into the kind of snare he was about to walk into for you? Of course you do. You're not stupid. You're almost too smart for this job. So I have to ask: what the fuck were you thinking?"

Doc stood aside to let him enter. "You're a lot more likable when you bring pizza."

"I got your pizza right here. You might have signed someone's death warrant the other night. And you're a shitty host, to boot. Just because I didn't bring pizza doesn't mean I should still be waiting for a beer."

"Beer's in the refrigerator. Drag your lazy Fed ass out there and get it yourself. One for me, too, while you're at it. I have urgent personal business to attend to."

Doc came back from the bathroom to find Keaton sitting in his recliner. "That's my chair."

"It's your house. Strictly speaking, they're all your chairs. Since I got the beer, I get the host's chair." Gestured to an open bottle on the coffee table. "That one's yours."

"Lite beer? I know I have real beer in there. I only keep this around when some poor, clueless SOB comes by who can't handle hi-test. I thought of offering some to you."

"You don't deserve good beer after what went down last night. Give us Feds some credit. When we fuck up that bad, it's a policy decision. You're out there making this shit up as you go along. It's unprofessional."

Doc drank the top two inches of beer. Swallowed and made a face. Drank the rest of the bottle in one long draught, came back from the kitchen with a can of Foster's.

"Whoa! Where'd you find that? All I saw was the Rolling Rock."

"Typical Fed. The Rocks are on the door, first place you looked. Couldn't be bothered to find the enormous goddamn oil cans behind the Tupperware salad thing. Bottom shelf, all the way in the back."

Keaton drank, rubbed his eyes. Considered what to do next. "Enough banter. Seriously, what were you thinking, getting up in Volkov's face like that?"

"I didn't think of it that way until things got noisy. I was looking to get in my boss's grill, make him understand the game he was playing wasn't free.

Show him how easy it was to shine a little light on what was going on, no matter how clandestine he thought he was being. I knew how Rollison would take it, and guessed right about Harriger. I'd hoped Yuri would laugh it off."

"He might have if your cousin hadn't busted his balls."

"Yeah, well, my cousin led me from Harriger to Rollison to Volkov, and he's the closest thing we have to a witness in the Wierzbicki killing. He does nice work, but you buy the whole package."

Keaton sat tapping his wedding ring against the beer bottle. "Must run in the family." Looked like he had more to say, in no hurry.

Doc said, "You really think Yuri might kill someone because of what I did? I figure he has Mannarino teed up already."

"Harriger might have bought Mannarino some time by forcing you to arrest him. Yuri could want to see what the courts do before taking things into his own hands. I suspect our justice system will seem to move much slower for him when he wants something to happen than it does when he's avoiding something."

"So no harm, no foul?"

"Don't get carried away. Yuri might have laughed you off as a small town inconvenience. Your cousin showed him up. He's not the kind who forgives that sort of thing. I was your cousin, I wouldn't sit with my back to any rooms for a while."

"He's going back to Chicago day after tomorrow."

"That helps, so long as he remembers there are Russians in Chicago, too." Keaton's beer was gone. He gestured toward the kitchen. "You mind if I have another?"

"Help yourself." Keaton went into the kitchen and Doc moved to the recliner.

Keaton walked straight to the couch with a fresh Foster's. Doc said, "Someone asked me earlier what happens now. I told her I really didn't know. What do you think?"

Keaton shook his head while he drank. "Too many variables. Our intelligence is pretty good as far as Mannarino and Yuri go, but we don't have a handle on what Sergei's thinking. For what it's worth, you might've killed Harriger's chance to be chief. Pointing him out like you did, and Yuri can't be too happy about how Mannarino keeps staying out of jail and aboveground. I still think they're going to retire your friend Napierkowski, but the new chief might have to come from outside now."

"He's going to kill Mannarino, isn't he?" Five beers at Edgecliff, the lite with Keaton, now the 25-ounce Foster's, a lot more beer than Doc usually drank in a night. "I'm thinking he thinks he has to."

"I don't know about that. I'm sure he wants to. That doesn't make Mannarino special. Yuri probably wouldn't mind killing him and you and your cousin. Maybe even Harriger, just for letting this drag on."

"What should we do?"

"I told you this before and you didn't listen, but here goes: nothing. Stay out of it, at least for now. I understand how you feel, and I can't say for sure what you tried to do last night was an altogether bad idea. He's had things too much his own way, get him off track, make him think about something else for a change. I could quibble about the execution," made a noise in his throat, part belch, part nose clearing, "what's done is done."

"I talked to Mannarino for you again. When I arrested him. Brought him in the scenic route so we'd have time."

"How'd he take it?"

"He knew he was being set up. Already had his lawyer cued up when I got there. He at least acknowledged I gave him a few courtesies."

"Such as?"

"No cuffs until we had to. Let him leave his wallet and keys in his office. Tried to get him in without the media, but Harriger beat me to that."

Keaton nodded. "That's good. I appreciate the effort. Now we wait. We'll hear from him, or we won't. No point rushing anything. Maybe I'll make contact in a week or so."

They talked about working for the Bureau and what it's like to be a small town cop. Why neither would want the other's job. Families and weather and if the US Open would come back to Oakmont anytime soon. Doc struggled to stay awake. This much beer could put him out faster than turkey and NyQuil combined.

Keaton stood to leave. Doc said, "You know the way. Nothing personal. I'm too comfortable to move." Reclined a few more inches.

Keaton paused at the door. "Something for you to think about. Everyone knows Stan Napierkowski's a stand-up guy, and respects him for it. You're on the radar, too. I don't want you to think you're on an island here. You have friends."

He left and Doc pulled a thin blanket over his bare arms. He was asleep in less than a minute.

[50]

Doc and Nick sat at the Edgecliff's bar.

"Night before I leave and you finally take me someplace doesn't look like the out-processing center at Stateville. The beer's even cheaper." Nick took a sip. "Colder, too."

"This is a farewell night out. No work talk, once I get this out of the way." Doc told Nick of Keaton's visit, to watch his back.

Nick spoke into his glass. "That wasn't my finest moment. I hope I haven't left you holding a steaming bag of shit when I go."

"I told you before, I'm a cop. Once Yuri settles down, he'll remember I'm more trouble to kill or injure than I'm worth. You're the one pissed in his oatmeal. Distance is a good thing for you. Enough about that. So, your mom's okay now? Good as new?"

Mom was fine and dad was fine and Nick gained five pounds on the visit, from not exercising and eating all the food Doc's mother sent over, then the food his mother made because she felt guilty for not feeding him herself. Time to get back to work.

"I meant to ask you about that. You've been gone quite a while. How's the shop stay open with you away so long?"

"Forte Investigations probably makes more money with me here than there. No shit. The woman I hired to run the office took over most of the computer work, and that's just about all we do now. Background checks, that sort of thing. We even have a girl comes in two-three times a week to help. A company does our accounting, frees up Sharon—she's the one that really runs the joint—to produce revenue. I got a retired Texas Ranger to share the field work, but even he prefers to stick around the office now that he's married and inherited two kids. Fact is, the margins are so good on the inside stuff, there aren't that many clients that can afford an old-fashioned, long-term investigation. I'd stop doing them altogether, but I hate to give up the stereotype of the hardened gumshoe."

"And you hate sitting in the office all the time."

"Oh Jesus Christ do I. That's why I don't want you to feel like you put me out the past couple of weeks. I had a ball."

"Glad I could be of service." Tore a coaster, rolled it into a ball, delaying the unmanly question. "You seeing anybody?"

"My mother ask you to do that?"

"Yours does that, too? Mine's on me all the time. No, actually it was my mom asked me to ask you. Either your mom asked her, or mine doesn't want to be out of the loop. She talks about you all the time since you came over that night."

Nick's turn to destroy a coaster. "Off and on. Nothing regular. You know how it is."

Did he ever. Barb Smith flashed through Doc's mind. Maybe pretty soon he'd have to remember how it is, not live through it.

Nick was still talking. "It's hard with Caroline. I don't get to see her enough as it is. No fault of Diane's, she's good with visitation, but there's no way you can be as good a father outside the home as inside. Can't be done. So I stay on call. Diane needs help, Caroline needs something, I drop every-thing and get over there. Work makes that hard enough, and I haven't met a woman lately who's good with playing second fiddle."

"Diane doesn't abuse the privilege?"

"Sometimes I wonder, but, no, not consciously. You've met her, she tends to forget other people have their own perspectives on things that might seem perfectly reasonable to her. I don't sense any malice. As divorced couples go, we get along great."

Doc hadn't spent so much time with Nick since high school. It felt good, bonding again, prompted him to ask a question he wouldn't under ordinary circumstances. "Ever think of having more kids?"

"No more kids." Nick took a coaster off the pile on the bar. "I don't have the kind of judgment a good parent needs. I defer to Diane on that stuff now and everyone's better off."

Doc knew Nick had taken his five-year-old son to a Bears game in bad weather against Diane's advice. The boy died in an accident on the way home, Nick not able to leave the hospital for the funeral.

"You and me haven't hung out together for a long time, Benny. Things happen. People change. I've changed. I think women sense it and it puts them off." Then, in a voice Doc had never heard, "I think it scares them a little."

Nick finished his beer in a swallow. Pushed the glass across the bar and signaled for two more. "Coupla shots, too, please." Turned to Doc with the unspoken question.

"Jack Daniel's."

"Some things never change. Thank God. Oh," he reached into an inside pocket. "These are yours." Laid the Special Deputy badge and carry permit on the bar.

"The badge I need back. Keep the permit. Souvenir. It expires in a couple of weeks, anyway."

The drinks came. The cousins touched glasses and threw back their shots.

Nick cocked his head until the drink settled. "Last I looked Johnnie Walker had red, black, green, gold, and blue labels. Some day they'll have plaid, won't even take money for it, have to get a tattoo or cut off a finger or something for a shot, prove how cool you are. Jack Black's good enough for me. Old school. Two more, please."

Doc started to demur. Nick pointed into his Pilsner glass. "Okay," Doc said, "but then I'm done."

"Me, too."

Denny Sluciak dropped off the shots with a smile. Doc and Nick toasted again, then dropped the full glasses into their beer. Natural boilermakers.

They each drank off an inch. Doc's face started to warm. "Mmmm. Been a while."

"Yeah. You don't think we might be getting too old for this shit, do you?"

"Maybe you aren't. I sure as hell am." Doc's cell vibrated in his pocket. He held up one finger for Nick to wait, flipped open the phone.

"Ben, it's Barb. I don't want to make too much of this, and I don't know what to think, so I thought I'd call you first."

"What's wrong?"

"Maybe nothing, but this car has been parked in the street outside my house since it got dark. There's a guy sitting in it. He's right under the street-light, like he wants me to see him."

"What's he look like? Can you tell?"

"Just that he's a white guy. Looks big. You want me to go out and get closer?"

"No. Stay right there." Made eye contact with Nick to hold his attention. "What about the car?"

"Dark Lexus. Looks like a four door. I can't see any of the plate."

"Wait one." To Nick: "There's a dark Lexus sedan parked under a street-light in front of Barb Smith's house. Guy in it's been there since it got dark. Could it be the car you saw the night Wierzbicki got clipped?"

"I know an easy way to find out. Work better with one more guy, though."

"I'm right with you." Spoke into the phone, "Stay put. Keep an eye on him. I have to make a phone call real quick, then I'll call you back."

He paused to think. "Is your piece handy?"

"In the closet."

"Get it."

[51]

Grabek lived in West Mifflin, too far to be useful. Rick Neuschwander's wife had the minivan. Stush would have come in a heartbeat, but his heartbeats were too unreliable for Doc's taste. He caught Eye Chart Zywiciel at home and scrambled him to meet them in a parking lot half a mile from Barb's house. Simple plan: Eye Chart and Nick parked near the corners of the cross streets either side of Barb's. Doc would make a routine traffic stop, they'd cut off the Lexus if it tried to run. Easy.

Everyone in position, Doc made his move. Attached the magnetic police flasher to the roof and lit him up. New York plates. Gave the driver a few seconds to make peace with situation, then got out.

He tapped the window with a knuckle, one hand on the grip of his gun. The window came down. Doc didn't recognize the man inside.

"Can I help you with something?" Russian accent.

"Detective Dougherty, Penns River Police. You mind if I ask what you're doing here?"

"Is illegal to sit quiet in car in Penns River?"

"You've been here for some time. It's a residential street. People are wondering what you're up to."

"Must be high crime area, people afraid of man sitting in car minding own business."

"Look, we can do this easy or hard. You want to bust balls, I'm game. Let's see your license and registration, just to get you in the mood."

The driver's eyes went to Doc's gun hand. "License is in pocket. I reach for it, I don't want to be worry about no itching trigger fingers."

Doc moved his hand a few inches, turned the palm up to show it was empty. The driver wriggled around in his seat, took a wallet from his back pocket, removed the license, handed it out. Pavel Unpronounceable. Brooklyn address.

"This is a little out of your neighborhood, Pavel," Doc said.

"Is old license. I am moved to Pittsburgh three, might be four months now."

"Supposed to have a Pennsylvania license within sixty days."

"I thought was ninety. My mistake."

"One last chance," Doc said. "What are you doing here?"

"Since you are asking so nice is only fair I tell you. I am waiting for my friend to give ride to."

"Your friend live around here?"

"Someplace close by, I think. He tell me to wait here for him."

"From what I hear, you've been waiting a long time."

"My friend is not always good about on time."

"Let's give him a call," Doc said. "See what's holding him up."

"Phone also is in pocket. No sticky trigger fingers again, okay?"

Doc showed his hands, the right ready. Pavel dug in his coat pocket and Doc stiffened when something hard pressed against his right kidney.

"Ah," Pavel said. "There he is now."

Yuri Volkov said, "Take your gun with two fingers and hand to Pavel in car."

"You think I'm handing him my own gun to shoot me with, you're dumber than I thought."

"You need shooting, I do it myself. Pavel, lean back in seat so bullet does not go through and hit you."

Doc lifted his gun from the holster with two fingers. Held it up so Yuri could see, tossed it over the car's roof into Barb's front yard. "Good enough?"

"You got big mouth, but you got balls and smart intelligence. Now keep keeping your head and no one will be hurt. Get into back seat so we can talk in privacy."

"This is a cop's house. She's already called the cavalry."

"Is no matter. We will be out of your—fucking shit, what is word for *pod-sudnost*?—your, uh, jurisdiction before they get here. Is lots of black Lexus around. Get in now, please. Is only time I say 'please.'"

Doc reached for the door handle and felt Yuri stiffen. The gun came away from his back and he heard his cousin's voice, very close.

"Good boy, Boris. Point it up where I can see it, and throw it away." Yuri did. "You in the car, don't think I'm not paying attention. Do anything I don't expect and you'll have to find out if the car wash down the Sunoco can get Boris's brains off the finish. Put your hands on the outside mirror." Pavel did. "Now let's have that talk you asked for, but let's have it at the police station."

Yuri looked over his shoulder at Nick. "Why is always Boris with you Americans?"

[52]

Grabek needed almost an hour to get in from West Mifflin. Stush made it in twenty-five minutes, his first appearance at the office since the heart attack.

"Don't say it, Benny. I can see you're having second thoughts just look-ing at you, but you did exactly the right thing calling me. We need someone in charge who wasn't involved. This is what they pay me for, no matter what some think."

A cue for Jack Harriger if ever there was one. He didn't disappoint, stand-ing in the doorway as Stush finished his thought. "I got here as soon as I heard. Is it good for you to be up and around so soon, Chief?"

"I'm fine, Jack." Stush looked tired. His color not as good under fluores-cent lighting, almost eleven o'clock at night. The shadows made his cheeks appear sunken. What seemed a healthy weight loss in sunshine was gauntness in artificial light.

"You're the boss. If you get tired, or don't feel up to it, let me know. I have the authority to act if needed."

"You're authorized to act in my absence, Jack. I'm here now. You want to stick around, have a seat. Or you can find some work in your office. Or you can go home. From what I hear, you might have a conflict of interest with this suspect."

Harriger reddened from his collar to his ears. Said, "I'll stay," took a seat to Stush's right.

"I know most of what's going on here," Stush said. "Someone catch me up on what the hell happened in Monroeville the other day, and over at Barb's house tonight. Anyone needs coffee better get it now. We might be here a while."

Doc wanted time to organize his thoughts, volunteered to make the run to the coffee room. Everyone wanted something but Stush.

"No coffee?"

"Not tonight, thanks. I'm only allowed to drink decaf and that's no god-damn good if you're only drinking it to stay awake. I'll have a can of V-8 from the machine if they have any."

Back in the office Stush shook his V-8 and said, "Let's start with Mon-roeville, Benny." Harriger started to speak. Stush cut him off, pointed to Doc. "I said Benny. That's him. I'll get to you, Jack."

Doc told how he got the call from Nick and what happened at Tor-rance's. Stush let him finish, said to Nick, "Lot of stuff seems to happen when you're around. Sounds like we owe you, how you rolled this up all the way to Yuri Volkov, maybe even a murder. The whole town's grateful how you stepped in tonight to get a police officer out of a tough spot. Remember one thing, though: your authority's limited. Be careful you don't overstep your bounds." Nick nodded, mumbled something that sounded like agreement and Doc started breathing again.

"Chief," Harriger said. His voice had only enough energy to get as far as Stush. "You said you'd let me tell my side, too."

"I will, Jack," Stush said. "I didn't say it would be tonight. We're a little pressed for time right now, and my wife's going to call in an hour or so and wonder where the hell I am. She might even threaten to come over here and take my fat ass home. Your side might have to wait until tomorrow." Then, to Doc, "Now. About tonight."

Doc told the story, grateful for the opportunity to describe something how he saw it, not have his interpretation and judgment questioned on every salient point. Stush sipped his juice, reminded Doc of some of the interviews they'd done together. Everyone in town thought Stush just another fat redneck, and he let them think it. Encouraged it at times. He knew how to listen, to make other people fill uncomfortable silences with things they would have been better off leaving out, never a menacing action or word from Stush.

When Doc finished, Stush asked Nick if he'd really threatened to blow Yuri's—called him "that man"—head off.

"Not in so many words, Chief."

"But that was the impression you wanted to give."

"If I felt either of us was threatened, yeah."

Stush looked for a second as though he might ask Nick if he would have gone through with it. Instead he said, "So right now we have Yuri Volkov dead to rights for assaulting a police officer with a deadly weapon. His friend Pavel's at least an accomplice." Stared a hole through Harriger. "Anyone disagree?"

Harriger wanted to, didn't dare. He was in deeper than he could have imagined, with no way out unless someone took pity on him, which was even worse than not having a way out. Doc almost felt sorry for him, caught himself just in time.

Stush drained his juice can. "Let's go see the big man."

"Chief," Nick said. "Do you mind if I tag along?"

Stush rose, looked at him, then Doc. Said, "You really don't have a place in there, son, but we owe you. I don't like to think what might've happened to my nephew if you weren't there tonight. You earned your way in, if you promise to behave." Nick nodded and they all left together, Harriger bringing up the rear.

At the door to the interview room Stush paused. "Benny, you know the most about this, you take him. Willie and Jack and me will watch from the booth. Nick, you still have that Special Deputy's badge? Go on in, then. You know how the 'Good Cop, Bad Cop' thing works, don't you? Well, you're the Mute Cop."

Yuri Volkov sat handcuffed to the table. Men waiting for buses looked more concerned. He greeted Doc with, "When can have night court so I am getting out of this shithole?"

"This is a small town. No night court here. You'll be charged when the judge comes in tomorrow morning."

"I spend night here? I sleep here?"

"I'm afraid so."

"Then you are the only one afraid. I have been to much worse."

"Have your rights been explained to you?"

Yuri laughed. "Many times."

"I mean tonight."

"You can do now. Lawyer is on his way."

Doc read the Miranda card, showed him where to sign the acknowledgement. "You can have them explained to you in Russian if you like, but a translator won't get here until tomorrow."

"I speak English plenty good. Give me pen to sign." Doc handed him a ballpoint. "So then. What questions do you ask?"

"You don't want to wait for your lawyer? He might advise you not to talk."

"I talk when I want. Who knows? In five minutes, maybe not want to. Better ask quick before I change my mind, police man. Someone tell me once I am volatile. I like that word. I am volatile."

You are peckerhead, Doc thought, kept it to himself. "Do you understand the charges against you? Assault with a deadly weapon?"

"Is not clear how is assaulting. I never touch you."

"That's battery. All that's needed for assault is to point the weapon, or make a threat while you do it."

"When did I threaten you?"

"When you told Pavel to sit back in case you had to shoot me and the bullet went through."

"Was not threatening to you. Was warning to Pavel."

Doc knew Yuri would run him around like that until it bored him, or his lawyer arrived. He'd make bail in the morning, whatever it was, and be as drunk as he wanted to be by lunchtime.

After ten minutes Doc let himself give in to the fatigue, losing interest in the interview while he was conducting it. Looked over at his cousin, slumped in the doorway like it was an imposition to have to be there. Whatever cues his body language sent, his eyes never left Yuri. He watched every movement, every dismissive flick of a hand or inappropriate laugh. Doc found himself more interested in Nick than Yuri, lost the thread a couple of times until Yuri accused him of trying to trick him. Yeah, that's right, you're too smart for me, Yuri.

Twenty minutes later the lawyer came and called a halt. Asked what the hell Nick was doing in there with no official capacity. Doc told him Nick was a sworn deputy and Nick showed the card. The lawyer said he'd be sure to mention it at trial, if it got that far.

Yuri paused next to Nick on the way to his cell. "What is this Special Deputy they are calling you?"

"Means I don't work for the city. I'm just helping out. Doing my public service."

"You are not police man?"

"Pisser, isn't it? Getting taken down by a civilian."

Yuri's smile was uneven and warm as Moscow in January. "So you are not even cop. Is good to know."

[53]

The weather got warmer every day, baseball season picking up as the hockey playoffs moved along. Pittsburgh a better baseball town than it got credit for—eighteen straight losing seasons takes the starch out of all but the most diehard fans—hockey the big spring sport now. With Sidney Crosby in town, every spring brought Stanley Cup ambitions. Crowds flooded the parking lot near the old Civic Arena to watch on large screens while those lucky enough to get tickets shook the Coal Mine—Doc's nickname for the Consol Energy Center.

Mike Mannarino always got the urge to pitch this time of year. He'd earned his nickname on ball fields, not meat packing plants. He could break off an honest-to-Bert-Blyleven twelve-to-six curveball any time he wanted from the age of fifteen, and for strikes. He kept a ten-inch mound in a small barn behind the garage, sixty feet, six inches from a legitimate home plate. Behind it a net with a ribbon woven through for a strike zone. Once or twice a year someone would piss him off and stand in for the net, tied to a backboard braced in front of the plate. Whatever message had been missed, get hit with fifty, sixty baseballs, even the dimmest bulb got the point.

Tonight Mike wanted nothing more than to strap that ball busting nigger Tookie Harris to the board and let fly. Police looking to bury him in jail, Yuri looking to bury him literally, that cop Dougherty talking about flipping, a hundred grand out of pocket for bail, and this narcissistic shine wants a personal meeting. For "contiguencies," that half-wit Butterfield had told Stretch. In case Mike goes away. Drug venture the only thing in Mike's life not turning to shit right now, and Tookie can't leave it alone.

"I should of told him to fuck off, Skipper. I'm sorry." Stretch had Mike's underworld power of attorney in most cases, could have told Tookie to piss up a rope. Walking on eggshells around Mike the past few weeks. Buddy, too. Not wanting to add to Mike's *agita*, they also didn't want to blow off what they thought was a nuisance and find out Mike wanted to know. The whole operation was fucked up.

"It's okay, Stretch. Really. It's always better to deal with something than let it slip and bite us in the ass later." Tookie would have to deal with Stretch. Period. He didn't like it, he could take his business to the Russians. Of course, that other Tootsie Roll taking his business to the Russians started all this. And Mike needed the money.

"What do you think about this spook?" Mike said. Stretch had a knack for sensing when people were up to something, caught gestures or tones of voice that didn't mesh with what was said. He lacked the smarts to figure out what they were up to most of the time so Mike handled that part, how he got to be boss.

"Something's not right," Stretch said. Mike waited. Stretch took a while to get ramped up. "He talks to me, I don't know. It's not like he's lying, exactly, but watching him talk and listening to him, it's like going to two different movies."

"You want a beer?" Mike said. Stretch nodded. Mike opened a couple of bottles of Iron and they sat.

Stretch said, "He comes out of nowhere, looking for us, working with a guy who knows the package has been coming from someone else. Has to hear the rumors we had the other guy clipped, comes up to us all respectful. You know, 'Mr. Mannarino this,' 'all due respect.' Shit like that. And no one knows him. Him and his retard buddy says he did a long stretch, just got back. Okay, maybe. But I ain't found no one could tell me anything about him from before he went away."

"Are you sure he was inside?" Mike thinking about things he'd only felt before, too much else on his mind.

"You mean sure, like willing to bet going inside myself on it?" Stretch took his time. "No."

"You do any checking?" Mike feeling guilty, like he was playing catch-up.

"Asked around is all. You want me to try to pin him down on where's he been? See who we know who might know somebody?"

"We should a done that already. That's my fault. Too much on my mind." Mike took a pull of beer. "What's that cop's name? The Polack down Oakland. Guy with the bad hair and a gambling problem."

"Kuzniak?"

"Yeah. He owe anybody right now?"

"Probably. He always does. Last I heard he was into Tommy Vig for a couple large. He works Oakland, though. Squirrel Hill, around there. He ain't gonna know this guy."

"I thought I remember him working Homewood, Polish Hill, around there when he was patrol. Been a while, but he might know of this guy from years ago. Even if he don't, he can check prison records easier than we can. See what he has. I'll buy the note off Vig if I have to."

[54]

Doc got past the receptionist at Hecker and Associates with his badge and a smile. The woman guarding Hecker's inner sanctum was made of sterner stuff.

"I'm sorry, Mr. Hecker is very busy. He couldn't possibly see you today." Frances Liebermann showed signs of having been attractive once upon a time. Some women grow into being handsome; Liebermann aged into becoming formidable. She had the warmth and naiveté of a prison matron. "There's time on his schedule next week. I'll see what I can do."

"What you'll do is get me in there in less than half an hour. I don't know what his boys are telling him, but he needs to see me before the wheels come off altogether in Penns River."

She asked him to take a seat, phone already in her hand. Doc prepared himself for the inevitable jousting with Security. She made two calls. No one came for him. A group of three men walked down the hall behind her desk. The phone rang twenty-six minutes after she'd put Doc off. He could go in now.

"I knew you had it in you. He wouldn't have you out here if you weren't good."

Doc's first time inside the Gulf Tower. Everyone his age and older remembered it as the building that forecast the weather, the pyramid at the top changing color in anticipation of rain or clear. Now only the very top did, and it only showed the current weather, which struck no one as cool. Even in Pittsburgh, people knew rain from not rain without having to be told.

The man who opened the door to Hecker's office didn't get much sun. Thin and well-postured, already going soft around the eyes and neck. His hand was dry but fleshy when Doc shook it.

"Detective Dougherty, I'm George Grayson."

"I know."

"Really?"

"I wouldn't be much of a cop if I didn't recognize Danny Hecker's right hand."

Grayson tuned and walked into the room, speaking to Doc over his shoulder. "We've been meaning to get together with your chief to see what can be done up there in Penns River, but, well, you know how schedules can be. Mr. Hecker will be right with you."

Hecker was, of course, on the phone, his back to the room. He talked and gestured as he looked out the window behind his desk. The view went past the fountain to the Point and down the Ohio, probably all the way to West Virginia. Doc wondered if anyone was on the line.

Hecker made a show of hanging up, pointed to the chair on Doc's left. "Detective, have a seat." He didn't stand, or extend his hand. He didn't offer a drink. Doc took the chair on the right. Grayson took the other.

"What can I do for you?" Hecker said. He rocked back in his chair, crossed his right leg over the left in a figure four. Arrogant wasn't a strong enough word for his smile. Doc wondered if there was an adjective for hubris. He tried to hide his distaste, knew he'd fail. Among the things he'd liked about Penns River was its lack of men like this, who knew how to make money and nothing else and believed they should be allowed to do anything they could afford.

"I don't think there's a lot you can do for me," Doc said. "I'm here to see if I can help you, maybe help myself while I'm at it."

"What do you have in mind?"

"Things are getting out of hand in Penns River. Yuri Volkov needs a governor put on him. His father might be able to do it. I want you to make it happen."

"Who's Yuri Volkov?" Grayson said. "And who's his father?"

Doc looked at Grayson, turned back to Hecker to speak. "Let's not do it like this. You're busy, and I took a big chunk out of my day to come down here. Please don't insult my intelligence and act like I don't know what I'm talking about when we all know I do."

Grayson started to object. Hecker cut him off.

"I know a Sergei Volkov, but not this Yuri you mentioned."

"He'll do."

"I should tell you I know *of* him more than know him, so I don't see—"

"Mr. Hecker, I'm here unofficially. I'm not taking notes and I haven't advised you of your rights, so nothing you say here could be used against you even if I thought you were guilty of anything. Which I don't. At least not in my jurisdiction."

It must have been a while since Hecker had been interrupted. His mouth stayed open, creating the impression he'd invited Doc in to speak, ready to resume what he wanted to say at the first opportunity. Doc kept moving to deny him the chance.

"Sergei Volkov is the source of most of the money that built the Allegheny Casino. He greased a lot of skids, too, after the bubble burst and you were overextended in Harrisburg. He's not a public figure—no one wants that— but you know him well enough to get him on the phone."

"What makes you think so?"

"It's not a question of what I think. We both know I'm right." Slight sideways smile to Grayson. *The men are talking now, kid.*

"Where do you get this information?"

"Does it matter?"

"You're a cop. Don't you consider the source when deciding how accurate information is?"

"I'll make you a deal. Soon as I say something inaccurate, you can ask the source."

Hecker not as smug and aloof as before, still nine on a scale of ten. "What do you want me to talk to Sergei about?"

"He needs to put a leash on his boy. Frankly, I'm not sure he can, but there's sure as hell no one else. So far we have him dead to rights on assault and attempted kidnapping of a police officer."

"Can't you, uh, put a leash on him for that? Sounds serious to me."

"He made bail with the money that falls between his couch cushions. We'll keep at it. We're close to placing him at a homicide."

"Do you mean the drug dealer they dropped on the casino's steps last month? I was under the impression someone else was under arrest for that."

"This is why I'm here. You're either not being told, or not paying attention." Hecker's smug dropped another two points. "The arrest we made last week was for a different homicide, a sloppy frame that'll never go to trial. No arrests have been made in *your* homicide."

"I was going to ask about that. It's been over a month. What are you waiting for?"

"Evidence. That was a professional hit, very well executed. What I'd expect from a man like Mike Mannarino. Nothing like the one he's been arrested for. That one's Yuri all the way."

"If you don't think Mannarino killed the other man, why did you arrest him?"

"You told me to." Down to a five now, a line of red crept from under Hecker's collar. "Not personally. But the word came down that Mike Mannarino had to go away. Someone said 'Move,' and Jack Harriger was already in motion by the time it occurred to him the direction might matter."

Grayson said, "You're over the line, Detective. That's a charge and you've not advised Mr. Hecker of his rights."

Doc turned only his head in Grayson's direction. "Mind your place. I don't talk to cut-outs when I have The Man in front of me." To Hecker: "He has a point. Say what you want now. If your lawyer can spin my comment as a formal accusation—and I bet you can afford one who can—you're home free for the rest of this conversation."

Hecker was at four and falling. "Get to the point."

"Harriger can't help you now. He was in too far over his head and botched everything he touched. He's not chief anymore, and he's not *going* to be chief. The politicians you cultivated are scared. They expected boom times and got dead bodies and police threatened on public streets. Let something like this get a little momentum and your little Las Vegas will have less action than the Vatican. I know people on the zoning board. They're ready."

"And you can fix this," Hecker said. "Now that Harriger's failed."

"No," Doc said. "That's why I'm here. The difference between Jack Harriger and me—well, *one* of the differences—is I know when I'm in over my head. I need someone to call off Yuri. Only Sergei... might be able to do that. You're the guy who can talk to Sergei. You don't, or if Sergei can't calm his boy down, then he and Mannarino are going to fight it out. A lot of people are going to get hurt, and not even Sergei will have enough money to keep the Gaming Commission from taking a very hard look at that license. Forget the table games. This gets out of hand, and people will remember that build-ing as where the casino used to be instead of the old Monkey Ward's."

Hecker thinking now, engaged at last. "What do you get out of it? Chief?"

Air leaked out of Doc. Hecker would never get it. He didn't want to. Fine. What bothered Doc was that Hecker didn't need to. He existed above all this petty human bullshit. "I grew up in Penns River. I want it to be a place worth living in."

"That's what we're doing. Your town needs money and the casino can de-liver it."

"Your casino needs a town, too. Mannarino and Volkov carve it up, there won't be much there. A grind joint like yours doesn't have much to offer if people don't feel safe."

It was "grind joint" that got Hecker's goat. His face reddened and Doc did-n't have time to close his mouth before it started. "You got a lot of nerve, com-ing down here to insult me and the only growth opportunity that shithole you live in's had in forty years. I should pull out and leave you and your friends to drink themselves to death like they've been doing since the first mill opened. I should, but I don't do business that way. I'll stay, which is more than I can say for any other business you've had for a long time. I'll make something out of it for you. In spite of you, and your nickel-and-diming politi-cians and holier-than-thou zoning board. I'll show you how things are done right."

"I hope you do. Really. You have to understand events are moving now, and you'll be in over your head with the rest of us if you aren't careful. And quick. Call Sergei. But don't wait too long."

[55]

"How do you have time for all this? I mean, I know you're retired, but still...."

Doc long ago took the array of handmade shelves, mirrors, picture frames and boxes, and ornamental birdhouses for granted. His father had made hundreds of them since before he retired—thousands of the birdhouses—to sell, at first, but mostly to give away when what was involved to sell them became too much like a job for a retired man.

They were new to his cousin. Nick was leaving in the morning, stopped by to say goodbye. Tom Dougherty wouldn't let him go without a shelf. And a mirror. A few dozen birdhouses he'd made and Ellen painted. Pick out the ones you like best. We have plenty.

"Understand," Tom said, "once you set the saws and drill press up and get the lumber, it's about as easy to make a lot as a few. Get the assembly line going for the parts and put them together at your leisure."

"I know, but damn, Uncle Tom, there are hundreds of them, counting the birdhouses."

"Old people accumulate things. I made a few for something to do in my spare time while I was still working. Retire and every day is spare time. I'm making them faster than I can give them away. Now I need to work on getting rid of them, or Benny and his brother will never get through all the shit we have down here when the time comes."

Doc studied a map of the places his parents had visited. This conversation came up more often every year; each time made him more uncomfortable. His parents' general health was good for people around seventy, but someone in good health for a seventy-year-old was less healthy than someone in good health for a sixty-year-old. Ellen kept a photograph in the living room, Doc next to his father the day he came home from basic training. Doc bigger by a few inches and twenty pounds. Fifteen years later, Doc only ten pounds heavier than his Army weight, and he dwarfed his father.

Tom had his eye on a small combination shelf, kick-knack drawer, and key hanger for Nick. "Here. Hold this and I'll reach that one for you." He leaned against a cabinet and all the lights went out. "Shit. That transformer down by Reid Fisher's is out again."

The phone rang once. Doc and Nick pulled their cells.

"No signal," Doc said. "Jammed."

"Take the upstairs," Nick said. "See to your mother." Gun already in his hand.

□   □   □

Doc found Ellen in the kitchen, slamming drawers until she found a flashlight. "That's twice in the last two weeks the power's gone out. All those computers and stuff. We never lost power this much when you were kids."

Doc moved so fast to take the flashlight he bounced off the door jamb. "Don't turn that on!" Sat it on the table and took his mother by the arm.

"What are you doing?" she said. "How are we supposed to see in here?"

Doc held the gun at his side so the limited light wouldn't reflect off it, pulled Ellen past him. "Go into Russell's bedroom and lay on the floor next to the bed. Pull a blanket over you." He kept his eyes on the side door, closest to where the phone and electrical lines came in.

"What's wrong? It's just another power failure. They happen all the time."

Doc locked the metal entry door. He didn't want to yell at his mother, or use the cop voice and manner to demand compliance. He didn't want to negotiate with her, either. Eased her into the middle bedroom faster than she wanted to move, keeping his back between her and the front of the house. "Mom, I can't argue with you now. Those guys we've been after might be coming for Nick."

"Oh my God! It's just the two of you here! Call for help!"

"We will, Mom, soon as we can. Please get down next to the bed." He tossed a pillow on the floor for her head.

"How can the two of you watch the whole house?" She went rigid. "Where's your father? Where's Tom?"

"He's in the basement with Nick. He's fine."

Ellen tried to claw her way past Doc, back into the hallway. "But Nick's the one they're after! Tom! *Tom!*"

Doc grabbed her shoulders harder than he wanted to. "Mom! Nick and I will take care of it, but we can't do it if we have to worry about you and Dad. Now get down on the goddamn floor and lay there until one of us comes for you. I don't have time to ask you nice."

Ellen let him back her into the empty bedroom, looking over his shoulder all the time. One window—small and well above eye level from outside—would force any bullets to the ceiling; the comforter he threw over her should handle any splinters or glass. She started to cry as Doc helped her to the floor and covered her.

"Keep this over your face. Leave a little gap here by the wall so you can breathe. Whatever you do, don't get up until one of us comes for you."

"Benny, be careful. Take care of your father."

"These windows are too high to get in through. I can see both doors from the kitchen. Nick will take care of Dad and watch the garage and the back. I need you to help me and stay where I know you're safe."

Ellen said something. Doc couldn't make out what, her voice covered by the rattle of automatic weapons and breaking glass.

□   □   □

Nick's idea of keeping Tom Dougherty safe differed from Ellen's.

Soon as Doc ran upstairs, he asked his uncle, "You have any weapons down here?"

"I keep Benny's old .22 by the door there to shoot coons when they get in the garbage. The shotgun I used to hunt rabbits with is down here somewhere."

"Flashlight?"

"There. On the desk."

Nick found the flashlight on his third reach. Shielded it the best he could, saw the rifle leaning against the wall. "Is it loaded? Ben's .22?"

"Yeah, but I couldn't tell you how many."

"More than one or two?"

"Maybe."

Great. "Where's the shotgun?"

"In the shelves in the corner somewhere."

"Here." Nick handed the flashlight to Tom. "Cover it as much as you can. I'll watch the door."

Nick opened the door into the garage. Tom's Buick, parked nose in, along with a table saw, router, and various other tools and workbenches. Both doors were closed, but the top half of the entry door was windows. Such is life. He found a spot behind the drill press where he could see and still have some cover.

Behind him Tom said, "Found it."

Nick heard his uncle rummaging around. "Loaded?"

"No, but the shells should be right here." More foraging among the boxes. "Here. Got a half dozen, anyway. Been a while since I used this, but they should be dry and if they're dry, they should shoot."

"You're a good man, Uncle Tom. Come on over here."

Tom walked to the door, staying inside the basement. Nick said, "Go over in front of your car. Move quick. I'll cover the door."

Nick stood in the gap his uncle had to traverse while Tom hobbled behind him to the front of the car. Eight seconds that seemed like twenty minutes.

"Now lay on the floor. Use the car for cover. Peek around the quarter panel and tire and shoot anyone who comes through the door that isn't me or Benny."

"I'd love to help you, but no way can I get down there. Not with these knees. I'll lean on the hood."

"No. You're too big a target that way. We don't have but a few seconds. Get down now."

"Now" still hung in the air when the firing started. Glass broke and the roll-up door convulsed. Tom hit the ground like a dropped bowling ball while Nick ducked behind the drill press. He took the rifle from the doorway and started up the stairs.

"Where are you going?" Tom said.

"Even the odds."

The garage was dug into a bank that fell away from the bathroom and Doc's old bedroom. Its roof started near the windows, sloped away until it almost met the ground. Nick opened the bathroom window, removed the screen, and climbed through.

A breeze pushed clouds in front of the half moon. The dark shingled roof absorbed what light there was, and Nick was above the four men gathered behind his and Doc's cars in the driveway.

They were late. Proper technique would have been to fire the opening fusillade as soon as the lights and phone were cut. Storm the house at the same time, use the shock to overwhelm whoever was inside. This group didn't know their tactics, or had underestimated Doc and Nick and expected them to be inside wetting their pants. Either way, Nick was grateful.

He lowered himself to the roof well back of the edge to hide his silhouette and crawled forward. Shifted into good prone firing position and looked across the gravel driveway when he heard movement. Two men came toward him from behind the cars, moving toward the garage, where stairs led up to the main kitchen door. A third broke away from the pack, around the back of Nick's car, and ran through the spotty light to the stairs that led to the door on the far side of the house.

Nick aimed for the one closest, right in front of him, no more than twenty yards. Remembered as he started to squeeze that Tom had the shotgun sighted on the door below him, and Doc had two doors to watch, plus his mother. He shifted his sights to the man at the far side.

He'd never fired a rifle in a hurry; never fired this one at all. Adrenaline slowed the action for him. A quick breath in, then out as slow as he dared. Fired for what he took to be center of mass.

The man stumbled and went down. Placed one hand on the steps to steady himself and take inventory. Nick shot him though the head.

He pulled away from the side as automatic fire ripped the shingles and gutter away. Men yelled in Russian. Nick rolled up the roof toward the bathroom window.

□　□　□

The sound of the .22 surprised Doc until he remembered where his father kept it. He didn't have time to wonder where it had been shot from, or who was shot when the automatics started firing toward the garage roof and he guessed Nick had decided to take the fight to them. He cursed through a tight smile and duck-walked toward the door to see if he could draw any fire away from his exposed cousin.

Halfway out of his crouch he saw through the broken windows a man hur-rying up the steps that came from the garage. Lighter outside than in the house, so Doc waited until the man was two steps from top before he shot him three times in the chest and watched him tumble back the way he'd come.

□ □ □

Tom Dougherty lay on his belly in the garage, far more worried he'd shoot one of the boys than about what might happen to him. Surprised at how good he felt—except for the elbow he leaned on to sight the twelve-gauge—alert and engaged. Tried to decipher what the sounds meant. Recognized the .22 as Nick doing what he could. Scared for the kid—forty now, anyone whose shitty diapers Tom had changed would always be a kid to him—when the Russians shot away half the garage roof. Wondered if his insurance covered gunfire. That gutter wasn't two years old.

The shooting let up and someone yelled. A name, maybe. Could have been "Pavel." Saw the head and shoulders of a man through the shot-out windows at the top of the entry door and buried the stock in his shoulder. Caught him-self before he fired, knew the door would catch a lot of the pellets, no point letting anyone know he was here. Wished he knew what was up with Nick.

The entry door banged open. A man backed in, dragging something. Tom leveled the shotgun and took his breath, but couldn't shoot him in the back. Said, "That's far enough," and the man reached back and shot the shit out of his Buick. The rounds went well over Tom, breaking glass and rock-ing the passenger compartment, and he decided he could shoot a man half in the back.

□ □ □

Nick had made it almost to the window when he heard the shotgun blast, then nothing. If they were past his uncle, he could stay on the roof and shoot them as they passed through the bathroom. That would leave his back exposed from the low side of the roof if there was someone he hadn't accounted for. Bet-ter to get back into the house and shoot them as they came up the cellar steps.

But... Tom's shotgun was the last weapon fired. Nick scrambled back to the edge and risked a peek over. Two bodies were piled like dirty laundry at the foot of the stairs next to the entry door. Not a sound, eerie after all the shooting.

He heard footsteps running away on the gravel. Saw a figure fleeing across the yard toward the woods to the south. Nick stood and ran down the slope of the roof to hop to the ground and follow.

□   □   □

Doc saw the man run, too. Obtained a sight picture before remembering the range was iffy for a handgun and he had more pressing matters. His mother's crying sounded more like fright than injury. He ducked below a kitchen window and opened the door.

Nothing happened.

He took the flashlight his mother had found and got on his belly, knew he'd take some glass in his hands. Pushed open the screen door hard to create motion and noise.

Nothing happened.

He crawled onto the oversized stoop where his father kept the grill. Froze when he saw motion, resumed when he realized it was Nick pursuing whoever was left, couldn't leave well enough alone. Returned to more immediate concerns and saw one man lying against the steps near the road side of the house. He didn't look like he'd be going anywhere, given his posture. Looked down the stairs toward the garage and saw a pile that had to be more than one man, could have been three in that light. Assumed a proper stance and started down one step at a time, ready to vault the railing into the yard.

Nothing moved. He heard motion through the brush fifty yards away—Nick and whoever—something else he couldn't identify. Soft and straight ahead.

At the bottom of the stairs he risked the flashlight. A man lay doubled over like the seat back in a two-door car. A chunk of his side big enough to be a shark bite was missing. Blood and viscera glistened in the light. The sound was coming from under him. Doc aimed and pushed the top body aside with his foot.

Yuri's man Pavel shuddered as the weight came off him. His shirt was drenched with blood. He looked in Doc's direction, his eyes already going glassy.

"You. You fucking shit town police man. I try to tell Yuri." Pavel's eyes closed and his body relaxed for a few seconds until he caught his breath. "Military, no? And the other. Your cousin."

"Both of us." Doc wouldn't have called for an ambulance, even if he could. He had no idea what kept Pavel alive. "Me more than him."

"*Da.* I knew all the time. You are hard men. Yuri thought you were cunts." Pavel took a long, slow breath. "Fucking Yuri." He breathed out and didn't move.

"Benny? Is that you?"

Doc turned and aimed in one motion. "Dad?"

"You're gonna have to get me out of here," Tom said. "No way I can do it by myself."

Doc holstered his gun as he stood and half-jumped over the pile of bodies in the doorway. "Are you hit?"

"No, I'm not hit. I'm just old. Help me up. My knees are killing me."

Doc walked past the car, crouched to grab his father under the arms. "Did I get him?" Tom said. "The asshole that shot up my car?"

Doc helped his father up, looked back to the doorway. "Oh, yeah. You got him."

□   □   □

Nick took his time through the woods. Whoever was ahead of him made enough noise for both, and Nick already knew where he was going. The grown-over trail led down into a little creek, then up to Reid Fisher's place, somewhere along the hundred-yard path Fish used for a driveway.

Benny knew these woods better, but Nick knew enough. They'd played here as kids. Army and cowboys, practiced their Scout trailblazing skills when it seemed to them the trees went on forever and getting back wasn't a foregone conclusion. A mound of dirt might be the foxhole they'd dug, parapet and firing step and all. Benny and Russell's old tree house was off to the left somewhere.

At the bottom of the hollow he stepped over the creek, not much more than soft ground in this weather. Couldn't see who was ahead of him and didn't have to. He'd come out into Fisher's property in a minute or so, and a light was always on outside the small barn that housed a truck and some snow removal equipment.

When Nick's eye level reached above the crest of the rise he saw the black Lexus he'd followed from Dwight Wierzbicki's sacrifice. The same one Yuri Volkov tried to force Benny into. It was a hundred feet from the tree line, half lit by Fisher's floodlight. Yuri Volkov stumbled toward it, halfway there.

Nick leaned against a tree, exhaled, and shot out the left rear tire. Yuri hit the ground and Nick shot out the left front. Had to be a real buzz kill, watching your escape settle onto its rims like that.

Yuri rolled over and fired three times from his ass. Nothing came closer than thirty feet of Nick. Yuri scrambled on all fours to the car, sat in its shadow and fired again, still not knowing where to shoot. Sirens sounded in the distance.

Nick let out another breath and shot Yuri in the right shoulder. The gun fell to the ground and Yuri groped for it. Nick aimed between Yuri's hand and the gun—let him see it, not reach it—pulled the trigger. Empty.

He left the rifle against the tree and stepped into the pool of light, Yuri still fumbling for his gun. Nick drew a M1911 ACP .45 from under his arm and shot out the driver's window. Walked toward Yuri in a straight line like he had all the time in the world.

Yuri struggled to gather his feet under him. "Okay, police man. I am only raising one hand, you see. You fuck up the other good." Braced his back against the car door to slide himself up. Reached his feet when Nick had covered half the distance. Extended his arms, wrists touching. "Okay, police man. I am giving up now. Take me to your jail. You catch me fair and square."

Nick continued his pace. Said, "You forget. I am the one who is not even cop," and shot Yuri in the face.

[56]

Doc walked into Stush's office as the chief hung up the phone.

"Coffee?" Stush said. Tapped a box with his finger. "I know you want a doughnut."

Doc took a chocolate frosted. "You supposed to be eating these?"

"I'm not eating them. You are. You think I'm going to let a mild heart attack kill a cherished Penns River tradition?"

Back two weeks, Stush worked fifteen minutes more every day, expected to be back full-time by Memorial Day. Seeing him in daylight now a lot less scary to Doc than how he'd appeared the night Yuri tried to bushwhack him.

"That was Sally Gwynn on the phone," Stush said. "Called to tell me they're not going to prosecute the Hook for Wierzbicki. Asked if she should expect anything from us on Broaddus."

"Not unless someone confesses."

"That's what I told her. Poke around in it once in a while. Make it look good if that asshole Hecker asks, but treat it as a cold case. Maybe that half-wit friend of Broaddus's—what's his name? Butterfield?—will grow a conscience."

"Didn't you hear?"

"Hear what?"

"Nelson Butterfield took one from long range last week. Him and some yo from Baltimore, tied to the business there. Can't remember his name."

"Where was it?"

"Hartwood Acres. By the amphitheater, I guess. Two of them laying on the ground next to a car, shot with a 30.06."

"Huh." Stush sipped a V-8, looked at the box of doughnuts the way a cat looks at an open can of tuna. "Anything to do with our case?"

"Too soon to tell. Rumor has it there was a shortage of heroin a week or so after Broaddus went down. I'm looking to see if anything similar happens with Butterfield out."

Stush's phone buzzed. Said, "Send them in," into the receiver, then, to Doc, "Grayson's here. Janine says someone's with him."

Doc stood at the side of Stush's desk when George Grayson came in with an older man whose eyebrows qualified for their own genus and species. "Chief," Grayson said. "This is—"

"Sergei Volkov," Stush said.

Grayson gave a confused, "You've met?"

"Wouldn't be much of a cop if I didn't recognize my town's biggest employer, would I?" Doc wiped a hand across his mouth to cover a smile.

"May we sit?" Grayson said.

"Of course." Stush swept an open hand over his desk. "Make yourselves comfortable."

The visitors sat and Grayson said, "Mr. Volkov would like to express his concern and, uh, acknowledgement of some activities that have occurred over the past several weeks."

"Mr. Volkov's sitting right there. He'd seem more genuinely concerned and, uh, acknowledgeable, if we heard it from him personally."

"Mr. Volkov is not a native English speaker," Grayson said. "Under the circumstances—"

"I think Chief Napierkowski and, especially, Detective Dougherty, deserve to hear from me personally." Volkov's English much better than his son's, with a hint of a British accent under the Russian. "You are, I presume, Detective Dougherty?"

"I am," Doc said.

"If the two police officers give me their word as honorable men that we are speaking unofficially, then I am happy to speak for myself." Stush and Doc nodded.

"As you know, I am an investor in the Allegheny Casino. I also invest in many other things. How I came to be in such a position is not... germane to this conversation. Agreed?" The cops nodded again.

"I choose to remain a silent partner in my investments. The reasons are my own, and are also outside this conversation." More nods. "Because of this, actions are sometimes taken without my approval. Sometimes without even notifying me, so I am unaware.

"I say 'unaware,' not 'blameless.' If I am to reap the rewards of my investments—which I surely intend to do—I must accept responsibility for the failures. Please understand, I am accustomed to the business practices of my country, where a... hidden investor may remain completely in the shado—background. It is different in this country. Please forgive me my inexperience." Volkov cleared his throat. "Excuse me, but may I have something to drink?"

Stush leaned toward his coffee maker. "Coffee?"

"Would it be possible to have water? I wish no offense, but American coffee does not agree with my system."

Doc left and returned with three bottles of water. Grayson accepted his with a nod. Volkov said, "Thank you, Detective. Your courtesy is appreciated."

Everyone took a drink and Volkov resumed. "In a venture such as a casino, there are sometimes, uh, a—a seal—a seal nary?" Volkov's voice trailed off as his eyes looked on the ceiling for the word he wanted. "Ancillary? Yes. Ancillary." The manual laborer he'd once been surfaced for a second through a sheepish smile. "I apologize. I am learning to speak better English. My wife says a businessman must not sound like a peasant, so I hire a tutor to teach me to be more... eloquent. Sometimes I think he is not very successful.

"Now, to ancillary businesses. These are unintended and are of no profit to the casino, but that's where the dog is buried. To be fair, they are also not unexpected. As a partner with a large investment, I should have been aware of this possibility. Mr. Hecker is a great man, but he is not experienced in such matters. I should have taken a more active part."

A sip of water. "God blessed me with three sons. Now, two." Doc looked for a challenging glare, got none. "Yuri was my oldest and, like many firstborn male children, my favorite. He did not have to start at the bottom to learn my business. He learned the benefits without knowing the sacrifices required. He saw opportunity in these ancillary businesses. This is not good or bad, but once becoming involved in these matters, he became greedy. This is not unusual for young men. They do not appreciate that enough is as good as a feast. He did not consult with me to see what is appropriate. As for me, I was living as if my house was at the end of the street and had no idea of his actions. That blame falls on me, and I pay a heavy price for my negligence."

Doc held his questions, less interested in his pound of flesh than in seeing where the old man would take his monologue.

"Yuri did things here that were mistakes. No, I am sorry for that, worse than mistakes. They were not only errors in judgment, but—forgive me, he was my son and my love for him may cloud my opinion—they were also errors of moral acuity. There is no excuse for ambushing Detective Dougherty," a nod in Doc's direction, "and for what was done to your father's home. May I be permitted to make restitution?"

"You'll have to ask my father," Doc said. He nodded toward Grayson. "He'll take it better if you speak to him personally."

"Yes, of course. Father to father is proper. Mr. Grayson will take me there immediately we leave here."

Doc smiled until Grayson made eye contact. *Oh, Georgie, warm up the car.* To Volkov he said, "Thank you. I'm sure he'll appreciate the gesture."

Sergei nodded. "I come here to tell you these actions were not condoned by me, or by Mr. Hecker. They were not even known to us. I am also here to assure you that no other such actions will take place. I am a man who is not comfortable with public speaking. I do not relish the spotlight. As you see, my command of your language is not so good. Because of this, I will remain in the background. I will make my effort to be better informed, and Mr. Hecker has personally guaranteed his oversight to all matters of the casino to ensure nothing of this type ever happens again. May we consider what was done by Yuri to be put to rest?"

Doc knew what Stush would say. Volkov still held the best cards. "Everything we know says your son acted as a free agent, following no orders. He's gone, and so is anyone we know of who was involved with him. I have to say this is a dead issue—" he cringed, "—unless new information comes to light."

"That is fair." Volkov rose, Grayson vaulting to his feet on first movement. "Thank you, gentlemen, for your time today. I know you are busy men."

"One more thing, Mr. Volkov," Doc said. "About my cousin."

"He is the private investigator from Chicago."

"That's right. No offense, but he shot Yuri in self-defense. We've given our word as honorable men that nothing said here today is on the record. I'd like your word as an honorable man that no harm or harassment will come to him, or anyone close to him, because of what happened with Yuri."

Volkov squared up to Doc. "I do not swing fists when the fight is over. Your cousin did what he had to do. What any man would do. There will be no retribution. I swear to it." He turned to include Stush in his comment. "Thank you again, Chief Napierkowski. This is a small town, but I see you have good people under your command. I commend you. And now I say *do svidanija.*"

[57]

The Den was in Fox Chapel, about a mile from the Pittsburgh Field Club. Doc didn't spend a lot of time this direction, half an hour and several income strata from his house. He heard about The Den from a woman he dated for a while then forgot about it, due in part to his haste to forget about her. She always wanted to go, said it was the most romantic place around. Two fire-places, the building set so you could look through the picture window to see the river below, the edge of a bluff hiding traffic on the Allegheny Valley Expressway.

Doc didn't know what made him think of The Den. A reference to a golf tournament at the Field Club, maybe. He cleaned himself up after his shift and ate a sandwich while he waited for traffic to thin out.

Only half a dozen tables occupied at seven o'clock on a Tuesday night; no one at the bar. Doc sat near the end farthest from the door, took a twenty from his wallet. The barmaid gave him a "one minute" gesture while she made something in a blender. Doc wrinkled his lips, waved for her to take her time.

She put an umbrella into each glass of what came out of the blender and handed them to a waitress. Walked over drying her hands. She had dirty blonde hair with highlights, gripped at the back of her head with one of those grabber combs. She had blue eyes and fair skin that hadn't yet become acquainted with the laugh lines around her eyes. She wore a white tuxedo shirt that presented her breasts well and with discretion. The fourth finger of her left hand was bare.

Doc ordered a Bass draft and slid the twenty across the bar. She brought the beer—she gave perfect head—and his change. He pushed two dollars back to her. She smiled and went about her business.

No television. The Den was a rendezvous, not a sports bar. Doc watched the door, rotated his seat to glance across the room, looking for all the world like a man killing time. He thought about Wilver Faison, who hadn't shown for the Pirate game. It felt good that David hadn't let Wilver's absence spoil his fun, Doc not yet ready to believe it was time to give up on Wilver and focus on David.

He didn't notice he'd finished the beer until he tipped it back and only a rumor of foam touched his lips. He slid the glass across the bar. Didn't gesture for the bar maid. She'd be over.

She closed out a check and nodded in his direction. He nodded back and she drew him another Bass on her way over. He pushed money across the bar for the beer and another two dollar tip.

"Thanks." She slid the extra two bucks into a tip glass. "You waiting for someone?"

Doc had the glass to his lips when she asked. Took his time finishing, said, "Actually, I'm here to see you."

"Really. And who told you about me?"

"No one. No offense, but I'm here to see whoever's working tonight. That seems really impersonal. You mind if I ask your name?"

"Kate."

"Hi, Kate. I'm Ben. My friends call me Doc."

Kate extended a hand. "Hi, Ben."

Doc smiled. "Relax. I'm not trying to pick you up." That didn't mean he might not under different circumstances. "I want to show you something and I don't want anyone else to see it. No, it's not that."

They half-turned their backs away from the room and he let Kate see his badge.

"It's nice," she said. "I've seen bigger."

He made eye contact so she'd know he considered several things to say and chose not to. "How long have you worked here?"

"About three years. Yeah, three years in July."

"The other women? The waitresses?"

"Jen just started last week. Dee's been here for over a year, I guess."

Doc saw the curiosity in her eyes, liked that she had control of it. Took the envelope from his sport coat's outer pocket. The photographs of Marian Widmer, Carol Cropcho, and David Frantz showed the wear of being presented every week or so at bars and lounges all over the Pittsburgh area. Doc had scanned copies on his hard drive at home, ready to make new ones when these wore out.

"Kate, you ever seen any of these people in here? Take a good look at the two women in particular. Would have been a year or so after you started."

THE END